# Kokopelli's Song

Four Corners
Fantasy Folklore

## Suzanne J Bratcher

Expanse Books

Published by Expanse Books, an imprint of
Scrivenings Press LLC
15 Lucky Lane
Morrilton, Arkansas 72110
https://ScriveningsPress.com

Printed in the United States of America

Paperback ISBN 978-1-64917-060-6

eBook ISBN 978-1-64917-061-3

Library of Congress Control Number: 2020943146

Cover by www.bookmarketinggraphics.com.

*[Scripture quotations are]* from the Revised Standard Version of the Bible, copyright © 1946, 1952, and 1971 the Division of Christian Education of the National Council of the Churches of Christ in the United States of America. Used by permission. All rights reserved.

Published in association with Jim Hart of Hartline Literary Agency, Pittsburgh, Pennsylvania.

*For Vaughn,*
*always ready for an adventure!*

# ACKNOWLEDGMENTS

Stories have distinctive life cycles. Occasionally a complete story materializes from the mythical birthing-ground of fiction, and the writer's job is simply to get it on paper. These stories, however, are the stuff of which legend is made. More often a part of a story emerges, leaving the writer to discover or invent the rest. A vivid character badgers her writer into discovering plot. A nagging conflict forces the writer to search for characters. Even a setting can grab hold, refusing to let go until the writer tells the stories that haunt that place.

The most difficult stories to write, however, begin with a title, leaving the author to uncover plot, characters, and even setting. *Kokopelli's Song* was that kind of story. Kokopelli, the flute player figure from ancient petroglyphs, is a popular icon throughout the Southwest. He appears in flashing neon, on letterhead, on T-shirts, and in scholarly tomes. I own a pair of Kokopelli earrings set with turquoise, a beautifully illustrated book of Kokopelli Ceremonies (Hill and Montoya, 1995), and a sandstone fragment carved with replicas of Kokopelli petroglyphs. Most people in the Southwest know Kokopelli, but as far as I know, no one knows what song he plays on his red cedar flute.

I don't remember when the title *Kokopelli's Song* surfaced, but the conflict began to tease me fifteen years ago when I first visited Chaco Canyon. (Read a more complete chronicle of what happened there in the *Author's Note* at the end of this book.) The characters came later, even going through name and age changes along the way. In that fifteen-year trek, many people helped this tale take its final form. Vaughn Delp and Marcia Coman camped overnight with me at Chaco Culture National Historic Park; The Hunters and the Killens provided me with a quiet place to write and friendship at *A Mountain Retreat* while I worked out the earliest draft; my friends Joy Ice and Ron Latimer hosted me multiple times on my trips through Santa Fe; a step-on guide named Lloyd Harper showed me the Hopi Reservation, including Old Oraibi; my friend and writing partner Mary Johnson critiqued early drafts; and my daughter Jorie Hoskins helped me develop contemporary teenaged characters.

More recently, my editor Linda Fulkerson accomplished the feat of streamlining prose I produced before I understood the conventions of contemporary fiction; my intrepid reader Marlene Lloyd picked up errors and oversights in the characters and the plot; and my MS care partner Rhonda Hall kept my me fed and my house running smoothly so I could meet tight deadlines. The phrase "it takes a village" leaps to mind, but this tale took a pueblo. My thanks to all the inhabitants.

As always, I offer my gratitude to the Spirit—above, below, ahead, behind, on my right, on my left, inside, outside—always leading.

# SERIES INTRODUCTION

## Introduction to the
### *Four Corners Folklore Fantasy* Series

Welcome to my new series! If you like majestic settings, present-day conflicts with roots in the past, characters who solve problems and learn something about themselves in the process—and if you'll believe for a few hours that magic might exist just out of sight—you've found stories I think you'll enjoy.

When I was growing up, my favorite book was a collection of fairy tales that belonged to my grandmother when she was young. An over-sized hardback with fraying edges, yellowing pages that cracked if I turned them too quickly, and an occasional colored illustration on shiny paper, it was filled with fairy tales from all over the world. I read all the standard stories like *Cinderella* and *Snow White*, but I also encountered lesser-known stories like *The Princess on the Glass Hill* and *Snow White, Rose Red*. As I got older, my love of fairy tales expanded to include folklore.

Fast forward to my late twenties. I moved to Flagstaff, Arizona, where I spent the next thirty years. I traveled all over the four corners states—Arizona, New Mexico, Colorado, and Utah—and I fell in love with towering mountains, wide-open mesas, ancient ruins, and towns with intriguing histories. I hiked in the Grand Canyon, the Rocky Mountains, Bryce, and Zion. I explored the Painted Desert, Santa Fe, and Chaco Canyon. I met native people whose ancestors lived in the four corners region a thousand years before the Spanish crossed the ocean to discover the "new" world as well as people descended from those explorers and from immigrants who made their way to Colorado during the 1858 gold rush.

Forward through another fifteen years, and we arrive at these stories. To create what I've dubbed *folklore fantasy*, I mix folklore, history, and present-day realism. I sprinkle that mixture with a bit of magic and life-threatening danger. Then I place in characters with everyday struggles into this world and see what happens.

For this first book, I blended my version of a few Hopi legends with bits of history and research about the ruins in Chaco Canyon. Next, I added what I learned on visits to six historical sites, a tidbit of archaeological speculation, and a hint of magic. I placed a young woman searching for her identity and a faceless villain into that world. *Kokopelli's Song* is the result. Because some of the words I needed to tell the story may be unfamiliar, you'll find a glossary at the end of this book. Teachers, book clubs, and readers interested in delving deeper into the story will find a free study guide at the end of this book.

Right now, get ready to meet Amy and run for your life!

*Suzanne J. Bratcher*

August 12, 2020

# I. SIPAPUNI [PLACE OF EMERGENCE OR DOORWAY]

Out on the windswept mesas of Hopiland and down in the pueblos dotted along the Rio Grande, storytellers preserve the history of the People in the times before our Time began. Each generation has its own storytellers, but the stories remain the same, passed from the old to the young.

Today, science books tell of a Big Bang, but storytellers gather the people around them and speak of music. They say the Creator sang the First World into being: the sun, moon, and stars, the oceans and land, the plants and animals, and, of course, the First People. When all was finished, the Creator taught the First People to sing. "As long as you sing the Song of Creation," he said, "the world will be in harmony, and you will be happy."

At first, all was well. The People sang as the sun rose in the East, while it shone directly overhead, and as it set in the West. They sang when the moon and the stars appeared in the dark canopy of Tokpela, the endless void. As they sang, they lived in harmony with Creation, and they were happy. Then came a time when some of them stopped singing, then more and more. When the People fell silent, they began fighting and killing—animals and

1

people alike. The First World fell into disharmony, and eventually, the thread of life ran out.

In the midst of the Chaos, the Creator called the last of the Singers together. Heaving a great sigh, he said, "I have decided to destroy this world and try again. To keep you Singers safe, I am sending you to the Ant People." When the Singers were deep in the earth with their brothers the ants, the Creator destroyed the First World with fire.

Then he sang the Second World into being. It was even more beautiful than the first, and the Singers were happy and multiplied. As long as they sang, the world was in harmony, and all was well. But then, just as before, some of the People fell silent, and disharmony crept into their hearts. And as before, more and more people forgot until finally, the thread of life ran out. Again, the Creator sent the last Singers to safety with the Ant People. And again, he destroyed the world—this time, with ice.

A third time the Creator sang the world into being, and a third time the pattern was repeated. But this time when the thread of life ran out, rather than sending the last Singers to the Ant People, the Creator sealed them in hollow reeds that could float. Then he destroyed the Third World with water. For many days, the Singers drifted on Endless Water. Their food ran out, and still they had not found the place of emergence into the Fourth World. Just before they starved, they found it—the Sipapuni.

Storytellers say the world those Singers emerged into is our world. They say this Fourth World is the last chance the People have to learn to live in harmony with Creation. They say it is our last chance to keep singing.

# CHAPTER ONE

*Santa Fe, New Mexico*

In her tiny room above the Delgado Gallery, Amy Adams punched her pillow for the third time. She flipped to her side and stared at the digital clock. Green numbers blinked three a.m. She needed sleep, but her mind trudged around the endless loop again. Grandmother Adams lied. Mahu was her twin brother. Taáta was her Hopi father. Grandmother Adams lied. Mahu was her twin brother. Taáta—

Pottery smashed on the ceramic tile downstairs. Not a small pot, one of the decorative water jars that reached her shoulder. Amy lay still, held her breath, waited for the next sound.

Mahu was down there, asleep, or maybe awake, on the long leather couch reserved for customers who wanted to consider an outrageously expensive purchase.

Amy listened for the next sound. Silence.

Heart pounding, she threw off the scratchy wool blanket and sat up. Fear like glacial runoff pumped through her veins. Not because she believed Mahu had broken a pot, but because she knew her twin was in danger. She felt it as surely as if the two of them had never been separated to grow up in different worlds.

Just like she knew Mahu was in danger, she knew whoever was with him meant evil. Her bare feet hit the cold floor. She ran out of the room, down the dim hallway. She shivered in the sleep shirt that reached her knees, but she didn't have time to care. At that moment, Amy was Kaya again, the older sister, the firstborn twin. The need to protect snapped at her heels, urging her to go faster, faster.

The narrow staircase cut straight down into inky darkness. Kaya Amy didn't pause to grope for the light. Instead, she threw herself down the steps, racing to get to Mahu before someone hurt him. Before she reached the bottom, she sensed she was too late.

Still, she ran through the gallery, darting through a confusion of light and dark, evading ghosts of tiny bronze cowboys riding tiny bronze horses, ducking around shadows of rugs hanging from the ceiling, swerving to miss chairs carved from twisted roots and iron tables laden with painted pots.

She found Mahu on his side under the long window, backlit by the streetlamp's watery light that illuminated the shop front. His flute and backpack lay beside him. For an instant, Amy thought she saw Kokopelli, the humpbacked flute player of the ancient petroglyphs. Then the vision was gone, and she saw her twin again.

One arm beneath his body, the other flung back, hand clenched into a fist. A ceremonial arrow with a turquoise-inlaid shaft protruded from his chest. Not shot from a bow, stabbed in like a knife. Blood seeped from the wound, soaking his shirt. Fragments of a huge ceramic vase lay strewn around him, the one she'd heard break, the one he must have slammed into as he fell. More blood seeped from his head, spreading onto the ceramic tile floor, gathering in a pool.

"Mahu!" she cried. "Mahu!"

4

No answer. Only silence—silence that scared her more than a groan or even a scream. Crouching beside him, she whispered, "Mahu. Mahu."

His long dark hair, as straight as her own, fanned out across his face. Tenderly, almost as if he slept and she didn't want to wake him, Amy pushed back his sticky hair. The uncertain light of the streetlamp flickered across his face, one moment revealing her twin's face, the next the face of a stranger. Not dead, she prayed. Please, please—not dead.

She wanted to find his pulse, needed to find it. At first she tried to move him, pull the closer arm out from under his body, but he was too heavy. Reaching across, she grabbed the other arm. His wrist felt warm. The fist relaxed, releasing a scrap of cloth.

The air behind her stirred. No sound, but a warning. She crouched there for the length of a heartbeat, clutching Mahu's limp hand, and held her breath.

Then fingers brushed her hair.

Amy grabbed the torn fabric and scrambled to her feet. She dodged a hand that plucked at her shoulder and lunged for the outside door. Too late, she remembered it was locked at night. But when her shoulder hit the glass, the door let her out as easily as it did customers hurrying for the next shop, dumping her into the snow-filled night with a cheery tinkle.

Cold slapped her face and sucked the air from her lungs. Ignoring the icy needles that pricked her bare arms and legs, Amy sprinted across the stone courtyard. As she passed the frozen fountain, her feet slipped. For one breathless moment, Amy thought she would fall. But she didn't have time.

Throwing her weight forward, she found her balance and kept running. She reached the tall wrought iron gate that should be locked. But like the door, it swung open as soon as she touched it. Behind her, the gallery door tinkled again—Mahu's attacker.

5

Slipping but never quite falling, she ran along the empty street past dark shops toward the hulking outline of St. Francis Cathedral. But the hope of sanctuary mocked her. Like the shops that hadn't been broken into, it would be locked.

The gate squeaked behind her, followed by footfalls. Not bare feet like hers, feet in boots. Snow swirled around the streetlamps, transforming the moonless night into a chaos of flickering orange and yellow light. Each breath of frigid air seared her lungs, yet she ran. Faster. Around the corner. Into an alley.

Mahu's battered pickup waited beside the dumpster. She had wondered when he tucked the keys behind the driver's seat. 'No one wants this bucket of bolts,' he said with the gentle smile that transformed the unfamiliar teenager into her five-year-old twin. 'Besides, I always believe in leaving an escape route.'

She thought he was kidding. Amy yanked at the door and wondered. Had he known he was in danger? Why hadn't he warned her? She pushed the thoughts aside—no time to wonder.

Amy jerked open the driver's door. The screech disturbed the snow's silence. Had her pursuer heard? The cab's overhead light shone like a beacon, signaling her location. She clambered in, reached for the keys with one hand and slammed the door with the other, extinguishing the light.

Her fingers found the ignition key, big and square. She slid it into the steering column and jammed one numb foot on the clutch and the other on the gas pedal. The engine coughed. For one frozen second she thought she'd flooded it.

It coughed a second time and then roared into life. As she pulled around the dumpster, a dark shape in a hooded sweatshirt reached for the passenger-side door. Simultaneously jerking the steering wheel and flooring the gas, she aimed the pickup at him with such force that he lost his grip and fell heavily against the dumpster.

Tires sliding on the snow, the truck lurched out of the alley into the street. Headlights could wait. She had to get away. Now.

Amy swung onto Old Pecos Trail, heading for the interstate where cinder trucks would be spreading precious traction.

Unless Mahu's attacker had parked in the same alley, she had a few minutes lead. She needed to reach the road first. Even if he figured out where she was going, there were enough exits from the highway to throw him off track.

Amy sped around one corner, passed the cathedral, and pulled on the headlights. Ice crystals danced in the yellow light, rushed at the windshield, momentarily blinding her. She drove recklessly, hoping to find a patrolman to pull her over, return to the gallery with her, get help for Mahu.

Nothing but snow. Snow the wipers pushed at ineffectually, snow that covered her tire tracks almost as soon as the pickup made them. The streets were empty and silent, trails through an invisible city. Up a hill, sliding back, down a hill, slipping forward.

At last, she saw I-25, as empty as the city streets. Amy steered madly up the entrance ramp, ignoring the engine's clatter and clamor, willing the old pickup to keep moving. Then she entered the highway, driving on cinders already disappearing under new snow.

She pressed hard on the gas. A quick glance in the rearview mirror showed nothing but darkness. Amy exhaled the breath she'd been holding and slowed to a less frantic speed.

Heading south, she would soon leave Santa Fe behind. Amy longed for the open highway with nothing but a few exits to a string of pueblos, all off the road, shut up, sleeping out the storm. She checked the gas gauge. Half a tank. Enough to reach Albuquerque, but Mahu was lying on the gallery floor, bleeding, dying. She had to stop, had to find help.

Amy took the next exit. Cerillos Road. At the bottom of the ramp, a darkened gas station occupied one corner. Across the street an all-night drugstore spilled light out into the snow. Amy parked in the deepest shadows, rested her head on the steering wheel, and tried to think.

Headlights on Cerillos Road briefly illuminated the cab, dumping her abruptly back into the present. Amy blinked. Sitting up, she pushed her tangled hair out of her face and looked down at herself. In the drugstore sign's dim neon light, she saw her nightshirt, stiff with blood. Mahu's blood. Panic welled up inside her. She couldn't go to the sheriff. Couldn't trust a man wearing a brown uniform. Something tugged at her memory. Something scary. Something she didn't have time to think about right now.

One thing was certain—brown uniform or not, the sheriff would say she was a runaway. He would say she belonged to Grandmother Adams until she was 18. He would call the house in Virginia, and Grandmother Adams would come for her. She couldn't go to the sheriff, but she could call 9-1-1.

She looked at her hands as if wishing for her cell phone hard enough would make it materialize. Her cell was in her jeans pocket, jeans that hung on the chair beside her bed.

Amy's right hand was empty. Her left hand still clutched the scrap of fabric Mahu had been holding. It must be important, but not now. She tucked it behind the seat where she'd found the keys and opened the glove compartment. Did Mahu have a cell phone? He had to have one. Everybody had a cell phone.

The glove compartment light was burned out. She rummaged in the dark, searching by touch rather than sight. A tire gauge, a tiny spiral notebook, a broken pencil, a twisted bandana. No cell phone. She groped under the seat. No cell phone. She ran the tire gauge along the narrow space between the seat and the back window. Still no cell phone.

She found it at her feet on the filthy floor under the rubber mat. An icon indicated a missed message, but Amy didn't care about messages. Hands shaking, she punched in 9-1-1.

"Santa Fe County Emergency."

Doing her best to sound like a grown woman instead of a

panicky teenager, Amy said, "I need to report someone badly hurt." A voice in her mind whispered, Please don't let Mahu be dead. Don't let him be dead. "At 121 San Francisco Street."

"Your name?"

"There was a break-in. Send an ambulance to the Rebecca Delgado Gallery." She grabbed a breath, hurried on. "Send it now. Before he dies!"

Amy heard the hysteria rising in her voice. Before the woman could ask any more questions, she broke the connection and turned off the phone. She knew cell phone calls could be traced, and she didn't want to be found. Couldn't be found. Not yet.

All she needed was a week. Five days really. Just until their birthday, hers and Mahu's. Once she was eighteen, she would have time to find the missing part of herself, the part of her Grandmother Adams had taught her didn't exist, the part that lived in her dreams. She could find out who she was, where she belonged, where home was. But Mahu had to live.

Amy dropped the phone in her lap and laid her head on the steering wheel. "Please, God," she whispered, "please let him live!"

Gradually the shock wore off, or maybe it started to set in. Amy shivered uncontrollably. Hands shaking, she turned on the engine and, without much hope, the heater. Lukewarm air stirred the winter air that leaked in around the windows, under the doors. Pulling her aching feet up under her, she tried to think. She needed help. Someone to bring her warm clothes and shoes. Someone to help her get away.

She didn't know how long it would take the sheriff to identify Mahu or how long to find his pickup, but she did know if she wanted to keep free from Grandmother Adams, she needed to get away from anything connected to Mahu.

But who? Who would help her?

# CHAPTER TWO

A my stared at the snow, somehow alien. Different from snow in Virginia—Virginia where all her friends were. Maddy would help her, but Maddy was in Williamsburg where the snow was softer. No one here would help her. No one here knew she wasn't eighteen.

A few weeks ago, with the red and yellow leaves still on the trees in Virginia, her grandmother shouted, "Santa Fe! That's where your tramp of a mother met that—that *Indian!*"

Amy had stepped back, repelled by the hatred in her grandmother's voice. Prejudice? From a woman who claimed to be fair-minded? Amy knew then Grandmother Adams wouldn't tell her anything more about her father. Shaken, Amy packed a bag and climbed on a bus headed to New Mexico. She hadn't run away—just left the grandmother who had lied to her for as long as she could remember.

She needed someone she could trust to help her. Becky Delgado. Why hadn't she thought of Becky sooner? She picked up the phone in her lap, punched in half the numbers, and stopped. Becky wasn't at the gallery, and Amy didn't know her home number. It was no good. Becky led her right back to the sheriff.

Who else?

She gulped air, held it, and exhaled slowly, desperate to halt the panic welling up inside her. Amy felt hope seeping away when another name popped into her mind. *Diego.*

Mahu had come to Santa Fe to show a friend something old and valuable he'd found, his friend Diego. Amy had also met someone named Diego, a college student a couple of years older than she was. Could he be Mahu's friend? Probably too much to hope for. Santa Fe was a big place. But any straw to grasp was better than sitting here paralyzed.

Amy turned on the phone and scrolled. She found the name in the contact list—*Diego.* She pressed the number, held her breath, and waited. One ring, two, three—

"Mahu? Sorry I missed you earlier, but hey, bro, it's 4:30 in the a.m."

She thought the sleepy voice belonged to the guy she'd met, not too deep and slightly scratchy. Not positive, but sure enough to try. She blurted, "It's not Mahu. It's Amy. Amy Adams. You might not remember me. I took one of your tours at the museum." *Too much information.*

"I remember you. Girl with long black hair. Looking at the pottery, trying to find your family or something." He yawned. "But why are you on Mahu's phone and why are you calling me at 4:30 in the morning?"

"I'm Mahu's twin sister. I need help. Mahu and I both need help!"

"Mahu is your brother?" He sounded confused, but the fuzziness of sleep was gone from his voice.

"It's complicated." Not far from where she sat, a siren wailed. "I'll explain later! Right now I need a ride. Can you come get me?" *Please—Please, believe me!*

"Where are you?"

Relief washed over her, relief so strong the tears she hadn't had time to cry filled her throat, threatened to choke her so she couldn't answer.

The siren, closer this time, wailed again. She had to move. The only place she could think of was the interstate. "The rest area on I-25. The one on the south edge of town."

"Amy, what's happened? It's more than a breakdown, isn't it? Is Mahu okay?"

"He isn't okay. He's not dead, but he's hurt. If you want to help him, help me. Please! I need clothes." She was shivering again, shivering so hard she could barely hold the phone. "Something warm—and shoes. I need shoes."

A long pause, so long Amy was afraid he'd changed his mind. Finally, like he was thinking aloud, he said, "I guess my mother has some extra things. She's out of town, but she won't care."

"How long?"

"In this snow? Thirty minutes."

An eternity. "I'm in Mahu's pickup."

This time, he didn't ask what was going on. Just disconnected.

Amy closed the phone, dropped it on the seat beside her. She put the pickup in gear, pulled on the headlights. The wipers struggled to shove the heavy wet snow that covered the windshield to the side. One pass, two. On the third pass, she could see enough to risk driving.

The tires slipped as she backed out of the parking space, but help was on the way. And she was moving. She was about to pull into the street when a fire truck, siren blaring, lumbered past, headed for a fire stubborn enough to blaze in snow.

Relief flooded through Amy, making her light-headed. Inhaling deeply, she fought the pickup out of the parking lot and headed toward the interstate. When she was finally up the ramp and following the single cleared lane, Diego's face came into her mind—skin the color any blue-eyed blond beach bum would kill for, intelligent black eyes framed by wire-rimmed glasses, and a mass of curly black hair.

She'd met him at the Museum of Indian Arts and Culture, MIAC, the second week after she arrived in Santa Fe. She visited several times, searching for an exhibit that might give her a clue, if not to her family, at least to her tribe.

After Diego's tour they sat on a stone wall in the shadow of a bronze colossus depicting a Native dancer and traded bits and pieces of their stories. The son of the director, he worked as a part-time tour guide showing exhibits of thousand-year-old pottery, contemporary weavings, and duplicates of sand paintings.

She hadn't known about Mahu then, but Diego sounded surprised when she told him Becky Delgado had given her a job.

'Becky's loaded,' he'd said, 'but she's not exactly quick to offer a helping hand. She must like you.'

A semi rumbled off the highway a few hundred yards ahead of Mahu's pickup, spraying snowy slush on the windshield and jerking Amy back into the present. The truck pulled into the rest area. She'd been concentrating on Diego, not on where she was.

Steering carefully to keep from sliding on the icy exit, Amy followed the semi. Except for the two of them, the rest area sat deserted. The big truck turned toward the oversized-vehicles lot, and she parked as far from it as she could, picking a space away from the two streetlights.

Turning off the motor, she took a deep breath and tried to relax. Out on the highway, a patrol car moved toward the rest area. Panic gripped her. She couldn't wait for Diego in Mahu's pickup. Even if the sheriff hadn't traced the plates yet, a teenager in a blood-soaked sleep shirt would attract attention. Taking the cell phone, she opened the door and slid out.

Freezing air pricked her skin, made her want to run, but that would attract attention. Ice and snow glazed the walkway.

Watching where she put her feet, she made it up the slight incline without falling. As the patrol car's headlights swung into the parking lot, Amy ducked into the women's restroom.

The fluorescent lights made her blink, but a quick check reassured her she was alone. She moved quickly to the farthest stall and perched on the old-fashioned toilet's closed lid with her knees pulled up under her chin.

The outside door squeaked. "Anybody in here?" A man's voice with the hint of a Spanish accent echoed in the empty restroom.

Amy held her breath. *No one you want!*

"Sheriff. Coming in."

The memory came suddenly, so clear it seemed to be happening right then. She was five. She was Kaya, and she and Mahu were sitting in her father's lap. Outside the adobe house, they looked up at tall white clouds suspended in an electric-blue sky. Taáta said, 'Mama and Baby are with the Cloud People.'

Kaya shook her head. 'No! I want Mama to come home.'

'She can't come,' Taáta murmured, 'but she can see us. She still loves us very much.'

'I want her!' Kaya said.

'Me too,' Mahu whispered.

A white car with red and blue flashing lights left the highway and turned onto the dirt road. It headed toward them. They watched for a little while. Taáta stiffened and stood the twins on their feet. As he got up, he said, 'Go inside, children.'

'Why?' Kaya demanded. Mahu took her hand and pulled.

Taáta, his voice harsh, said, 'Into the house. Now!'

Grandmother Iso came to watch from the doorway. Kaya and Mahu stood behind her, one on each side, clinging to her long soft skirt. The car stopped in front of their house. An Anglo woman with red hair like Mama's got out of one side. A man dressed in a brown uniform got out of the other.

In the restroom, two stall doors banged. The patrolman was

checking stalls. His footfalls came closer. He pushed the door to her stall, but she'd locked it. The flimsy lock held. Through the tiny crack at the door's edge, Amy watched him bend over and check for feet.

*Please! Please*, she prayed. *Don't let him find me. All I need is five days.*

"Out of order," he muttered and moved away. "Always at least one."

Amy allowed herself a shallow breath, but she didn't move until the outside door squeaked open and swung closed. Putting her bare feet on the floor, she took a deep breath, followed by two more. Her heart raced. Dots danced in front of her eyes. She couldn't pass out. Leaning over, she put her head between her knees and waited.

Through the wall, she heard two voices in the men's restroom. Suddenly, she was afraid the truck driver had seen her. After another minute, the voices stopped. A toilet flushed. The outside door opened and shut. Twice. Then silence. Wonderful, safe silence.

She heard an engine start and wheels crunch on the snow—the patrol car leaving. The semi still rumbled in the background, idling the way trucks idle, sometimes for hours, while drivers sleep. She waited for what seemed like a long time, listening with the extra intensity she'd heard a blind person develops. Nothing.

Amy stood and left the stall. She was headed for the door to risk a peek out when the cell phone rang. Not music or bells, a buzz that ripped the silence she had begun to trust, announced her presence to the truck-driver or anyone who might have crept on foot into the rest area.

*Diego—Please don't tell let him have changed your mind!* Holding her breath, she put the phone to her ear.

"His phone *was* in the pickup. I thought it might be."

Not Diego's voice. Not a voice she recognized. A muffled

voice, a man's voice. "A very organized person, our Mahu. Are you an organized person, Amy Adams?"

Shock, as much as the need to keep silent, made her mute. Besides Diego, only one person on the planet could know she'd taken Mahu's pickup.

Mahu's attacker, the man who had chased her to the pickup and grabbed the door handle. How did he know her name? She trembled. Not her arms and legs, but her insides.

"I need the rest of the lienzo, Amy. You shouldn't have taken it."

*Lienzo?* "I don't know what you're talking about," she whispered.

"Don't bother lying to me, Amy. It tore when I tried to take it from him, and you have the other piece. You ran away, but I'll find you. I found Mahu, didn't I? Now, what do you say we make a little plan?"

Fighting the urge to throw up, Amy disconnected and turned off the phone. Every nerve screamed at her to run, but she forced herself to stay in the restroom. He couldn't know where she was, couldn't trace the cell phone without specialized equipment. And Diego was coming, would be there soon.

She waited, forcing herself to breathe. Calm in: one ... two ... three ... Fear out: one ... two ... When at last she could breathe normally, she forced herself to think. Mahu's attacker was after the scrap of cloth, the lienzo behind the seat of his pickup.

*What was it and why was it worth stealing?* An image of the arrow in Mahu's chest flashed her mind. *Was the lienzo worth killing for?*

A thousand or maybe only a hundred breaths later, she heard tires crunch on the snow. Her pursuer, the patrolman again, an unsuspecting tourist, Diego. One chance in four, but she had to know. She pushed the outside door open carefully so it didn't squeak and looked out.

17

The semi, its motor still idling, sat shrouded in snow. Mahu's pickup was where she had left it, covered with snow so that only the corner of the orange abandoned vehicle sticker the patrolman had placed on the windshield showed. A snow-dusted Jeep had pulled in beside the pickup.

The chances were down to one in three—her pursuer, a tourist, or Diego. The driver's door opened. Light glinted briefly off a pair of glasses. Suddenly the odds were good enough that Amy ran down the sidewalk, away from the confusion and fear of the last hour, toward help.

Diego stared at her and took a step back.

With a sick feeling she pictured what he saw—a barefoot girl in a darkly stained sleep shirt that hung to her knees. Long dark hair so matted and tangled it hid her face, both hands clenched into fists.

He looked confused. "Amy? Where's Mahu?"

She stopped just short of him, terrified he might turn away and leave her there. "He's hurt." She held out her hands with the phone to reassure him she wasn't armed. "I called 9-1-1."

"I thought he'd be with you."

"He was at the gallery." Her entire body trembled. "I guess he's at the hospital by now."

"You guess?" His tone sounded skeptical. Angry, even. "You didn't stay with him?"

"I couldn't! You don't understand." The tears she'd been holding back escaped, ran down her cheeks, mixed with snow, froze on her skin, stuck to her eyelashes. "I tried to help him. But the guy came after me. He's still after me!"

"The message on my cell—" Diego yanked open the passenger's door and half-helped, half-shoved her into the Jeep.

The dots returned. Amy put her head between her knees as Diego shut the door. Then he got in the other side and slammed his door. The motor started. Warm air rushed onto Amy's frozen feet. Ignoring the wave of dizziness that gripped her, she raised her head, dropped the cell phone, held out her hands to the heat. "The cloth." Her voice shook. "It's in Mahu's pickup, behind the seat."

"You have the lienzo?"

"You know what it is?"

"Yep. I know." Diego was already opening his door, letting in the cold that fought against the heater's welcome blast.

He returned in a heartbeat. Silent and grim, he handed her the scrap of cloth and swung the Jeep around to head for the interstate.

In the east, the sky lightened, not yet with sunrise but with predawn gray that pushed the snowflakes farther apart. Two exits later, Diego pulled into the parking lot of an all-night café. He turned off the motor but left the heater running. "Tell me what happened."

She couldn't tell him because she didn't know, not really. "I was asleep. Mahu was downstairs in the gallery."

Amy put her hands to her temples and pressed, trying to drive the image of Mahu curled in his own blood out of her head. "He fell and hit his head on a tall pottery vase. Someone stabbed him with an arrow. It wasn't from the gallery. I'm sure of it."

Diego frowned. "This is my fault."

# CHAPTER THREE

"If I'd gotten Mahu's call." Diego sighed. "If only I'd picked up his message, I could have met him at the museum. We could have locked the lienzo in my dad's office. None of this would have happened. You have to take it to the sheriff, Amy."

"No! He'll send me back to Virginia, and I'm not going."

Diego gave her a puzzled look. She wouldn't meet his gaze, refused to explain.

After a moment, his face cleared. "You're Mahu's twin. Mahu isn't eighteen yet. You're a minor. A high school kid—a runaway."

"I'm not a runaway! I graduated from high school last spring, and I'll be eighteen in five days. I came to Santa Fe to find my family, to find Mahu …" Her voice trailed off. Despite the heater, she shivered violently. She tried to stop but shivered even more.

"Okay. Remember, I'm one of the good guys." Diego reached in the back for a bundle and dropped it in her lap. "Mi madré is taller than you are, so these are going to be too big. But, hey. Anything's better than what you're wearing now, right?"

Amy made a sound that was somewhere between a sob and a laugh. She clutched the bundle to her chest.

"There's a sweatsuit, a coat, a pair of athletic shoes, and extra socks. I looked for mi madre's boots, but she must have them with her."

She wanted to thank him, but she was afraid she'd lose control if she spoke, descend into hysteria. All she could do was nod. She hoped he understood.

Diego opened the glove compartment and removed the plastic sleeve that held the car registration. He replaced the paper with the scrap of cloth.

When the lienzo was safely in the plastic, he slid it into his heavy leather jacket pocket and turned off the motor. The heater stopped, and when he got out, a quick blast of cold air rushed in.

"We'll talk more inside the café." The door closed, and he was gone.

At first, Amy sat in the dim vehicle, trying to comprehend where she was, who she was with, whose clothes were in her lap, and what had happened in the gallery. But it was no use. She was still completely disoriented, so she gave up.

She tugged on the sweatpants, shoved her feet into the two pairs of socks, and then slipped on the shoes. They would have been too big, but the extra socks helped. Replacing the blood-soaked sleep shirt with the clean sweatshirt was a relief beyond words. With a shudder that seemed to start somewhere around her heart and radiate out to her hands and feet, she shoved the sleep shirt under the seat.

The coat was green wool, a heavy car coat with deep pockets and a hood. Green and purple weren't a combination she would have chosen, but Amy was grateful for the warmth. Scooping Mahu's cell phone up off the floor, she dropped it into the coat's pocket and got out.

Snow still fell, but not as hard as it had earlier. Amy held her face up to the gray sky, letting the cold, wet flakes melt on her cheeks. They felt like tears, but they calmed her. Because the sky was crying, she didn't have to. Leaning down, she gathered handfuls of snow to scrub her face and matted hair. It wasn't a bath, but it helped. When she felt marginally cleaner, she pulled the hood over her wet hair and went into the café.

Diego waited on a bench near the door. When he saw her, he rose to his feet, tall and lanky. Under his leather jacket, his T-shirt was inside out. Dark stubble accentuated his jawline and upper lip. His glasses balanced on the bridge of his nose at a precarious angle, and his curls were so tangled Amy wouldn't have wanted to try to drag a comb through them.

"You look a lot better." He jabbed at his glasses and took her arm. "I got us a booth, and I ordered oatmeal. My mother always says oatmeal is good in emergencies."

Amy didn't want oatmeal, but she didn't tell him. What she said was, "I'll pay you back." It was a silly thing to say. She could never pay him back. Maybe for the oatmeal, but she could never pay him for believing her, for coming to get her, for not forcing her to go to the sheriff.

"Forget it." He slid into an empty booth already set with silverware rolled in paper napkins and brown plastic glasses of water.

Speechless and shaky, she sat across from him and reached for her glass. The water cleared her head, brought her out of the shock, at least a little bit. After a moment, she looked across the table. "What's this about, Diego? What is a lienzo?"

"A manuscript from the 1500s. Paper was scarce and didn't last, so the Spanish conquistadors wrote on linen or cotton." He took the plastic folder out of his pocket and carefully removed the scrap of cloth.

He spread it out gingerly, a frayed rectangle a little bigger than a three-by-five note card. Cramped handwriting in badly faded ink filled one side. Stylized stick figures covered the other.

"Pictures in a manuscript?"

"Not pictures. Pictographs. I'm almost afraid to say what I think this is." Diego's voice was so low she could hardly hear his words, but his body language shouted that he suddenly knew why this scrap of cloth was important enough to cause someone to follow Mahu and then attack him for it.

"What is it?"

"I'm no expert, so, I could be wrong."

"You could be right too. What do you think it is?"

"Pictographs on one side, Spanish writing on the other. What if this is a Spanish *translation* of a pictograph panel?"

"I don't get it. How can anyone translate art? Aren't pictographs and petroglyphs just pictures of life as it was? Or markers where there's water? How do you translate that?"

Diego looked up. "You're saying what most people think. Many serious researchers, including my dad, believe the petroglyphs are stories written on stone—like the hieroglyphics in the Egyptian pyramids. If the two sides of this manuscript say the same thing, this lienzo would be like the Rosetta Stone. It could unlock the meaning of the stories in the rocks."

"It's really valuable then."

"Yep."

"I wish your dad were here and we could lock it up! Whoever followed Mahu and attacked him is still after it. He's determined to get it."

"You say that like you know for sure. Did someone follow you to the rest area?"

Amy was finally warm. She shrugged off the coat. "He called me on Mahu's cell phone. He said he'd found Mahu and he would find me."

"Mahu's attacker called you on Mahu's cell? He has the number?"

"That man's number—" Amy pulled the phone from the coat pocket and turned it on. "Maybe it's in the list of calls."

The waitress, a tired-looking woman with gray hair, appeared with their order, but Amy didn't look up. The phone was different from hers, but she found the recent calls. *Unavailable.* Frustrated, she tried calling it. Nothing happened.

"No good?"

She shook her head.

"It was worth a try. Have some oatmeal. It's not as good as what mi madré makes, but it's not bad."

Amy closed the phone and put it back in the coat pocket. She gazed at the gray oatmeal. Without tasting it, she knew she couldn't eat it. In fact, she didn't think she could ever eat again. Drink more water maybe. "I can't eat. I have to know how Mahu is."

"You have to eat," Diego said. "I know it doesn't look too good, but it's okay. Cover it with raisins and try it."

"No thank you, Grandmother." Picking up her water glass, she drained it.

"We've got enough problems without you passing out from low blood sugar."

"I told you I can't eat! I have to know how Mahu is."

"At least take a few bites." Diego put down his spoon. "While you eat, I'll call the hospital. Deal?"

Amy rolled her eyes. "Deal. But I'm not promising any number of bites."

"Whatever."

Covering the oatmeal with brown sugar, Amy watched Diego get out his cell. She poured milk while he searched for the hospital's number. She ate two bites and heard him say into the phone, "Has Mahu Sekatewa been admitted?"

Amy stared at Diego. *My last name is Sekatewa. Not Adams —Sekatewa.* A long name but it tiptoed through her mind, softer than Adams. Se-ka-te-wa. Seka-tewa. She stopped eating, held her breath. Still, the name whispered to her. Sekatewa. Kaya Sekatewa.

Diego frowned. "I know you can't tell me anything about his

condition, but surely you can tell me if he's there. I'm his brother!"

A young busboy carrying a plastic pitcher headed for their table. As the tired-looking teen refilled their glasses, Diego put down his phone. "Nada."

"They wouldn't tell you anything?"

Diego shook his head. "I thought if the hospital could tell me he was there, we'd at least know he's alive."

Amy watched the retreating figure of the busboy. "He's alive. He's hurt. I don't know how bad it is, but I know Mahu is alive."

She felt Diego studying her, but she refused to look at him. He didn't believe her. His silence told her that. When the silence was unbearable, she forced herself to look at him. "What?"

He shrugged. "Isn't it obvious? How do you know? Mental telepathy or something?"

"Not mental telepathy. I just know I'd feel it if Mahu died. All those years, Grandmother Adams told me he didn't exist, but I dreamed about him. Mahu and I have a bond I can't explain. But I'm sure if he died, I would know the instant it happened. Argue all you want. I'm not changing my mind."

Diego held up his hands in mock surrender. "I don't want to argue. I believe you. I don't know why, but I do."

"Okay, then. You have to go to the hospital and get in to see him. I can't go because of the sheriff, but you can."

Diego shook his head. "I have to find X."

"X?"

"The creep who did this."

Amy started to object, say that was the sheriff's job. But she knew what he would say if she brought up the sheriff. "It's not your fault."

Diego was eating again. Between bites, he said, "Maybe it is. Maybe it isn't. The point is I'm going to find the guy. Mahu saved my life once. I owe him."

She heard it and wondered, but there wasn't time for a story.

"You owe him support at the hospital, not some wild goose chase after a criminal."

Diego gave her an exasperated look. "What could I do at the hospital? I doubt they'd even let me see him. Besides, I have a plan—a good one. While I was waiting for you to change clothes, I figured out where to start. But it's a long drive, so you'd better eat while you can."

Amy looked at the oatmeal, considered it, and pushed it away. "What are you talking about? Where are we going?"

"Old Oraibi. To see your grandfather. White Bear is a shaman. He might know what's going on."

*Old Oraibi. Home. White Bear. Ikwa.* Like her name, the words slid effortlessly through her mind. Except the words turned her internal world upside down and inside out.

Diego was still speaking, and she forced her attention back to him. "White Bear will want to' see you, Amy. And you have to tell him what happened to Mahu."

Suddenly nervous, she said, "I'll call. Let him know we're coming."

Diego shook his head. "Old Oraibi is a very traditional place. No phones. Not even electricity. We have to go. Try to eat a little more. I'll go pay."

The oatmeal was cold, but she ate a little. *Ikwa.* The name made her feel safe. Ikwa will know what to do. A memory or a promise? Either way, the thought gave her courage. She slid out of the booth and headed for the door.

The snow had stopped, and as Amy and Diego climbed into the Jeep, the sun was a brilliant gold ball balanced on the Sangre de Cristo Mountains. Something almost like hope whispered in Amy's mind. Mahu was badly hurt, but he was alive. She was in more trouble than she'd ever imagined, but Diego was here to help. Neither of them knew what was going on, but they would ask White Bear, her grandfather—*Ikwa.*

Diego turned the key in the ignition and looked at her. "It's about an hour to Albuquerque and a couple more from there to Gallup. All interstate. Try to sleep."

Amy let out a long breath and tried to release the sense of emergency. She leaned her head against the rest. She was safe, she was fed, she was clean. She was so tired.

As Diego backed out of the parking space and headed for the highway, she closed her eyes. For a few minutes, she drifted. Then as she began to sink toward sleep, the picture came—

Mahu on the floor, blood on his head and chest, blood on the floor, blood on her hands, on her sleep shirt.

She opened her eyes and sat up. Blacktop stretched ahead of them, a smooth ribbon of road flowing down a long hill that dropped from the mountains to the desert. But studying the vista spread out before her didn't help. The image still lingered, like a smear on a glass she struggled to see through. "I keep seeing him lying there," she said.

"Think about something else."

"Like what? Like that gruesome arrow?"

"No. Not that. Tell me how you met Mahu yesterday. When he and I were first getting to know each other, he told me he had a twin who was taken away by a strange grandmother when you were both little. Then a couple of weeks ago, he told me his twin would show up for their eighteenth birthday. But he didn't know how it was going to happen. How *did* it happen?"

"He knew I would be back?"

"Yep."

Amy leaned her forehead against window's cool glass and forced her mind back twenty-four hours—not even twenty-four hours, only about fourteen. The music. The haunting line of notes from a red cedar flute that wasn't a song. Tiny bits of sound she somehow knew.

"I was crossing the plaza, heading back to the gallery after making the bank deposit. He was sitting under the portico at the Palace of the Governors playing his flute. He had a few jewelry pieces spread out on a square of canvas, but all the shoppers had gone home. I stood and listened for a while. The music pulled me, so I walked over to him. He looked up, and when he saw me, he said, 'Kaya.'"

"*Sister.* He knew you as soon as he saw you. Did you know him?"

"It was so strange. I didn't know who he was, but when he said 'Kaya,' I said 'Mahu.' I didn't know who he was or why I said that name—it just came out of my mouth. Then he said, 'Twin. I knew our grandmother couldn't keep you forever.'"

"And you remembered what happened."

She shook her head. "Not then. I remembered that later. But I remembered *him*. Not the way he looks now, of course, but *him*." She paused with no idea how to explain.

"Like when someone comes into the room behind you and covers your eyes. You can't see them, but you know who it is."

Surprised, Amy turned and looked at Diego. "Exactly like that. How do you know?"

Diego grinned. "Mahu told me he thought it would be like that when you showed up. Of course, he remembered he had a twin, and he was expecting you sometime soon."

"Why did he think I'd be back for our birthday?"

"He said something about a prophecy White Bear taught him. He tried to explain it to me, but I was having a hard time with the idea of a twin sister, and I didn't listen as well as I should have. Moon Twins or ..."

*Moon Twins.* The shadow of a memory flitted across Amy's mind.

Diego was still talking. "... any idea what he meant?"

Amy reached for the shadow, but it vanished. She shook her head.

"Okay, then," Diego said. "The two long-lost twins recognized each other. Then what?"

Amy searched her mind for shadows. *Born for a destiny.*

"Hey, girl! You still here?"

Amy started. "What?"

"Did you and Mahu sit there and talk or what?"

Amy gave up on the shadow. "I had a million questions. I asked him to come to my room at the gallery. He told me about Taáta trying so hard to get me back ..." Her voice trailed off. After a moment she said, "Sorry. I can't think."

"Maybe you can sleep now."

"Maybe."

"I'll sing to you. Close your eyes and think about little lambs jumping over a fence."

Amy groaned. "It'll never work."

"Of course, it'll work. Brahms's lullaby always works. And before you object to my singing, I'll have you know this tenor has been heard in some of the finest churches in Europe."

Amy laughed.

"Don't laugh! You'll hurt my feelings. Besides, it's true. The youth choir at my church went on tour my junior year of high school." Reaching across the gear stick, he put his hand over her eyes and began to sing, "Lul-la-by and good-night ..."

Amy gave up. It was stupid. It would never work. But she was so tired. Diego's voice faded. She drifted, not quite dreaming, remembering. The mesa was quiet. The rain had stopped, and in shallow puddles, tiny frogs croaked tiny frog songs. "Not lambs," she murmured, "frogs."

## II. TAVANGWA [WEST]

Storytellers say when the People emerged from the Sipapuni, Masaw, guardian of the Fourth World, was there to greet them. "Welcome to this world," he said, "the most beautiful of all worlds. Here you can finally learn to live in harmony with each other and with Creation."

"We have tried three times before," said the oldest of the Singers, "and we have failed three times before."

Masaw nodded solemnly. "This time, you must follow the Plan of Creation," he said. "The clans must migrate to the Four Directions. Some of the clans will travel first to the West. When you reach the páso at the far edge, you must turn South and repeat your migration. At that páso migrate East. From the East, travel North.

"Other clans will travel first to the South, others to the East, and the rest to the North. When all the clans finish migrating, you will meet at the Center, the place of Harmony. There the sun, moon, and stars pause in their restless wanderings across the sky. Rain, snow, and wind breathe softly across the land, nurturing life. At the Center hunter and hunted dream together. Life is in full flower, and the harvest of prayers is collected. At the Center all of Creation sings in harmony."

31

*Masaw paused, and the people looked around at their neigh-bors, searching for their clan members. But the guardian wasn't finished. "This is World Complete," he warned. "The farther you travel on the Road of Life here, the more difficult your journey will become. At every crossroad, evil will whisper in your hearts, but you must resist the wrong choices. This is your last chance. This is the Fourth World, the last world the Creator will sing into being."*

*"How can we resist if evil whispers all around us?" someone asked.*

*"You must listen for the Song of Creation," said Masaw. "It will lead you."*

*"In the first worlds, the People forgot the Song," someone else said.*

*"In the Fourth World, you will have a helper," said Masaw. "The flute player will go with you. When you are in balance with one another, with nature, and with the universe, you will hear the Song, and you will know which way to go."*

# CHAPTER FOUR

A phone rang, a sound in Amy's nightmare, a sound that went on and on. Then someone shook her shoulder. "Wake up!" said Diego. "That's Mahu's phone! If it's X, I want to hear his voice."

Amy fought her way to consciousness, but Mahu's phone was in the green coat, and the coat was in the back. She unlatched her seatbelt and twisted awkwardly to reach it. The phone wasn't in the pocket she tried first. As her hand closed around it, the ringing stopped.

"Check the number," said Diego. "Maybe—"

Even before she could look, the phone rang again.

Diego held out his hand. "Give it to me. If X knows Mahu well enough to have his cell number, maybe I know him too. Maybe I'll know his voice."

"If you know his voice, he'll know yours. I'll answer. You listen." She punched the phone on and held it out so Diego could hear.

"You know why I'm calling," purred a whispery voice. "You still have the lienzo, don't you, Kaya honey?"

X knew *both* her names. Somehow that made her more vulnerable. She couldn't breathe, much less speak.

"It's time to make a plan. We can do it the easy way, or we can do it the hard way. You found Mahu, so you already know the hard way. You're too young to die, so maybe you're ready to try the easy way."

"You're threatening me!" said Amy. "What's so special about a scrap of cloth that you'd be willing to kill for it?"

"You don't need to know that," said the voice, harsh now. "All you need to know is an address: P.O. Box 2719, Santa Fe. Put it in an envelope and mail it to Boxholder. I want it tomorrow, which means you have two hours to find a Post Office."

"And if I don't?"

"You're a smart girl, Kaya honey. You figure it out." The connection dropped.

Amy shivered. "The only good thing is he doesn't know where I am."

"Let's make sure it stays that way," said Diego. "Turn off the phone, and we won't use it again. I doubt he has the equipment to trace calls, but I don't want to take the chance."

As they entered Albuquerque, Diego turned west onto I-40.

"Did you recognize the voice?" Amy said.

He shook his head. "Too disguised. It could have been a man or a woman."

"I know X is a man. He chased me to the pickup."

"But you didn't see his face?"

"It was too dark. There wasn't time."

"How big was he?"

Amy shrugged. "The only time I really got a look at him, he was reaching for the pickup's door. He wasn't remarkably tall or short, and he was wearing a bulky coat and a ski cap, so I don't know how heavy he is or what color hair or anything like that."

"So, you wouldn't recognize him if you saw him again?"

"Not a chance," she said. "Do you think he was just trying to scare me, or do you think he'd really try to kill me?"

"We don't want to find out. While you were asleep, I kept thinking about what must have happened. First point: The security alarms didn't go off. So, either X had the codes, or Mahu let him in without tripping the alarm. Second point: X stabbed Mahu—probably after he fell. If all X wanted was to put Mahu out of commission, there was pottery everywhere. He could have just knocked him out. X must have had half of the lienzo when Mahu fell, and yet he took the time to stab him with an arrow, an arrow that means something. That means that X had two goals—to get the lienzo and to kill Mahu. You saved your twin's life by getting downstairs so fast."

"But why would anyone want to kill Mahu? And why threaten me?"

"It has to be because the Moon Twins are somehow related to whatever's on that lienzo. Have you remembered anything about what you two are supposed to do?"

Amy shook her head. "While I was sleeping, I had a nightmare. The moon wasn't a beautiful silver disk in the sky. It was a hole in the universe, and something scary wanted to come through it ..." Her voice shook, and her body trembled. It was too much. Moon Twins, weird dreams, a murderer after them.

Diego put a gentle hand on her arm. "We have to stay calm, Amy. Think about something else."

"What does that help?" she blurted. "Pretend everything's okay and it will be?"

Diego winced. "Thought control is an esssential skill in dangerous situations. You don't ignore the problems—you just quit staring at them.

"Direct your attention to something else and take in the problem sideways. If you can do something about the problem, look at it straight on and do it. If not, focus on something small, something you *can* do something about."

"I thought you were studying archaeology, not psychology, Professor."

This time he didn't answer her. Finally, Amy took a deep breath and said, "I'm sorry. Sarcasm is my cure for everything."

He cleared his throat. "Here's the thing. I had a sister once. For about ten years. When she was eight, she was diagnosed with leukemia. For two years my parents and I watched her sort of fade away. After Lily died, my mother got really depressed.

"She went to counseling, and she learned skills to keep from going crazy. She taught my dad and me. Sometimes people take it the wrong way when I suggest things like that."

"I'm sorry," said Amy softly. "Sorry your sister died and sorry for my bad attitude. I'll do better. Something small. Like what?"

Diego thought for a moment. Then he said, "Your hair. It's a mess. I think there's a comb in the glove compartment."

"That might not be small." Amy laughed. "That might be medium, but I'll give it a try." She found the comb—under the lienzo. Suppressing a shudder, she retrieved it and set to work, pulling and unsnarling.

"Now sideways," said Diego. "You work at the Delgado Gallery and live upstairs. Tell me how you sweet-talked the Ice Queen into that arrangement."

"The Ice Queen?"

"Rebecca Delgado. She's one of the big donors to the museum, so I've known her for years. She's not exactly a warm, fuzzy person, eager to help out kids in trouble."

"So, you call her the Ice Queen?"

"Not me personally—the underlings of my ilk who scurry around trying to please her."

"Becky's been nice to me."

"I know she has. Explain."

Amy dropped her head and separated her hair into three handfuls. "I went to the museum looking for something that might give me a clue to who I was. It was before I met you—my first visit."

Raising her head, she braided her hair. "I was coming out, going down the steps, and Becky was coming in, going up the steps. She had a load of pottery storyteller dolls she was taking to the gift shop to sell. She caught the heel of her shoe. I grabbed the box before it fell. She said I saved her a thousand dollars."

Diego whistled.

Amy crossed two strands of hair and reached for a third. "Becky bought me lunch at the museum café, and we started to talk. After lunch, she invited me to the gallery. She asked if I needed a job and a place to stay."

Diego frowned but didn't comment.

Amy finished her braid. "I hope you have a rubber band."

"Maybe in the glove compartment. Why did she want you to come to the gallery?"

Amy found an ancient rubber band around an even more ancient car manual. She twisted it around the end of her braid, carefully so it wouldn't break. "She wanted to show me her magic collection."

"Now we're getting somewhere. How did that come up?"

"I don't know exactly. She said something about the story-teller dolls being good magic and what a tragedy it would have been if she'd broken them. I said something about needing a little bit of good magic myself.

"I didn't mean anything by it. I don't believe in magic or anything like that, but she thought I was serious. She said she's studied magic all over the world and asked if I wanted to see her special room. I went."

"I bet she kept after you about the magic."

Amy shifted uncomfortably and pulled at her seatbelt. He was more right than he knew, but she didn't want to admit to playing along to keep her job. So, she didn't answer directly. "Becky's kind of a fanatic. Have you seen her collection?"

"Nope. I've certainly heard about it, but you know how rumors are. I haven't known what to believe. Some people say she's a witch."

Amy forced a laugh. "There isn't a single bottle of dragon's scales or eye of newt."

"But, something bothers you."

Amy sighed. "The pieces are all beautiful—a gold and black head of Nefertiti, a little marble statue of Artemis, and a carved eagle dancer. She's got some jewelry—a gold ankh, a silver medallion designed like the Aztec calendar, an old pawn squash blossom necklace. There isn't one specific thing that makes me uncomfortable ... unless it's the painting of Mami Wati."

"Who or what is *Mami Wati*?"

"The painting is of a beautiful black-skinned woman with wild hair. She's dressed in a patchwork of blood-red, white, and emerald green, and she has an enormous snake looped around her waist, her left wrist, and across her shoulders. Becky told me she's a Brazilian high priestess or an African water deity or a reinvention of the Egyptian goddess Isis."

"Long life."

"What?"

"All the things in her collection symbolize long life. The Ice Queen had open-heart surgery a couple of years ago. That's when she really got into the magic stuff."

"I didn't know that. In a way, it explains things. She's too young for heart trouble. Mr. Delgado is older, but she's in her late twenties."

"The Ice Queen is thirty-one."

"Don't call her that! Even if she is a bit nutty, Becky has always been nice to me. And not just me. She was nice to Mahu too."

"Mahu?"

"Becky was leaving the gallery when we got there. I intro-duced them, and she stayed to talk a minute. She recognized his name and invited him to bring some of his jewelry to show her some time."

"So, the Ice—Mrs. Delgado knows your story?"

"Not all of it. When Becky hired me, I told her I was an orphan trying to track down my family. She was excited that I'd found my twin."

"Does she know you're not eighteen?"

"I'll be eighteen in five days!"

"Hey, I'm just asking if she knew you weren't eighteen when she hired you."

"I'm not stupid, Diego."

"Just a little bit dishonest."

"I suppose you always tell the truth, the whole truth, and nothing but ..."

"Yep."

"You don't!"

"Do!"

"Don't!"

"Do!" But he laughed. "Lighten up, girl. I'm not criticizing you. I'm just wondering how long it will take your boss to find your grandmother to tell her about her injured grandson—and discover that legally you're an underage runaway. Did you give her your Virginia address?"

Amy was about to answer when the wail of a siren cut her off. Twisting to look over her shoulder, she saw a patrol car, lights flashing, rapidly catching up to them. "Diego!"

Shrugging, he slowed and pulled onto the shoulder. The patrol car sped past. A mile or so ahead, a second patrol car crossed from the other side of the divided highway and roared after the first one.

Amy shuddered. "I thought the sher—"

"It's too soon," Diego said. "Besides, the sheriff doesn't know to look for you with me."

A semi rumbled past, then a pickup hauling a horse trailer.

Finally, there was a break in the traffic, and Diego pulled onto the highway. When they were up to speed, he spoke again. "Did you give the Ice Queen your grandmother's address?"

Amy shook her head. "She didn't question me about my background. She seemed to think I'd been sent to her."

"When the teacher is ready, the student will come."

"What?"

"You know the saying 'When the student is ready, the teacher will come'? Maybe she thought of it the other way around. She was ready to be a teacher, and you showed up."

Amy considered. "You might be right, but you can't have it both ways. An Ice Queen wouldn't want to teach anyone anything."

"No, but a witch might."

"Stop it!" Amy reached to turn on the radio. "We've got enough problems without imagining witches on our trail."

The choice of music was country western or country western, but it got them down the road without any more disagreements. At Grants, Diego pulled into a truck stop. "I want to fill up," he said. "The gauge on the Jeep isn't exact."

Amy unhooked her seatbelt, stretched, and got out. The air was warmer than it had been in Santa Fe. It felt good to move. The women's restroom was empty. She took extra time, splashing warm water on her face and washing her hands and arms up to the elbows.

Diego waited for her by the outside door. His dark curls were damp, and his T-shirt was right side out. "Hungry?"

Amy smiled and shook her head. "That oatmeal stuck to my ribs. I'm thirsty, though."

"I bought a case of bottled water." He opened the glass door and held it for her. "I like to keep a supply when I'm traveling." Then he was gone, loping across the parking lot.

Amy followed more slowly, watching his quick movements. She wondered if his girlfriend was a runner. Surprised, she realized she didn't know if he had a girlfriend. Or what kind of girls he liked.

When she climbed into the car, he handed her a water bottle and gave her a searching look. "You okay?"

She shrugged. "I keep thinking I should be at the hospital. It's been so long since I knew Mahu, but the bond is there—just like we were never separated."

Diego turned on the engine and headed for the highway. "Mahu's a strong, determined guy. We can help him more by finding out who did this and why."

Traffic was sparse but moving fast. They passed a battered station wagon filled with restless kids and a pickup hauling water. A new Cadillac with tinted windows passed them.

In Gallup, Diego pulled into the parking lot of a big grocery store, busy with Sunday customers from all over the reservation.

"Food?" asked Amy.

"Nope. A mailing envelope and stamps."

"You think we should send the lienzo to that P.O. Box?"

"It's the safest thing to do."

"Maybe. Maybe not. What if he takes it and still comes after me?"

"Any suggestions for motive?"

Amy unhooked her seatbelt and shifted nervously. "I don't know. Maybe trying to keep the Moon Twins from turning eighteen in five days."

"White Bear's prophecy. Have you remembered it?"

She shook her head. "All I remember is a serious feeling about being a Moon Twin, something important we had to do when we grew up. I want to ask Ikwa what he thinks we should do. If he thinks we should mail it, we can do it tomorrow."

"A day late."

"So? X will spend tomorrow trying to figure out where I am."

41

Diego reached for her shoulders and turned her to face him. "Maybe X won't wait for Tuesday to see if it comes."

"Maybe not." She pulled away. "But I don't care. When Mahu found it, the lienzo became his responsibility. Now it's mine."

"Maybe so, but I'm pretty sure Mahu wouldn't want you to take any more risks for it."

"He took a big risk bringing it to Santa Fe."

"That was different."

She shook her head. "To be Moon Twins, there have to be two of us. He's one. I'm the other. All I'm doing is following Mahu's lead."

# CHAPTER FIVE

Diego frowned. "Following Mahu's lead is dangerous, Amy. X practically threatened to kill you if you don't put the lienzo in the mail right now."

"I don't care! I want to show it to Ikwa and ask him what he thinks we should do."

Still he sat in the Jeep, not turning on the engine to get back on the road or opening his door to enter the grocery store.

Amy crossed her arms. "You set out to find out who did this to Mahu and why and I came along. We already knew X was dangerous. We can't quit because he's making more threatening phone calls."

She held out her hand. "Give me the keys. I want to go on, and I want to drive."

"You don't have your license with you."

"I need to *do* something, Diego. I feel absolutely useless. You need rest as much as I do. I'll stick to the speed limit, and I won't get pulled over."

He shrugged. "I could use a break, I guess."

They switched places. After she got them safely out of the parking lot and on the highway, he put his glasses in the glove compartment. "We won't see won't much traffic on this stretch of road but watch for livestock. Hitting a cow or a sheep is complicated—and expensive—on the rez."

"I'm a good driver. Go to sleep."

Diego let his seat back. "All you have to do is stay on 264. We cross into Arizona about twenty-five miles from here near Window Rock. From there, it's about a hundred miles to Keams Canyon. If I'm still sleeping when we get there, wake me up."

She nodded and glanced at him. "Want me to sing to you?"

He closed his eyes. "No need."

Within a mile or two, his breathing had slowed, and shortly after, Amy heard soft snoring. It felt good to drive. As the miles slipped by, she relaxed enough to notice her surroundings. The sky shone the same intense blue she had dreamed for twelve years. Nothing else looked familiar.

The long empty stretch of blacktop wound up low hills dotted with pinyon pines or dropped into dry flats where she saw an occasional dust devil spinning. Here and there, a deeply rutted dirt road took off into open land. Eventually, she saw a stoplight in the distance changing from green to red and back to green. Just before she reached the light, a sign said, "Leaving New Mexico. Please come again."

Arizona. Was she home? The stoplight turned red. The empty highway continued west, but a sign pointed right to Window Rock, one of the landmarks Diego mentioned.

She turned. A couple of miles later, they reached the capitol of the Navajo Nation. It was noon. Dusty pickups appeared from nowhere, depositing passengers at a laundromat, a convenience store, and a various fast-food restaurants. Then the town was behind them. Amy saw an immense stone window worn through red rock by wind and sand. Without warning, the memories began.

Kaya looked up at a red rock tower that reached into a bright blue sky. Mahu was there, and Mama and Taáta. In the distance, they saw other free-standing monuments rising abruptly from the flat desert floor. Taáta pointed and said the names—Left and Right Mitten, Ear of the Wind, Gray Whiskers.

Mama laughed at herself, at the way she struggled with the names that rolled so easily off the children's tongues. 'I'll get it, Wilson,' she promised. 'I'll learn to speak Hopi without a trace of an accent. Even your family will forget I'm an outsider.'

Taáta leaned over and kissed Mama. 'You're not an outsider. You're my wife, and I love your accent. The way I love everything about you.'

The Jeep caught up with a red Ford pickup at a stop sign. A little girl riding in the back with three boys waved. As the pickup turned right, she saw three adults in the cab—Dad, Mom, and Grandma. The family was going home.

In her memory, the sky was gold and peach. Taáta said they were going home.

A word whispered in Amy's memory. *Nima,* going home. Was she going home now? If so, which way? The pickup had gone toward Sheep Springs. The road to the left went to Sawmill.

Straight ahead, she saw Ft. Defiance High School. Diego hadn't mentioned any of those towns. With no other vehicle in sight, Amy considered. Overhead the sun had passed its midpoint enough that she knew they were headed north, not west.

The stoplight! Diego said they would go by Window Rock, not through Window Rock. She'd mixed up the directions. Making a U-turn, she headed back.

*Ni-ma, nima, nima!* The word chanted in her head, and as she listened, a window opened in her mind. Or not a window, a door into a forgotten room, the room where Kaya could always find Mahu, the room Grandmother Adams had convinced her was only her imagination.

The door stood open, inviting her into a space of copper-

45

colored earth, brilliant blue sky, and dry wind, a space once filled with home's warmth and safety. Now a place where Mahu dreamed the song of a flute. She drove, knowing her twin slept.

With Ganado far behind them, Diego opened his eyes and stretched. He woke as abruptly as he'd gone to sleep. "How are you doing? Want me to drive?"

She shook her head. "I'm fine. " She didn't want to talk about her twin and his dreams, so she said, "I remembered things. Just bits and pieces, but memories from before Grandmother Adams."

Diego found his glasses and reached for his water bottle. "Good ones?"

"Mmm. It's strange to be able to remember that far back. Up until now, it's like I was born when I started school."

Diego twisted off the cap and drank. "In a way, you probably were. The transition from reservation to town was over. Your family, your language, everything familiar was gone." He drank some more.

When she didn't speak, he continued, "You were assimilated. Your memories were confusing, especially when your grandmother contradicted them. So, you let them go. You were reborn as the child your grandmother wanted."

She gave him a curious look. He caught her eye and laughed. "That information was from a report I wrote in fifth grade on brainwashing during the Korean War. Take it for what it's worth."

"It's worth a lot." Another memory came. Grandmother Adams was scolding her. 'You're too old for an imaginary playmate. Not another word about this Mahu, or you'll go to bed without supper.'

Without knowing it, Diego interrupted Grandmother Adams. "You were kidnapped, Amy. Unfortunately, a lot of that happened in the past, and not so long ago. States took Native American children away from their families, shipped them off to boarding schools in strange cities, and tried to eradicate their cultures—including their languages."

Diego took another long drink of water. "Why didn't your grandmother take both of you? Mahu is as much her grandchild as you are."

"I don't think she wanted her grandchildren. What she wanted was to replace my mother. She needed a girl for that."

Diego made a disgusted sound. "That couldn't happen today. It was illegal for an Anglo grandparent to take a child from the rez when you were little, but once it was done, your father would have had to file a lawsuit. Courts take time."

"I'm sure she found a lawyer to make her case to a judge, and I'm sure the judge gave her what she wanted. No one ever stood up to Grandmother Adams."

"Not until her granddaughter decided to find out who she was."

Amy felt him studying her, and suddenly she was embarrassed. "I was desperate."

"Or determined. Like now."

"Desperate usually makes me determined."

"Good. Does anything look familiar?"

She shrugged. "Not really."

"It might start feeling like home when we get up to the mesas. If you want me to drive so you can concentrate on the landscape, there's a good spot to pull off coming up."

Nima. Sing or cry? Too confused to explain, she shrugged. "Sure."

They pulled off at the turn to Keams Canyon. Diego nodded at the road. "An outpost of Hopi land in the middle of Navajo land. One of the so-called compromises of the Navajo-Hopi land dispute."

Hopiland. A strange excitement filled Amy Kaya. *Nima!*

At first, the road cut straight across an expanse of grassland. It crossed a dry wash, identifiable as a streambed only by the

47

ribbon of sand that snaked north. Then the road climbed into blue-white sky that stretched to infinity. A low and flimsy guardrail bordered the road offering no comfort as the desert floor dropped away.

At the top, the mesa spanned horizon to horizon. They drove through villages with strange-sounding names—Polacca, Mishongnovi, Shungopavi. They passed flat-roofed pueblos strung together like a one-story multiplex. They passed free-standing houses marked with signs that told tourists where they could buy silver jewelry.

But nothing looked familiar, nothing looked like home. The excitement she'd felt in Keams Canyon gradually gave way to an emptiness as vast as the grassland they'd crossed.

It was early afternoon when Diego said, "White Bear isn't expecting us. I don't want to go into Old Oraibi unannounced. I'm going to stop in Hotevilla at the Hopi Cultural Center to see if someone knows where we can find him."

"Why? If he's not home, can't we just wait?"

Diego shook his head. "Remember I said Old Oraibi is very traditional? Folks there take a dim view of visitors. The village is closed to outsiders. Whenever I've been here before, I've been with Mahu. It'll be better if we can find White Bear before going in."

He slowed and pulled into a graveled drive that skirted a large Cultural Center sign and took them into a paved parking area. The lot was full, but he found a spot between a silver Airstream and a pop-up tent trailer.

Beyond the vehicles in the sparse shade of an alligator juniper, a Hopi woman who might have been twenty or forty had her wares spread out on a table. Familiar with the museum-quality pieces sold in Becky's gallery, Amy immediately knew these necklaces and bolo ties were inexpensive imitations, cheap souvenirs of "Indian Country."

A middle-aged man in a yellow knit shirt picked up a T-shirt and held it out for his wife to see as they watched. The printing on the shirt said, Don't worry. Be Hopi.

*I'm not Hopi. When I was little, when I was Kaya, I was Hopi. But now?* "I don't belong here! I don't even know who I am. Am I Amy Adams, tourist, or am I Kaya Sekatewa, Hopi? Either way, I'm an outsider, and I won't be welcome in Old Oraibi. This was a mistake, Diego."

"Maybe so, but it's too late to change our minds now. Besides, the folks here like tourists *and* Hopis, anyone who'll spend a little money."

She laughed, and for that moment, everything was okay. Amy Kaya opened her door and got out. It was early afternoon, warm enough to leave the coat behind, but cool enough she was grateful for the purple sweatshirt. Soon she'd get some clothes of her own. But not a T-shirt that said, Don't worry. Be Hopi.

The modest Cultural Center complex sat beyond the parking lot. A small museum, a one-story hotel and restaurant, and an ancient stone wall created a small plaza dominated by a large chunk of black basalt. Diego took her hand and started toward the hotel. Her hand relaxed in his, just as it had when he'd taken it in the Santa Fe restaurant.

Like they were a couple of kids. Okay for now, but maybe someday something more. Maybe.

The lobby seemed almost dark after the bright midday. Diego crossed the room without hesitation. He approached a long counter labeled Hotel Check-in and hit the small metal bell. Amy followed more slowly, grateful the wooden benches along the walls were empty except for several copies of well-read newspapers.

A young Hopi woman emerged from a back room. She wore a dark woven dress that set off a striking silver and turquoise necklace. Her long black hair was twisted up at the nape of her neck and secured with a silver and turquoise comb. She saw

Diego and smiled warmly. "Hupko, brother, it's good to see you."

"Helen." Diego returned the smile. "It's good to see you too."

A flash of jealousy pricked Amy, but she pushed it away. Now was not the time. Someday maybe. But not now.

"Is Mahu with you?" Helen looked expectantly toward the door.

"No." Diego's smile vanished. "I have his twin with me."

The other girl looked at Amy, comprehension dawning. "Kaya," she said with a sort of wonder. "Mahu's been talking about you for months. He said you'd be back for your birthday. But if he's not with you, where is he?"

"In the hospital in Santa Fe," Amy said slowly. "Dreaming."

"It's a long story," Diego said. "He was attacked early this morning."

"The lienzo," Helen whispered. "Ya-Ya."

"You know about it then?"

Helen sighed. "We all know about the lienzo. Heavy rains shifted some big rocks near Flute Spring last week. Mahu found an old Ya-Ya cave no one knew was there. He found the lienzo inside with some other stuff. But the lienzo caused all the controversy. A few traditionalists wanted to burn it, but Mahu insisted it was an important archaeological find. He wanted your father to take charge of it. He went to Santa Fe to find you."

Diego frowned. "He was attacked before we connected,"

"Do you know who attacked him?"

Diego looked at Amy. "A man," she said. "That's all I know. We've come to tell my grandfather."

"Helen," Diego said, "do you know where we can find White Bear?"

"I'll ask."

She ducked into the back room. Diego looked at Amy. "We haven't had much to eat today. The restaurant here is good."

Amy shook her head.

Helen reappeared. "White Bear and some other carvers went for cottonwood roots." "They should be back soon. Have you had lunch?"

"I could eat a horse," Diego said, "but Amy's not hungry."

"Never mind." Helen picked up menus and rounded the counter. "One bite of our mutton stew, and you'll be hungry. The best on the rez."

She led the way into the bright dining room. Log beams crisscrossed the ceiling. Booths with high wooden backs ran around the walls, and tables with hand-carved chairs filled the center. Like the parking lot, the restaurant was comfortably full. Helen stopped beside a booth carved with stylized semi-circle clouds and perpendicular rainfall. "A good luck table," she said.

"We need all the luck we can get," Amy said.

Helen caught Amy's eyes and held them with her own. "Mahu told me you'd be back for your birthday, Kaya, and here you are. He'll be here too. He may be hurt, but he's strong."

Kaya nodded.

As Helen turned away, Kaya looked for the door in her mind.

It was still open. *Be strong, Mahu!* Wishing him her twin strength, she suddenly remembered how it felt. A long time ago, she had wished Mahu her strength. He pushed away a bully twice his size. It felt like that now. Except the bully wasn't a person. It was death. *Push it away, Mahu.*

Diego slid into the booth and looked up at her curiously. "You okay, Amy?"

Kaya pulled herself back into the restaurant and gathered up the threads of Amy.

"What?" he said as she sat down.

She searched for words. Finally, she said, "I don't know how to explain it to you, but I can sense Mahu again. It's been happening a little bit at a time. When we were little, we always knew what the other was feeling. I forgot."

51

He studied her and then reached across the table for her hands. She put hers in his and felt her tension drain away. Kaya or Amy, it didn't matter to Diego. Almost as if he were Mahu and sensed her thoughts, he said, "What am I going to call you, girl?"

She smiled and shrugged. The waitress, a teenaged girl with a friendly face and a comfortable figure, appeared with water and silverware. "You two ready to order?"

Diego released Kaya Amy's hands. "Hi, Bea. Mutton stew for me."

Mutton stew for supper, remembered Kaya. But never at Grandmother Adams's house.

"Miss Kaya?"

Kaya smiled and nodded. Bea left, and Amy turned toward Diego. "Did Mahu talk about me so much that everyone knows who I am?"

"Nope. But everybody remembers your story. It's an archetype. Child carried off by evil beings—gypsies, fairies, kidnappers. In your case, a prejudiced Anglo—unfortunately, another archetype on the rez. Your reappearance is the 'happily ever after' ending."

Kaya sighed.

"Diego James!" The voice was loud and angry.

They looked toward the doorway. A powerfully built man in his late twenties bore down on them. His frown matched the tone of his voice.

"Who is that?" whispered Kaya.

Diego grimaced. "Yukioma. He's an old-style preservationist who preaches keeping anyone who isn't full-blooded Hopi off the reservation. He hates my guts."

"Why?"

"You'll see."

Yukioma towered over them. "Diego James," he growled. "You know you're not welcome here. And if you think you're going to go to Old Oraibi, think again. We haven't got the reservation closed yet, but that village is off-limits."

"You must have spies everywhere," said Diego. "I've only been here a few minutes."

The big man grunted. "No spies. I was working in Special Collections at the museum. I heard the Conquistador and the other half-breed twin were here for stew."

Diego got to his feet, almost as tall as Yukioma but only half his weight. "I know you don't like me," he said, "and it seems you've decided not to like Kaya without bothering to get to know her. But like us or not, we have the right to be here. We came to see White Bear."

"To tell him the meddler is in the hospital? Someone else can do that."

Diego stepped closer. "Are you the one who put him there? Helen said there was a controversy, and wherever there's a fight, you're in the middle of it. You probably wanted to burn the lienzo."

Yuki snorted. "Anything connected with Ya-Ya should be burned. But you're missing the point, Conquistador. The point is we don't want you or your friend here."

"Yukioma," said Helen, who had come up behind him unnoticed, "this is a restaurant, not a place for public debate. If you want to eat, find a table. If you don't, you need to leave."

Yuki looked down at Helen. Amy saw the frustration on the big man's face and knew when he decided to give up. "It's not over, Conquistador," he snarled.

Helen put her hands on her hips. "It's over here, Yuki."

Yuki gave her a hostile glare but turned and stalked off.

"I'll talk to him." Helen followed Yuki out.

"Just stay out of his way," said Bea, who had been waiting at a nearby table. As she put their bowls of steaming stew in front of them, she added, "Yuki doesn't have any real power."

Kaya Amy let out her breath. "He sure talks like he does."

"Nah," said Bea, turning away. "Whenever it comes to a vote, he gets voted down."

When she was gone, Kaya Amy said, "Do you think Yuki could be X?"

Diego shrugged and scooped stew with fry bread. "I don't think it was him on the phone, but the voice was so disguised, I can't be sure."

"But, you accused him."

"I was mad, and it sort of fit into the conversation. Yuki's a bigot and a bully, but I'm not sure he would attack Mahu."

Diego took another bite of stew and sighed. "Hungry or not, girl, this is good. What do you say we forget him and eat?"

She didn't think she could forget Yuki, but the aroma of the stew—the tang of mutton, the rich smell of tomatoes, the sweet scent of onions—pulled her home. *Nima* ...

## CHAPTER SIX

Amy took a tentative bite of the stew, expecting a new flavor. Instead, she remembered ... She stood beside Mama in the plaza, watching a kachina dance. The dancers, all wearing brightly colored costumes and bells on their shoes, handed out gifts to the children. Kaya was learning their names, so she knew a Mudhead kachina handed her a fat red carrot. 'Yum,' Mama said. 'We can put your carrot in some mutton stew.'

Diego's soft voice brought her back to the stew in her bowl. "More memories?"

Kaya smiled. "Maybe coming here wasn't a mistake."

"Ready to go on?"

"Soon. But, Diego, what is Ya-Ya?"

He pushed his empty bowl away and leaned back. "Nobody talks about it, especially not to outsiders, so I don't know much. All I know is the tribe outlawed the ceremony years ago. Supposedly it was forgotten, but every now and then, people whisper that witches still perform it. Ya-Ya has sort of become a synonym for witchcraft."

"So, since Mahu found the lienzo in an old Ya-Ya cave, Yuki thinks it's tainted by witchcraft and should be burned?"

"Yep."

"But that's a lot of superstitious nonsense."

"Depends on your perspective, I guess. But don't worry about Ya-Ya. With Yuki's determination to get rid of anything remotely associated with Ya-Ya, we won't run into any witches around him."

"I'm worried about X, not witches."

Diego indicated her empty bowl. "If you're done, let's go see if White Bear's home."

"Okay. The stew was delicious. I'm glad I ate."

He smiled at her—a warm, uncomplicated smile. Her heart turned over, and she felt a blush warm her cheeks. *Not now, not now!* Too late.

Diego practically jumped to his feet. "I'll pay. Why don't you go on out?"

Wishing he hadn't noticed, she followed Diego to the cash register. He stopped, but she kept moving. He was cute and smart and sweet, but this wasn't a date. And it was no time to fall for him.

The basalt in the center of the plaza drew her. She looked closer. Petroglyphs covered the surface, the largest a white line that snaked around a center point in decreasing concentric circles until it seemed to disappear into the stone. Or maybe it started in the center and swung out.

On one side of the circle petroglyph, a handprint was scratched into the stone, lower down a goat and a snake with a square head. But the glyph that held her attention was the flute player. She could almost hear the music. She listened and knew Mahu dreamed notes that climbed the scale and slid back down. With one finger, she traced the crooked shape.

"Kokopelli." Diego stood beside her.

"What song does he play?" A silly question, but Mahu's music intrigued her.

Diego took her question seriously. "No one knows. Archaeologists think he might have been a trader. The hump was his pack, and the flute let villagers know his approach was peaceful."

"Sometimes, I've imagined Mahu dreams Kokopelli's song."

"Maybe he does. Once he told me Kokopelli plays the Song of Creation."

Determined to put things between them back on the right footing, she looked up at him—sister to brother. "What's the Song of Creation?"

He met her eyes and shrugged. "No idea. Mahu didn't say."

Things were okay again.

Amy examined the haunting little figure. "Maybe it's the song of how life was meant to be. Friendship, beauty, peace."

Diego pulled the keys out of his pocket. "The things we're going to restore for Mahu."

Walking slowly, Amy followed Diego toward the parking lot. For the first time, she actually looked at their vehicle—a Jeep Cherokee so old the original paint had faded from green to almost white. When Diego picked her up at the rest area, she was so relieved to get away, she hardly noticed his vehicle.

Even when she took a turn at the wheel, she only noticed it was a stick shift and easy to drive. The Jeep wasn't beautiful, but Diego took care of it.

"It isn't far." Diego turned the key in the ignition.

They'd only gone a couple of miles when he turned into the paved parking lot of a pink cement block building. The words "Art Gallery" marched across a plate glass window, followed by smaller letters that spelled out "Kachinas" and "Jewelry." A world apart from Becky's gallery, but Amy wondered if some of the pieces Becky sold came from here, considerably marked up.

Except for a metallic blue Lexus, the lot was empty. Diego

didn't park. Instead, he drove around the building, off the pavement, and bounced them into a vacant lot, a stretch of bare dirt where three beat-up pickup trucks sat parked beside a scraggly juniper.

He turned off the motor. "We'll walk from here. No cars allowed in Old Oraibi." He got out, opened the back of the Jeep, and removed something.

Still, Amy sat. He opened her door, but she didn't move.

"Something wrong, girl?"

She stared at the barren landscape ahead that was supposed to be home. Sparse, thirsty-looking gray-green plants topped the hard-packed ground. Tumbleweeds proved something the size of a small bush grew somewhere on the mesa, but not here.

The warm feelings she experienced eating the mutton stew vanished. "Nothing looks familiar. I can't imagine a child being happy here."

Plopping a heavy net bag in her lap, Diego reached across her and unhooked her seatbelt. "Fight it," he said, retrieving the lienzo from the glove compartment. "Focus on something small. Your job is to carry the oranges."

For the first time, she looked down at them. "Where did they come from?"

"The truck stop. When I bought the water, I got them as a gift for White Bear."

She thrust them back at him and got out. "They're from you. You do the small thing and carry them."

"Okay. You're going to see your grandfather, but you're pouting about it?"

She crossed her arms over her chest and glared. "Yep."

He laughed. "Whatever."

They followed a footpath that wasn't much more than a line in the red dirt. After several hundred yards, it intersected a road, a dirt road that might have been a wagon track. It had to be the road Grandmother Adams came down when she took her away, but Amy couldn't remember it. Everywhere she looked, the landscape was alien. No telephone poles, no electric cables, no propane tanks. A rag fluttered from a stick. Weathered two-by-fours propped up crumbling red adobe walls.

Diego pointed to a crude ladder that went down into the earth. "That's the entrance to the kiva," he said, "the most important gathering place in the pueblo—an underground room dug out generations ago with stone tools."

"Why?" she demanded. "Why live like this?"

"Simple. The residents want to protect the old ways. The Bear Clan settled in this spot when they completed their migrations, so this is an extraordinary place. Sort of like Plymouth Rock—except about 800 years older."

*Nima* whispered in her mind. "The Bear Clan. That's why my grandfather is named 'White Bear.'"

"Yep."

"Mahu's clan. My clan."

"Nope. You and Mahu don't have a clan. Hopis are a matrilineal culture."

She put a hand on his arm to make him stop walking. "You're saying because Mama wasn't Hopi, we don't have a clan? I guess prejudice works both ways."

"It's more complicated than that, Amy, and I refuse to pit kidnapping against a sociological pattern that's been functioning for thousands of years."

"Stop!" she blazed. "Stop talking like a professor. I was right. I don't belong here!"

Juggling the oranges to free a hand, Diego pushed his glasses up on his nose. Frowning, he snapped, "We're not here because you're a member of the Bear Clan. We're here because you're Mahu's twin and you want to ask your family for help solving this mystery."

She stared at him. Amy knew he was right but resisted. Finally, she gave up and looked away. "My head is a mess. One minute I feel like I'm home, and the next, I feel like an outsider. I don't mean to take it out on you."

He didn't answer with words, just smiled, and held out the oranges.

As she reached for the bag, she heard the flute—a low sustained note with a hint of vibrato, a high note that chirped suddenly like a bird, a middle note weaving in and out of the other two. *Nima.*

"That path up there!"

Then she ran. Kaya ran home.

The path took her to a low adobe house attached on both sides to others like it. Ikwa sat in a sunny spot beside a hand-made ladder that led to the flat roof—an old man with iron-gray hair corralled by a yellow bandana twisted into a headband. Feeling suddenly shy, she came to an abrupt stop.

He was whittling, and under his knife, the oddly curved cottonwood root took on a new form. As the metal blade flashed in the sun, images of tihu flashed in her memory, small flat pieces of wood she used to learn the names of the spirits who came to dance. She and Mahu both loved the brightly colored figures, but he was the one who remembered the names easily.

In the silence, the flute song continued, tiny bits of sound following one another up and down the scale, echoing in a song that couldn't be sung. Gradually the names came back to her. Butterfly Maiden, Mudhead, Black Ogre, Eagle Dancer ...

White Bear looked up and saw her. Putting down his whittling, he rose stiffly to his feet. He wasn't as tall as she remembered, but his back was straight. "Come, Moeyha," he said, opening his arms wide. "All day I have waited for you."

Moeyha, little grandchild. Not Kaya. *Moeyha.* Smiling and crying, she ran into his arms.

He held her until the smiles won. Then he kissed the top of her head, released her, and turned. "Welcome, Diego James."

Diego handed him the bag of fruit. "Thank you, sir."

With the twinkle Moeyha remembered, White Bear said, "Please come inside. I have some oranges to offer you."

As soon as she stepped over the threshold, her mother's voice came from somewhere deep in her memory, softly reciting the mantra that had been like a lullaby. 'The flat roof above covers us as Father Sky covers us while we walk life's trails. The dirt floor beneath cradles us like Mother Earth cradles when we lie down to die.' Kaya Moeyha felt warm. And safe. Nima.

The room looked exactly like a room should look, an uncluttered space brightened by patterns of sunshine. A faded flowered sheet partitioned one corner. The furniture consisted of an ancient woodstove, a stack of mattresses leaning against a wall, and a metal table with four metal chairs. "Is Iso here?" Kaya Moeyha looked for her grandmother.

Ikwa shook his head. "She went to Cochiti. To make a little Christmas money from the pottery storyteller dolls the tourists like so much."

Damp clay. She breathed in the smell. The smell she'd missed for so long.

"Some of your grandmother's pottery is in the Smithsonian," Diego said. "These days, everyone wants one of her storytellers."

The beginning of another lecture, but she didn't hear it. Mahu was there, all around her. The little boy, the flute player under the portico, the terribly injured twin lying in his own blood. Amy Kaya Moeyha shivered and hugged herself. "Ikwa, I have some news. Terrible news. Mahu is hurt." She put her hands over her heart. "I know in here he's not dead. But he's not awake. I think he dreams Kokopelli's song."

White Bear gestured to the table and sat. "My heart has been both light and heavy all day. Light because I knew you would be here soon, Moeyha. Heavy because of what you are going to tell me now."

She sat beside him and swallowed a sigh. "I heard him playing his flute in front of the Palace of the Governors." She told the story with all its details. When she got to the attack, she said, "I reached for his hand, and I found the lienzo."

The old man sighed deeply. "When Mahu found that lienzo, he showed it to me. I knew it would bring trouble. We decided to lock it away in your father's museum, Diego James."

Diego frowned. "If I'd gotten his call, Mahu wouldn't have been hurt."

"Destiny is never a straight line," White Bear said. "Destiny is a line with twists and turns, a path both good and evil tread. The traveler steps and then missteps, goes the wrong way and then the right way. You did not attack Mahu."

White Bear shifted his gaze to Amy. "Now, Moeyha, you have told me about your twin. Tell me how you found your way home."

"My grandmother told me about Santa Fe."

Her grandfather shook his head. "Tell me what stirred in your heart to bring you here now."

Nima. She hadn't thought about it that way before, but she knew as soon as he asked. "I dreamed," she said. "Things that aren't in Virginia—an azure blue sky, patterns on clay, a little boy, and the song of a flute. Always the song of the flute."

"You see? Even your Grandmother Adams could not block the destiny of the Moon Twins."

"I'm here, but Mahu isn't."

The old man nodded and pushed back his chair. "I must go to a place I know and think."

"Sir," Diego interrupted, "before you go, please tell us what you know about this." He took the lienzo from his pocket and put it on the table.

White Bear sighed and settled back in his chair. He looked at the plastic sleeve but didn't pick it up. "I don't know what the Spanish says. The letters are strangely made."

Very carefully, Diego took the manuscript from its protective covering and handed it to the old man. "The figures on the other side look like glyphs to me. Do you know what they say?"

The old man frowned. "This is torn—only half of the lienzo Mahu found in the Ya-Ya cave."

"That's what X meant," Amy Kaya said. "He told me he wanted the rest of the lienzo."

"Never mind that," Diego said. "We need to find out why someone is willing to kill for it."

White Bear shrugged. "When my grandfather was a very old man, he told me about a lost kiva where ancient shamans painted a sacred panel. Maybe this is a copy of that panel."

"Panels tell stories," Diego said. "What is this story?"

For the second time, White Bear pushed back his chair, but this time he stood up. "The Tokpela Moon is almost full," he said. "I must think now. I will return at sunset."

They let him go because they knew they couldn't stop him. When the door closed, Diego took two oranges from the bag and handed one to Amy Kaya.

He peeled his orange. "We've got a couple of hours. Why don't we go to Special Collections and see what information we can find about the lienzo? Since Mahu found it at Flute Spring, it's been on Third Mesa for a long time. If anyone's seen it before, it would have been here."

"Isn't Special Collections where Yukioma said he was working?"

"Yep. If he's there, we might finish our little chat."

"You think that's a good idea?"

Diego got to his feet. "In a dark alley, maybe not. In broad daylight in the museum, yes. We'll be safe enough."

They went out into a golden afternoon. Suddenly, Kaya remembered a crumbling wall at the edge of the mesa. She said, "Instead of going to the museum, I want to go to a place where Mahu and I used to play."

He looked surprised. "Sure. Where can I find you later?"

"Farther down this road, beyond the inhabited houses. Come before sunset."

"Okay."

Kaya Amy watched him lope back toward the village, hoping he wasn't headed for a confrontation with X. With a shrug, she turned and started toward a spot she didn't know if she could find. The path took her away from the row of houses across an empty stretch of the mesa.

The wall she'd remembered was there, but she kept walking. In her mind, five-year-old Mahu said, 'I found a place just for us.'

She entered a part of the pueblo abandoned generations before. Many roofs and walls had collapsed. Two houses in the middle still stood, leaning against each other as if for support. She remembered an empty room—and a treasure box.

The doorway of the second house drew her. The right height when they were five, now she had to duck to get under the wooden crossbeam. Once inside, she could stand. As she waited for her eyes to adjust to the dim light, she inhaled the place's clean dry scent, like autumn leaves under a cottonwood tree.

When she could see again, she studied the tiny room. The crumbling adobe walls didn't seem to be in immediate danger of falling. Dust and small chunks of brick covered the floor almost to her ankles. She explored, moving around the walls, looking in the corners, sticking her head through a doorway that connected the house to its neighbor.

Then, she saw it. A rusting metal box the size of a shoebox. The hinges squeaked when she lifted the lid. Her fingers brushed a silky feather. She remembered stretching out her arms, a feather in each hand, stomping her feet like an eagle dancer. She pulled out a pointed arrowhead, and Mahu was beside her stripping bark from a stick to make a shaft. She ran her fingers over a smooth stone, a stone she used to grind kernels of dried corn on a flat rock she pretended was a metaté.

Somewhere in the distance, children shouted. Kaya Amy put the treasures back in the box and went outside.

She walked back to the wall and the red and brown desert far below. Sitting with her legs dangling, she ate her orange. Juicy sections filled her mouth and took her back to a turquoise pebble Mahu made into a bracelet, a tiny pot Iso helped her paint, a cloud in the shape of a lizard.

"Hey, girl. Has your twin telepathy signaled any change with Mahu?"

Kaya looked up at Diego and shook her head. Mahu still dreamed the song of a red cedar flute. "Did you find out anything about the lienzo?"

He dropped to the wall beside her. "Nada. I looked through vertical files, old journals, and three crates of crumbling newspapers. I even listened to a couple of oral history tapes. Not a single reference to a lienzo or a Ya-Ya cave. It seems this is the first time our lienzo has surfaced. It really could be the Rosetta Stone I think it is."

"What about Yuki? Did you see him?"

Diego's frowned. "Yuki's working at convincing his Committee for Cultural Preservation to come after us and demand the lienzo. If we want to keep it, we need to hide it. The glove compartment is no good. It's the first place they'll look."

"I know a place." She looked at the empty path. The only sounds came from a long way off. She pointed to the house. "I found the box Mahu and I kept our treasures in. The lienzo will fit."

"Sounds pretty vulnerable."

"I found things from twelve years ago in that box."

"That'll do. We only need a day or two, not years."

She showed him, and they tucked the lienzo away. Then they sat side by side on the wall again. The silence caught them. They watched a hawk float on an air current, drift over a vast expanse painted with the shadows of restless clouds.

After a time, Diego said, "When my family first moved to this part of the country, I couldn't understand why the Hopis have been so determined to live on these barren mesas. But after sitting here looking out at infinity, it's not so hard to understand."

Suddenly the hawk pulled in its wings and dropped into a sharp dive. It hurtled toward the earth and then pulled up abruptly, a tiny bird caught in its beak. Heart pounding, Kaya whispered, "We're the prey ... but who is the hawk?"

# CHAPTER SEVEN

T he sun dropped below the horizon, briefly gilding the edge of a far-away mesa. Diego put his arm around Amy Kaya and pulled her close. "Listen to me, girl. We are *not* prey. We're hunting the hawk."

She wasn't convinced, but she felt safe leaning against him. It was silly. What could Diego do to protect her? She couldn't protect Mahu. Still, it was a moment of comfort. Deliberately pushing away her doubts, she pretended the moment would go on forever.

Too soon, he dropped his arm and stood up. "White Bear said he'd be back at sunset. Let's go see what he says."

They didn't hurry, watching night gather like an indigo shadow on the desert floor and climb slowly into the evening around them. Halfway up the sky, the lopsided moon gradually brightened from pale white to silver.

"What is it about Moon Twins?" she asked. "What have twins got to do with it?"

"Twins have special power in Hopi lore. Especially male and female twins. I think the brother-sister bond represents all humanity, giving twins strength to accomplish great tasks."

"I'm afraid, Diego. Even if I could believe what you're saying, my twin isn't here."

He took her hand and squeezed it. "For now, I guess you'll have to settle for me."

As they got closer to the house, they could see White Bear, silhouetted by moonlight against the adobe house. "Moeyha," he said, "it is time to tell you the prophecy my grandfather told me. To hear, you must become Hopi again."

A breeze whispered against Amy's face. She wrapped her arms around herself to stop the shiver that was more than a physical chill. "I can't. It's been too long."

It was as if she hadn't spoken. "We saved your mother's clothes, Moeyha. Go inside and put them on."

She started to object again, but Diego's hands were on her shoulders. Turning her toward the door, he gave her a gentle push.

Memory or dream, Kaya knew where she would find the clothes. In a wooden crate behind the curtain. Three strands of turquoise and a necklace of cedar beads decorated a black wool manta trimmed with two narrow bands of red and yellow around the hem. Her mother's ceremonial clothes waited twelve years for her to remember who she was and come home.

When she lifted the lid and looked inside, the dusty perfume of rose pods pulled her out of the confusing present back to a time when she knew who she was—Kaya Amy Sekatewa, sister of Mahu, daughter of Wilson and Brenda, grandchild of White Bear and Eleanor. The crate held memories too, one linked to the next like the string of beads.

A kachina dance they were going to … Mama settled the black dress on her shoulders, tied the black and white woven belt around her waist, looped the string of turquoise beads and the cedar necklace around her throat, and pulled on soft white leather boots that came to her knees. 'You'll have a dress like this when you're grown, Kaya.'

Amy Kaya carefully lifted the manta from the crate. Not a dress *like* this, Mama. This same dress, your dress.

She pulled off the purple sweatsuit. Tears ran down her face. Good tears, tears that connected Amy and Kaya, and helped them both remember Mama. The soft undergarments brushed her skin, and the supple boots cradled her feet. The dress was only a little too big, easily sashed to fit.

Amy found a brush and pulled it through her tangled hair. A silver barrette caught it off her face. She'd forgotten about the silky rabbit blanket, but as she pulled it around her shoulders, she felt warm and safe, like a child in her mother's arms.

The warmth was only physical. Cold, hard questions hammered her heart. *Can I still be Hopi? Or am I just a little girl copying my mother? Am I Kaya only because I'm Mahu's sister? In my heart, am I still Amy—Grandmother Adams's little girl?*

As soon as she stepped outside, White Bear answered all the questions. In a voice so low it was almost a whisper, he said, "Moongirl." Her ceremonial name. She had forgotten it, but in some unexplained way, it settled her identity. Moongirl was Hopi.

White Bear, Moongirl, and Diego walked east through the village toward a white moon not yet at the top of the sky. They passed houses unoccupied for a hundred years and walked around rubble undisturbed for centuries.

Near the edge of the mesa, they reached a natural plaza swept clean by the wind. At each of the four cardinal directions stood a prayer stick—two reeds and two feathers bound with a cotton cord—four páhos brushed silver by the moonlight.

White Bear moved into the center of the square and motioned for them to sit, Moongirl on the South and Diego on the North. As they took their places, the breeze, colder now, played with the feathers, giving the páhos an eerie kind of life.

Facing West, White Bear sang, a low meditative chant with words Moongirl didn't know, words that might not be words at all, but syllables meant to keep the rhythm. As he sang, stars emerged in the black expanse of night. One star, then another, and another. Sometime later, he turned to the East and sang. When the sky filled with stars, White Bear fell silent.

Turning back toward Moongirl, he lowered himself stiffly to the ground. "Every eighteen years, the moon, the one we call Wandering Man, journeys from his northernmost rising place to his southernmost rising place and back again. At each end of this journey, the moon divides time in two, a standstill in his wanderings.

"When Wandering Man has completed fifty journeys from North back to North, a door opens between past and present, between our Fourth World and the worlds that have gone before. We call that door Tokpela Moon."

"Tokpela," ventured Diego, "endless space."

White Bear nodded, his gray hair threaded with moonlight. "Four nights from now, we will see the Tokpela Moon, a sight no one has seen for a thousand years."

Moongirl looked up. Overhead, Wandering Man, showing only half his face, had climbed to the top of the night sky. Soon he would be three-quarters, then full—the phases of the moon counting time.

White Bear spoke again, his voice so quiet it seemed to be part of the night. "My grandfather told me I would live to see Tokpela Moon, and he gave me this prophecy. 'Powáqas from the time of the Ancestors will try to enter the Fourth World through Tokpela Moon. Powáqas from our time will try to help them.

'These days will be filled with danger, for the universe itself will balance on the fulcrum of time, waiting to tip the future toward chaos or toward harmony. Powáqas will push toward chaos, toward uncreation, but Moon Twins will leave childhood behind to sing the harmony of the Song of Creation.'

The old man fell silent, and Moongirl thought the void

between the stars, which is Tokpela, moved restlessly, the way thirsty soil moves when a dust devil passes. If the Moon Twins failed, what then?

The door in her mind swung open. Instead of the red cedar flute's song, she heard a great roar—a cacophony of terror, the bloody jubilation of a thousand lions after a thousand kills, the indifferent battering of ten thousand hurricanes against ten thousand islands, the malignant whine of a hundred thousand missiles descending on a hundred thousand cities.

Then silence, a malevolent silence that wrapped her with long tentacles, choked every thought, suffocated every feeling, forced her over the edge of insanity.

As she catapulted into the abyss, White Bear's voice broke through. "... *blessing* ..." She grasped the word, pulled it to her, pushed it against the door until it finally closed. In the center of the páho square, White Bear rose awkwardly to his feet. "It is time. Moongirl, Moonboy, take my hands for the blessing."

Moongirl grasped White Bear's outstretched hand as desperately as she had grasped the word in that awful silence. He stood firm. She struggled to her feet. "Moonboy isn't here," she whimpered.

"But Moonboy's brother is," White Bear said.

Diego shook his head, but Moongirl stretched out her hand to him in a gesture of entreaty. Sighing deeply, he stood.

When the three of them joined in a circle, White Bear looked at the star-studded sky. "Creator," he said, "maker of this Fourth World, place the Song of Creation in the hearts of these Moon Twins. Let it guide them as they seek harmony in chaos."

In her mind, Moongirl heard the haunting tones of a red cedar flute and knew it was the song Mahu dreamed. As she listened, the Song of Creation swept away both sound and silence, replacing them with the deep calm of destiny.

Diego's hand relaxed in hers. She wondered if he too had heard. When the night joined with Creation and began to sing,

White Bear released their hands. For a moment or an hour or a lifetime, they listened and were comforted.

Then a coyote howled. Another cry, and a third. It was as if she'd never heard the Song. Part-way down the western sky, the white moon appeared as a tear in the black sky, an opening which would grow each night until it was large enough for ancient evil to slip through. Fear darker and deeper than she'd known existed engulfed her.

Shivering violently, Moongirl, who was Moeyha, who was Kaya, who was Amy, stepped out of the páho square. Her voice too loud for the silent plaza, she said, "I'm going back."

She hurried through the silent pueblo, wondering how to escape the terrible prophecy, how to get loose from her grandfather's nightmare. She heard Diego, but she couldn't slow down.

A few steps more, and he caught up to her. Putting his hands on her shoulders, he turned her to him. "Kaya—Amy, whatever this is, we can't run away from it."

She looked up at his shadowed face. He hadn't heard it. He didn't understand! Grasping for the last shreds of her sanity, she pushed Moongirl, Kaya, Moeyha away. "It's nonsense," Amy insisted. "It must be!"

"I don't pretend to know what it is we've landed in the middle of, but whatever it is, it isn't nonsense. If White Bear believes this prophecy, we have to take it seriously."

"A thousand-year journey of the moon? Ancient beings powerful enough to throw the entire universe into chaos? And we're supposed to defeat them?" To keep from dissolving, she put her forehead against his chest. Solid, warm, the scent of his leather jacket.

Diego sighed, and his ribs moved out and in. "I don't know what that's about, but whatever it is, clearly White Bear believes we're in a pitched battle with evil powáqas. He's a shaman, a wise man, so I can't dismiss his beliefs, strange as they are to me."

Diego might want to believe, but she didn't. She couldn't. She was Amy, and Amy didn't understand. Pulling away, she started walking again. "What are powáqas anyway?"

"Witches."

"Not witches again! I quit believing in witches a long time ago."

"Do you believe in evil?"

She sighed. "I don't think I know what it is. Define your terms, Professor."

"Fair enough. Bad things happen all the time. But not everything bad that happens is evil. A friend loses control of a car and crashes. That's bad, but it's not evil—it's physics. My sister gets leukemia and dies. That's bad, but it's not evil—it's disease. I think evil happens when someone uses power to purposely hurt someone else."

"Black magic?"

"Yep. Witches."

But noise and silence, both deadly? wondered Moongirl. "I think I'm going crazy," Amy said.

They reached the house, and Diego pulled her to him. Turning her so that her head was under his chin and they could look up at the sky together, he took her hand. Tracing the outline of a group of stars, he said, "See the four big stars? Those are the shoulders and hips of Orion, the hunter. The three little ones in the middle are a sword hanging from Orion's belt. You can see Orion from anywhere on the globe, except Antarctica. Those stars are the same tonight as they were a thousand years ago when the last Tokpela Moon rose and set."

She sighed. "Okay, Orion is unchangeable. How does that help us?"

"Maybe it doesn't. But when I feel overwhelmed, I look up at the stars, and things settle back into perspective."

Moongirl didn't speak, just looked up at the endless void where there was no sound, no silence.

White Bear's voice came out of the darkness, startling them. "You need to eat."

Diego let her go and took a step back. He pushed up his glasses. "You sound like my mother, sir. 'Eat, children, and all will be well.'"

Amy, who was Kaya, who was Moeyha, laughed, a shaky little sound, but a real laugh. "What's for dinner?"

"Beans and tortillas." In the pale moonlight, White Bear turned his face to the breeze and considered. "I think we will eat out here under the stars. You two build the cooking fire while I get the food. Diego, the wood is around back. Moeyha, the matches are inside."

It was good to have a small task, like carrying oranges. The fire cast a golden glow against the night, diminishing the moonlight and stars. White Bear settled a cast-iron pot filled with beans to warm and then squatted on his heels.

"What's this about, White Bear?" Diego dropped to the ground and sat cross-legged. "Witches and the moon?"

White Bear grunted. "The professor wants the facts." Harsh words, but a gentle tone.

"Please, sir. What is the story behind this prophecy?"

"Ah. The elders say a thousand years ago, a group of two-hearts took power. Their greed disrupted the harmony of the People, spreading chaos and violence."

Moeyha, standing in shadow just beyond the firelight, said, "Two-hearts?"

"Powáqas, witches. Two-hearts because they have the human heart they were born with and the animal heart they nurture in secret."

"Ya-Ya," Diego said.

"Mmm. A ceremony of great power given by the Animal People to help the Ancestors hunt. Then a few selfish men turned the ceremony's power to their own selfish purposes, twisting something good into evil, becoming two-hearts. When the door of Tokpela Moon opened, the first Moon Twins performed a ceremony that sent the two-hearts into endless space."

White Bear slapped a tortilla on a paper plate and spooned beans. Motioning to Moeyha to sit beside him, he offered her the plate.

She took it and folded the tortilla around the beans. "The páho ceremony?"

Her grandfather shook his head. "A special ceremony for a special task."

"Teach us," Moongirl whispered. They needed a ceremony to stop the noise and speak to the silence.

White Bear spooned beans onto a second tortilla. "The Tokpela Ceremony has been forgotten. The only record is the panel in the lost kiva where it was danced."

Diego accepted the plate White Bear held out to him. "The figures on the lienzo?"

"Mmm," said the old man, spooning beans for himself.

"So, we have half of the ceremony," Moongirl said. "X has the other half."

"Eat," Her grandfather nodded. "All is not well, but food will give us the strength to face what we must.

Despair so thick in her throat she thought she would choke, Moongirl Amy took a bite. The burrito was hot and juicy. Eating was a small thing—one bite and then another. Silence surrounded them, broken only by the crackle of the fire. Her heart settled back in her chest, and she began to breathe again.

A log broke, sending a stream of sparks up toward the stars. She jumped. "Even if we can get back the other half of the lienzo and learn the ceremony, Mahu isn't here. I can't be the Moon Twins alone."

"No, not alone," murmured White Bear. "Four shamans to help the Moon Twins."

"What about Mahu? Will he be here in time?"

"I can't see the future, Moeyha. I will go to Mahu tomorrow

75

to add the healing I know to the Anglo doctors' healing, but I don't know what will happen or when it will happen."

"Then, I might be alone!"

"White Bear shook his head. "You think this man you call X has more power than the Creator who plans destiny? If Mahu can't fulfill the destiny shamans saw a thousand years ago, someone else will be given the choice to fulfill it or not."

"You mean me," Diego said.

"Are you not Mahu's brother? Did you not accept his blessing in the páho square?"

The fire burned low, so Diego's nod was a small movement in the vast night. "He saved my life. I accepted his blessing, but I can't fulfill his destiny."

"Ah, Diego James, you still don't understand. Moonboy pulled you out of the flood beneath a December moon. You are a spiritual Moon Twin."

"It was broad daylight when Mahu rescued me!"

"The Wandering Man rises at different times on his journey." White Bear said in a calm voice. "That day the moon rose in the afternoon. You didn't see it, but it was overhead."

Diego groaned softly, an admission of defeat.

Moongirl looked at him with soft eyes. He was afraid. Just like she was. Folding her empty plate, she put it on the fire. Instead of bursting into flames, it scorched and curled at the edges.

"The Fourth World is World Complete, Diego James. It is a world of choices. You have the choice of following this destiny or of turning away from it."

"You had the choice to help or not when I called you," whispered Moeyha, who was Moongirl. Her plate, now nothing more than a circle of ashes, floated away a bit at a time.

Diego took off his glasses and held them out to the firelight, catching prism colors. "So, I stepped into Mahu's destiny when I decided to help his sister?"

"You had another choice in the páho circle," White Bear said.

Diego put his glasses back on and jammed them against the bridge of his nose. "So I stepped in a second time."

"You will keep getting choices. Destiny is never just one choice."

"What about X?" Moongirl said. "Is it his destiny to try to stop the Moon Twins?"

White Bear shook his head, making his shadow move restlessly. "The Creator plans only good, so evil is never destiny. Like everyone, X chooses each day what he will do. When he chose to hurt Mahu to get what he wanted, he was drawn into evil. Trouble is, the more one chooses evil, the easier it gets."

"You mean he'll try again, don't you?" Diego said.

"Mmm."

Moeyha fought to breathe. "How can we defeat this evil, Ikwa? There are too many questions. Who is X? Who are the modern powáqas? Why do they want to let in this terrible evil? How do we perform the ceremony that will protect the universe? Where is the lost kiva?"

"Hush now, Moeyha. You must trust. When you are following the path of destiny, you will hear the Song of Creation. You heard it when you found your twin. You heard it inside the páho square."

A song. How could a song uncover the secrets of the Tokpela Moon? She searched in her mind for Mahu, but the room where she had found him before was silent.

Taking Diego's plate, the old man put it with his own and laid them both on the glowing coals. The fire hissed, flamed briefly, and settled back.

# III. TATKYAQW [SOUTH]

Storytellers say the Old Ones built their great kivas deep in the earth to dance the ceremonies that keep the world in harmony. To remember the Four Worlds, the Builders set four massive stone disks at the four directions. To remember the journey across Endless Water in hollow reeds. On the disks, they set four pillars made from bricks interspersed with wooden poles.

To remember the fire that destroyed the first world, the Builders placed a sunken fire pit in the center of the room. To remember the Sipapuni, they dug a small hole beside the fire pit.

When they finished, the Builders roofed their kivas with ninety tons of tree trunks they carried from mountains a hundred miles away. In the roof, they made an opening for a ladder.

Storytellers say the Old Ones climbed down ladders into dark kivas lit only by firelight. There they danced their ceremonies, ceremonies that mirrored the slow dance of the stars to the Song of Creation. As the Old Ones danced, they held in quiet minds the majestic wheeling of the constellations across the midnight sky month after month, year after year. For a thousand years, dancers have kept plant, animal, and human life in harmony.

The first ceremony of the year begins when the November

moon is new and still dark. As winter descends on the mesas, kiva members begin the sixteen days of Wúwuchim. On the first three days, they make páhos from red-willow sticks and eagle feathers to carry their prayers to the Creator. After they set the páhos at each of the four directions, they go into the kiva to dance the sacred dances.

At sundown on the fifteenth day, the priest emerges from the kiva to make a circuit around the village. He goes West, then South, then East, and then North, claiming all the earth for the Creator. As the priest travels, the Flute Player breathes the Song of Creation into his red cedar flute, calling the People back to harmony.

As midnight of the last day approaches, the seven stars of the Pleiades appear in the ladder opening of the roof. In firelight, the priest recounts the People's journey on the Road of Life. Just at midnight, star-masked figures, spirits from the past and from other worlds, climb down the ladder to sing seven songs for seven stars.

Thus, they restore harmony to the earth for another year.

CHAPTER EIGHT

A my woke to the sound of voices in a shadowed room.
At first, she couldn't remember where she was. The
room was empty, but the door stood open, a gray
rectangle in the darkness. She was lying on a mattress on a dirt
floor wearing a thin slip, covered by a tightly woven blanket.
Another mattress, empty, lay on the floor a few feet away. A
third leaned against the wall.

The voices, not quite angry, sounded hostile—two male
voices. Gradually memory came. One voice belonged to Diego,
Mahu's friend, her friend. She was in her grandfather's house,
but the other voice wasn't White Bear's.

"It's Mahu's decision," Diego said quite clearly.

"It's *my* decision."

"I don't know whether the Committee on Cultural Preservation has jurisdiction, but even if it does, this isn't your personal
decision, Yuki."

"I'm the chairman, and I say it is! You're not even Hopi.
You're a descendant of Conquistadors."

Someone spat. Yukioma.

Flinging off the blankets, she scrambled to her feet. A chill

81

filled the adobe house, and Amy Kaya shivered as she pulled her mother's wool manta over the thin slip she'd slept in. The pounded dirt floor felt like damp clay as she stood first on one foot and then the other to work on the soft leather boots. Grabbing the rabbit fur blanket, she flung it around her shoulders and hurried to the door.

Dark shapes stood in the predawn shadow light. Yukioma, a little taller and much heavier, loomed over Diego.

"What's going on?" she demanded. "Where's my grandfather?"

The sound of her voice must have surprised them. The two figures turned toward her.

"Not here," Yuki said, his tone just short of gloating. "I've come to get the lienzo."

"You're not going to burn it," Diego said. "If there is such a thing as black magic, it resides in the two-hearts, not in a scrap of cloth."

Yuki spat a second time and took a step closer to Diego.

Amy Kaya took a deep breath, glad they'd hidden the lienzo. "White Bear is a shaman. We'll do what he tells us to."

At White Bear's name, the big man glanced over his shoulder, a guilty movement that put his face in the light for a moment. His expression, a determined glower, frightened her. *Good twisted into evil? A good thing to uphold tradition—but at what cost?*

"One hour. I'll be back. If White Bear is here, I'll listen to him. If not ..." Spoken or not, the threat was clear. Yukioma turned on his heel and strode away.

"Where is Ikwa?"

Diego shrugged. "I woke up when Yuki came to the door. White Bear was gone. We've got to find him. It's a pretty sure bet Yuki's gone to get the members of his committee. If they come back and White Bear's not here, we won't be able to control the situation."

"They won't find the lienzo unless we tell them where it is."

"Don't be so sure. Yuki's a smart guy. He's lived here his whole life, and he knows where the kids play. He also knows you were a little kid when you left. It might take him a while, but if he gets everyone on the committee to look ..."

Moeyha Kaya Amy nodded and looked anxiously into the gray dawn. "Ikwa said he was going to see Mahu today. Would he go without waking us?"

"It's time for morning prayers. You check the páho plaza. I'll see if anyone saw him leave Old Oraibi. Meet back here as quick as you can."

Then he was gone, loping toward the village. She took a moment to visit the outhouse and to splash cold water on her face. Then, pulling the silky blanket closely around her shoulders, she started across the mesa. As she picked her way around rocks and over uneven places, early purple dawn erased the edges of night.

When she reached the place where the páhos still stood, the last of the stars faded into a mother-of-pearl sky. A faint rim of light smudged the eastern horizon. No sign of White Bear.

Just below the mesa, a coyote yipped, and somewhere close a raven cawed. A night sound and a day sound. Sounds that shouldn't be heard together. An omen. But what it meant, she had no idea.

Intent on spotting the animals, Amy moved closer to the mesa's edge. As she neared the side to look, someone grabbed her blanket and forced it over her head. Rabbit fur covered her eyes, her nostrils, her mouth. Strong arms pinned her own to her sides, making escape impossible.

She fought for breath.

A low voice whispered in her ear, "The hunt will be successful."

She tried to scream, but only managed a croak. Beneath the blanket, rough hands grabbed at her.

*X. The lienzo.* Amy wanted to tell him she didn't have it, but her fur filled her mouth. Bright spots pricked the darkness behind her eyelids. She felt herself spinning. She was going to pass out. Or suffocate.

Hovering on the edge of consciousness, she thought she heard a shout and running feet. Ikwa, Diego, Mahu? But Mahu was in the hospital. Maybe it was her imagination. She felt herself being lifted off her feet and swung around. Toward the edge of the mesa—a thousand-foot drop. With one final desperate burst of energy, she kicked wildly. Her right foot connected. She kept fighting, using her knees, her elbows, her teeth, but swathed in rabbit fur, nothing helped.

"Let her go!"

The voice was close, close enough she could identify it. Diego.

Her attacker dropped her. Not over the side of mesa into the eternal abyss, but hard, onto the ground. So hard the impact knocked the wind out of her. She lay for what seemed an airless eternity, wondering if even now, the rabbit fur would suffocate her. But her arms worked, and Amy finally fought her way out of the blanket.

Taking great gulps of the cool air, she was dimly aware of Diego, helping her sit, putting the blanket around her shoulders, holding it off her face. Once, she felt him stroke her hair. Gradually her heart stopped banging in her chest, and the dots that swam before her eyes receded. Still, her lungs ached for air.

"What happened, Amy?"

When she tried to talk, she coughed. Somehow though, between gasps and coughs, she managed to tell him.

"Can you walk?" Before she could answer, he pulled her to her feet. "We've got to get the lienzo and get out of here." He had her hand. They hurried—through the sleeping pueblo, up the path through the scrub, into the makeshift parking lot behind the pink concrete block gallery—hurried so fast she didn't have breath for questions.

When they reached the Jeep, Diego opened the passenger's side and half-lifted, half-pushed her onto the seat. "Lock the doors. I'm going after the lienzo."

He slammed the door and left, not loping this time, running. She locked her door and made sure his was locked. Only then did the shock subside. Quivering began in her core and spread outward to the rest of her body.

Doubling over, she put her arms under her knees and hugged tight. She had to stop shaking. X was here. He meant to throw her off the mesa. Over and over, the same thoughts, almost as if her mind trembled.

A sharp knock on the driver's side window made her look up. Diego gestured urgently. She leaned across, unlocked his door. She had barely withdrawn her arm when he jumped in, relocked his door, shoved the key into the ignition, jammed the clutch into the floor.

The motor turned over. He shifted into reverse and swung the Jeep around. Skidding and throwing rocks, the Jeep bounced around two pickups and onto the road. He turned east, just as a blinding sun peeked up over the straight line of the horizon.

Shading her eyes with one hand, she said, "Yuki?"

"Yep. He saw me running toward the parking lot. Our only chance is to get out of here before he can get to his car."

"You think we can outrun him?"

"Nope, but I know a road he won't expect us to take. It goes straight down the side of the mesa. He'll expect us to stay on the highway, and he'll follow us that way. If we can get to the turn far enough ahead of him, we can get to the Navajo Reservation before he figures it out."

Just ahead, she saw a dirt road on the right. Diego slowed, and with only a slight bump, guided the Jeep off the pavement. The way was even steeper than the switchbacks they'd climbed from Keams Canyon without a guardrail in sight. As she looked out into pink sky's wide expanse, she remembered the hawk dropping like an arrow to snatch its prey from the air. And she remembered the rabbit fur in her mouth and nose.

"You saved my life."

"Like Mahu saved mine."

"Three spiritual Moon Twins? It doesn't make sense."

"None of it makes sense, but at least now I know what to call you."

She looked at him curiously. He'd pulled off his leather jacket and wore a different shirt, deep wine velveteen open at the neck, probably one of Mahu's. The dark stubble on his chin, two days growth now, looked almost like a beard in the early morning light. In profile, the glasses almost disappeared. He looked good, like an adventurer.

Unaware of her scrutiny, he continued. "I haven't known what to call you since we came to the rez. *Amy* doesn't quite work because you're different out here. *Kaya* is Mahu's name for you, but it means 'older sister,' and I'm older than you are. *Moeyha* means 'precious grandchild,' so that doesn't work."

"But now you know?"

"Yep. When Mahu saved my life, I became his brother. When I saved your life, you became my sister. I'm going to call you *Hermana*."

"*Sister* in Spanish?"

"Yep."

Biting her tongue, she pushed away the objections that rose to her lips.

Diego studied the rearview mirror. "We're below the rim of the mesa," he said. "Unless we left a trail of dust, I don't think Yuki will realize we turned off."

She twisted in her seat and looked behind at the empty road. "The sun will be in his eyes."

Diego let out his breath. "Yep. I think we're safe for the moment."

"I can't believe Ikwa left us to face Yuki alone!"

"He didn't. When I was looking for him earlier, I met another member of the committee. He told me White Bear asked them to wait on their decision until he could see Mahu. I guess he believes Mahu will be better soon. The committee agreed to wait. Yuki acted on his own."

"So, he grabbed me. When I didn't have the lienzo, he was just going to push me over the side with no one the wiser?"

"Maybe Yuki, maybe someone else."

"Couldn't you see him?"

Diego's silence was an answer she couldn't interpret. Turning to look at him, she demanded, "What? What did you see?"

"I don't know." Diego kept his eyes straight ahead.. Finally, his voice unhappy, he said, "Maybe I saw a powáqa."

"A witch?"

"Ya-Ya powáqas get their power from the animal kingdom, from horned animals—deer, elk, antelope. I saw a man with an antelope's head."

"He had on a mask?"

Diego shook his head.

"I don't understand."

"Neither do I."

She didn't want to talk about something they couldn't understand. "We're running away from Yuki so we can keep the lienzo. Where are we going?"

"To El Morro, to see someone who can translate the lienzo for us."

"You mean the Spanish?"

"Yep. And the pictographs. Just before I dropped off last night, I thought of Dr. Montoya. She's a linguist my dad consults sometimes. I heard him say she's working at El Morro this year."

"So, what is El Morro—a school of some kind?"

He shook his head. "It's a National Monument. *El morro* means *the bluff.* In this case, el morro is a red rock butte that sticks up out of the desert. There's water there, so over the centuries, it's been an important landmark for travelers.

"When they stopped for water, most of them left a record of their visit. Some of the petroglyphs go back 1,000 years. There are Spanish inscriptions from the 1600s and carvings from a railroad survey in the mid-1800s. Dr. Montoya hopes El Morro will provide the key to understanding petroglyph writing."

"We have witches after us, and we're going to consult a linguist?"

"Do you have a better idea?"

She shook her head and looked out the window. At the empty road. At a dry wash that slashed the red brown earth like a scar. At a tumbleweed caught in rabbit brush. At a dead dog swollen stiff and covered with flies. At a mangled hubcap. Suddenly, it was all too much.

Amy felt completely disoriented, an alien in this country. She didn't know the landscape. She didn't know the history. She didn't know Diego. She didn't even know her twin brother. She had come to find out who she was, where she belonged, where her real home was.

Instead, she had been dragged into a melodrama of moon phases, witches who were part animal, and indecipherable lienzos. Her twin lay in the hospital. She was lucky she wasn't in the next bed or worse, at the bottom of the mesa.

With an odd sense of being separate from her body, she heard her voice say, "I want to go home."

"You want to go home?" Diego's tone was incredulous.

She couldn't blame him, but she knew it was true. Twisting in her seat, she faced him. "I want to go home. I can't do anything for Mahu. The last time I was in Hopiland, I was five years old.

"I didn't know what White Bear was talking about last night. I don't know who grabbed me this morning, and I don't have any idea why we're going to see a linguist! Even if we find out what the lienzo says, what good will it do?" She felt herself getting hysterical, but she was helpless to hold back the flood of emotion.

Diego took his foot off the gas and the Jeep slowed. "Hey, Hermana, take a deep breath."

"Don't call me that! My name is Amy! And I want to go home!"

"Okay, okay. Where do you want me to take you?"

"I don't know! Just stop the car and let me out!"

He pulled the Jeep off to the side of the road. Even before the motor stopped, she opened her door and climbed out. She walked, back up the road, and turned into the wash.

Home! She wanted to go home. Not to Santa Fe. Not to the one-room apartment over the Delgado Gallery. That was just a stopping off place. Not to the college dormitory where she didn't fit in.

She climbed over a boulder and kept going. Not to Grandmother Adam's house. She had run away from there. Not to Old Oraibi. Mama and Taáta were dead.

A terrible sense of isolation engulfed her, and she stopped walking. She knew she should take a deep breath and go back to Diego. He was Mahu's friend, and he wanted to help. But Diego knew who he was. He wouldn't understand.

Then she heard the flute. A red cedar melody sang her out of her confusion. *Mahu?* Sitting on a nearby flat rock, she put her head in her hands and listened.

As she listened, a picture took shape in her mind. Mahu and Kaya walking hand in hand, little children. Then they were teenagers, still walking hand in hand. The young man Mahu she'd spent one evening with and herself.

The panic she'd felt in the car dissipated, panic floating away on clear notes that called her back into the bright morning. Getting to her feet, she walked back down the wash. Across the road, Diego sat cross-legged on the ground reading.

She sat beside him. After a few minutes, he put the book down.

"Studying?"

"Ancient history of the Southwest."

"Maybe I'll take that class sometime."

"Does that mean you're not going home today?"

She picked up three small stones and shook them in her hand. "I don't know where home is. Worse, I don't know who I am. Am I Moeyha Kaya Sekatewa come to rejoin what's left of her birth family? Or am I Amy Adams, a freshman at the College of William and Mary come to find her roots and return to her sensible Anglo life?"

Diego held out his hand. She dropped the rocks in it. He juggled them as she had. After a while, he said, "Maybe you're both. Maybe you're more than both. Like me."

"Like you? You mean genetically half and half? That's not me. For me, it feels like I have to be one or the other."

He shook his head. "It's both *plus*. Like amalgams in chemistry. Two elements that join to make something new. Some people are amalgams. People like us. My mother is Chicana, Mexican American. My father is British American."

"So, you think I'm Hopi and Anglo? Kaya Adams or Amy Sekatewa?"

"Not or. That's crazymaking. Listen, I'm not half and half. And neither are you. I'm all both, all of the above. Something new. Me."

"So, I'm Kaya Amy Adams Sekatewa? With a little bit of Moongirl thrown in?"

"Moongirl is a destiny, a task, not an identity. You're *you*, and you have the choice to be Moongirl or not."

"It's crazy, isn't it?"

Diego shrugged. "White Bear is a brilliant man, a shaman. If he believes the prophecy, I guess I'm afraid *not* to believe it. If he's wrong, the worst that happens is we end up feeling stupid. But in case he's right, we have to try."

Her heart sank. Still, she knew she agreed with him. Sighing, she said, "So how far is El Morro, this place where your linguist is working?"

"Between four and five hours."

She got to her feet and looked up and down the road. Still empty. Not a single car had come this way. But there was something in all the emptiness, something that made her uneasy.

"I feel like someone's watching us," she said. "Do you feel it?"

"Yep."

"Maybe it's just nerves."

"It wouldn't be exactly surprising."

"It couldn't be a witch!"

Diego didn't answer immediately. After a moment, he spoke slowly. "The Seeing Eye is one of the magical powers Ya-Ya claims."

# CHAPTER NINE

As the Jeep crept down the last switchback onto the desert floor, Amy Hermana pushed the Ya-Ya Seeing Eye out of her mind. In the distance, a dust devil whirled briefly and then dissipated. The road straightened out, following a wide wash that dropped gently toward what—the Gulf of Mexico? "Are we off the Hopi reservation?"

"Nope. Another twenty-five miles or so."

"So, if Yuki catches us here, we're in trouble."

"He won't. We know he's not behind us, and I think we can see at least twenty-five miles ahead. Do you see a red pickup?"

"I don't see anything except for lots of rocks and a few cedars."

"Right. I think you can relax, girl."

"It's okay if you want to call me *Hermana*," she said softly. "For now, anyway."

Diego grinned. "It's really not so bad being my sister."

She let that pass. "So, this linguist can read the lienzo, and she'll tell us what it says? You know her well enough that she won't think we're just two crazy kids who ought to turn the lienzo over to her and go back to school?"

Diego shifted uncomfortably. "I don't exactly know Dr. Montoya. Not personally. She's a member of my dad's research team. He says she's one of the good guys. We'll think of what to tell her by the time we get there. Dad sent us—or something like that."

She didn't want to think about being without a plan, so she changed the subject. "This is Monday, Diego. You're a college student. Shouldn't you be in class?"

"Plural. I should be in classes. Today I have Principles of Cultural Anthropology, Geology of New Mexico, and Navajo language class. Tomorrow I have Navajo again plus Intro to Astronomy and a meeting with my advisor about an independent study I'm doing on archaeoastronomy."

"Archaeology and astronomy?"

"Yep. I want to study how ancient peoples watched the sky. See which civilizations knew which bits of information and what they did with the data they had. The Greeks named the constellations after their gods and goddesses, the Aztecs made a calendar, but the Ancestral Puebloans worked out the complicated cycle of the moon more accurately than any other culture we know about."

"Tokpela Moon following a thousand-year path

Diego nodded. "Even if we weren't somehow involved in White Bear's prophecy, I'd be fascinated. One day I might ask permission to research it for a master's thesis."

"You've got to get your bachelor's degree first. It's pretty late in the semester to be skipping classes. What are you going to do?"

He grinned. "Students with straight A's can sometimes get special dispensations. When we get to a phone, I'll make a couple of calls to let my profs know I'm hot on the trail of a research project. Finals are coming up, and we're heading into reading week. As long as I get back before exams next week, I'll be okay. What about you?"

94

She shrugged. "I withdrew." That made her leaving sound planned. In reality, she'd simply ditched school, ditched her Daughters of the American Revolution scholarship, ditched her French major. "When I figure out who I am and what I want to be when I grow up, I'll go back to school." Maybe. "What about Mahu? Is he finishing high school?"

Diego shook his head. "He's apprenticing with a famous silversmith from Second Mesa."

"None of us are traditional students, are we?"

"Nope. Have you declared a major?"

French was ridiculous when she needed to learn—or remember—Hopi. "I'd like to be a potter, but that's not exactly a college major."

"You could major in art, but if it's pottery you want to learn, your grandmother would be better than any college instructor."

"Some of her pieces really are in the Smithsonian?"

"Yep. Eleanor Naranjo's storytellers are the finest in Cochiti, and Cochiti is where the form originated."

*Naranjo! Eleanor Naranjo.* It was like when Diego first said *Sekatewa*—a name she she'd forgotten, suddenly familiar.

"In the gallery," she said slowly, "pottery figures of adults with children. Sitting with their mouths open. One figure was a man with a row of children on each of his legs. Another was a woman with her arms filled with children, ten I think. They were signed, E Naranjo."

"You didn't know that was your grandmother?"

She shook her head. Not far ahead the road widened to two distinct lanes, and in the middle distance she saw pavement. "Where are we exactly? I know we're headed south to El Morro, but how do we get there from here?"

"At the moment we're on a reservation road, Indian Route 2. It's the back way to I-40. In about fifteen minutes, we'll pick up an Arizona state road at Leupp. Winslow and I-40 are about thirty minutes farther. At the interstate we cut east to Chambers and then drop south again to El Morro."

"Somewhere along the way, I suppose we need to eat."

Diego gave her a quick grin. "Getting with program, are you, Hermana?"

She laughed. "You bet. Eat, children, and all will be well."

They passed an electrical substation with heavy wires and huge transformers. A police car marked with the Navajo Nation seal pulled out of a side road and followed.

"You're not speeding, are you?"

"Nope."

"It always makes me nervous to have a police car following."

"Especially when they turn on their lights."

"What?" Amy Kaya twisted in her seat and saw red and blue lights flashing. "What's going on?"

"I don't know." Diego kept the Jeep at a steady speed. "Get the lienzo out of my coat pocket. Put the car registration back in its sleeve and put the lienzo under the floor mat."

"You think a *policeman* is after the lienzo?"

"I don't think anything. But this is weird. I don't want to take any chances."

Moving quickly, she made the switch. The siren wailed behind them. "What are you going to do?"

"Find a place to pull over where there are people around. This may be nothing, but just in case, I want an audience."

"Pull over!" came a voice over a loudspeaker.

Diego rolled down his window and pointed toward a convenience store a few hundred yards ahead.

The siren wailed, the voice repeated, "Pull over!"

Diego kept driving. By the time he pulled into the parking lot, an old Navajo man and a young boy stood outside the store. Lights still flashing, the police car pulled in close behind the Jeep.

More quickly than she would have thought possible, the policeman, a solidly built Navajo with an angry expression, emerged from his car and stood beside Diego's open window. He wore a brown uniform, reminding Kaya of the flashback that kept her from going to the sheriff in Santa Fe. A nameplate on his pocket said *Henry Begay*.

"What's this all about, officer?" Diego, said, his voice steady, his tone mildly curious.

"License and car registration."

"I'm sure I wasn't speeding."

"License and car registration."

"My plates are current."

"Suspicion of a stolen vehicle," snapped Begay. "Step out of the car."

Diego reached in his back pocket for his wallet. As he did, Begay pulled out his gun. "Step out of the car!"

Diego held up one hand and opened the door with the other. "Just getting my license."

Thoroughly frightened, Kaya Amy looked desperately toward the convenience store. A middle-aged man and woman had come outside. Where there had been two onlookers, now there were four. Reaching in the glove compartment, she retrieved the plastic sleeve with its car registration. Diego got out of one side of the Jeep, she exited the other.

"The car isn't stolen," she said to the group of watchers. "It belongs to my friend—*Diego James.* Here's the registration to prove it."

"Henry," the old man said, "put that gun away and stop scaring these kids."

"Stay out of this, Sam." Officer Begay slammed the driver's side door as if he thought Diego might jump back in and drive away. "This kid's been defying me ever since I put on my lights. Ignoring a direct order from an officer is breaking the law."

"Just being a smart-aleck," said Sam, limping toward the Jeep. "Sorta like you Henry. What's Chief Tsosie gonna say when I tell him you were waving that gun around on a routine traffic stop?"

Begay growled, but he holstered his gun. "All right, young lady," he barked. "Let me see that registration."

He studied it with what seemed like excessive interest, even pulling it out and looking inside the sleeve as though he expected to find something else. The lienzo?

Practically snatching the license from Diego, he compared it carefully to the car registration. "I guess this looks okay," he said grudgingly. He handed both documents back to Diego, then walked around the Jeep, examining it suspiciously. When he got to the back, he opened the door and stuck his head in.

Before the powerful man reached her side and the floor mat, Diego said politely, "If you tell me what's going on, Officer Begay, I'll be glad to explain. But if there isn't anything else, my friend and I need to be on our way."

"The kid's right, Henry," the middle-aged man said. "If you've got a burr under your saddle, tell him what it is."

"Not that it's any of your business, Leonard, but I got a report of a stolen car, this make and model. Just doing my job."

Diego, still polite, said, "My car's not stolen, Officer. If you need confirmation, I'm sure the Santa Fe Sheriff's Department will run the numbers through their computer for you." It wasn't exactly a threat of a harassment complaint, but it was close enough.

"All right," Begay growled. "I'll let you off with a warning this time. But when a police car turns on its lights, pull off the road right there. No driving around until you come to a spot that appeals to you."

"Yes, sir," Diego said, his door already open. Matching her speed to his, Amy Hermana climbed into the Jeep. By the time she had her seatbelt fastened, they were moving.

For fully the first mile neither spoke. Finally, she risked looking back the way they'd come. No sign of a police car. "What's happening? I'm sure he was looking for the lienzo, but he can't be X!"

Diego let out a long breath. "No, but maybe we're dealing with more than one X"

"What do you mean? Only one man chased me."

"Yep. But Hermana, think about the voice on the phone—neither one of us could be sure if it was a man or a woman. And was whoever, or whatever, that grabbed you on the mesa, the same or different as the man who attacked Mahu and chased you?"

Kaya Amy Hermana was silent for a long moment. Then she said, "Ikwa said powáqas. That's plural. You think there's a group after the lienzo?"

"It's the only thing that makes sense."

"What are we going to do,? We can't escape an entire coven of witches or whatever you call a group of powáqas."

"We can if we get some sort of official help. My dad's not here, but Dr. Montoya is."

"You think she'll help us?"

"El Morro is a lot closer than Santa Fe. If the witches think we're going to the Park Service, maybe they'll leave us alone. We have to find out what the lienzo says, now more than ever. Unless you have another idea? And I'm not being a smart-aleck. I really mean it. If you have another idea, I'm listening."

"No," she said softly. "El Morro is the next step. But I'm scared."

"Smart girl."

They rode in silence. Soon, they reached the interstate—cars, vans, pickups, semis streaming by at 80 mph. Oddly reassuring. Even as Diego guided the Jeep onto the entrance ramp, the idea of fleeing from an organization of powáqas seemed unreal.

By the time they reached Winslow, the Hopi world faded,

and the Anglo world was reality. An hour later when they reached Holbrook, she had lost her tenuous grasp of Diego's amalgam. She was sufficiently Amy again to feel conspicuous in her mother's Hopi manta.

"Breakfast time!" Diego pulled into the fast food plaza. "Taco Bell, Wendy's, or MacDonald's?"

"I don't care."

"Egg McMuffin and French toast sticks it is, then."

Anglo or Hopi, she was hungry. Pushing aside her doubts, she followed him inside. The woman behind the counter was Hispanic. Both cooks were men, one Anglo, the other Navajo. The man and woman in line in front of her were Japanese. No one seemed to notice her. Here, at least, it didn't matter who she was or what kind of mix. She ordered a scrambled egg and pancake platter and joined Diego at a table by a window that looked out onto a children's playground. She was taking her first bite when a tenor voice said, "Jim Jim! Mind if I join you?"

Diego flushed. Amy looked up at the newcomer. Tall, blonde, late twenties. Tight jeans, open-necked polo shirt, denim jacket with hammered silver buttons. The green of his shirt brought out the green of his eyes. So calculated a match, she wondered if he had a whole wardrobe of shirts that color.

"Walker," Diego said. "Would you go away if I said, 'Yes, I mind'?"

The man laughed and sat down in the empty chair next to Amy. "Nah. I'd sit at the next table and talk to you from over there. Don't be so unfriendly, Jim Jim."

"What do you want?"

"For starters you can introduce me to this pretty lady."

Amy's resistance, already high, ramped up a notch. She hadn't had a shower in two days, and her hair was a tangled mess.

"If you're trying to pick her up, Walker, forget it. She's with me."

Her heart skipped a beat. Hermana means sister, she told herself sternly.

"If it's like that, how about we trade info, Jim Jim? I heard—"

"Stop calling me that, Walker."

"Si, si, amigo. But one of these days you're going to have to learn to take a joke. That one's going to follow you the rest of your life."

"Since I was in preschool."

"Jim Jim?" Amy said.

"*Diego* is Spanish for *James*," said Diego shortly. "Get to the point, Walker. Are you here just to spoil our breakfast?"

Walker stretched out his legs and draped his arm over the back of Amy's chair. "I hear Mahu Sekatewa found something interesting. I'm on my way to Hopiland to find out about it, and I see your unique Jeep, not in Santa Fe where it belongs, but on the highway I'm on. You're tight enough with Mahu to make me curious. What gives?"

"It took more than that to bring you all the way out here on a Monday morning. You tell me what gives."

Walker shrugged. "All I've got is rumors. That Mahu was at Flute Spring when a rockslide opened up a cave the elders used to tell stories about. That he found something really old. Conquistador gold or something like that."

"Which, no doubt, you plan to turn over to your boss as soon as you find it."

"Hey, amigo, this is a friendly conversation. I'm just curious. Any find like this is news. I could use the publicity to market quality reproductions, little brass bound chests filled with chocolate wrapped in gold paper."

"Come off it, Walker."

"Set me straight. I'd bet big money you've talked to Mahu, and I'd bet just as much you're either on your way to meet him or on your way back."

"If you want to bet so badly, go to Vegas. I've got nothing to say to you. We're here to eat breakfast—alone."

Walker turned his attention to Amy. Offering her his hand, he said, "Gabe Walker. If the grapevine's got it right, you're Kaya Sekatewa."

The name startled her. She stared at the man, wondering how he knew who she was.

"Come on, honey. Your boyfriend doesn't like me, but I'm really a good guy. I just tease Jim Jim because he gets so riled up. Shaking my hand won't kill you."

Reluctantly, she took his hand. A big hand.

"Quite a coincidence," he said, not releasing her hand, "you turning up with this budding archaeologist. Where's your twin?"

She jerked her hand out of Walker's. "How do you know who I am?"

Walker laughed. "Same way I heard about Mahu's discovery. Where is our explorer, anyway?"

"Time's up." Diego got to his feet. "If you want to know where Mahu is, check with your source. I'm sure you can get all the information you want."

"You can get more flies with honey than with vinegar, Jim Jim." As lightly as he said the words, to Kaya they sounded like a threat. After a strained moment, he rose to his feet and left them.

Diego gave his glasses an angry jab and sat down. "I do *not* trust that guy. My dad swears Walker's boss is an honest trader, but I bet good old Gabe does some business of his own. Like today."

"You think he's after the lienzo? What could he do with it?"

"Sell it on the black market. Big money in illegal antiquities."

"Do you think Walker could be X?" She closed her eyes and tried to remember the hands that had brushed her hair in the dark gallery. Big hands. Walker had big hands, but so did Yukioma. And the powáqa who'd grabbed her. Strong hands, so strong.

She shivered and opened her eyes. "Walker or Yuki?"

A troubled look crossed Diego's face. "Or someone else, someone we haven't seen yet."

# CHAPTER TEN

Kaya climbed back in the Jeep after their interrupted breakfast. She tried to push X out of her mind, did her best to recapture Amy's skepticism of Moongirl's destiny. A tiny lime green car with a leather top sped past, a vehicle squarely in the present. "What is that?"

"A BMW Z." Diego explained what a Z was, who bought them, how many car companies manufactured them, and how much they cost.

She half-listened, wondering if X—faceless, part human, part witch—haunted him as he did her. In her mind, Kaya tiptoed to the room where she could find her twin. The door was open, and her twin was there. *Mahu! You saw him, talked to him. You know who X is. Tell me!* No answer came. Mahu dreamed on.

Diego's voice cut through her reverie. "Penny for your thoughts."

She didn't want to talk about X or her twin's dreams. "Tell me about Mahu. I still feel the twin bond, but he's a stranger. We only had Saturday evening to reconnect, and we spent most of that filling in the obvious gaps in our stories. I loved his jewelry.

You told me he's apprenticing with a famous silversmith. That means he's good."

"He's beyond good. Last summer, Mahu won first prize for New Artist at Indian Market. He's already sold a couple of pieces to a Santa Fe gallery."

"The pieces I saw were silver cut out with black designs showing through. I've seen jewelry like it in Becky's gallery."

"Hopi overlay. But Mahu's made the technique his own. The shapes of his pieces echo the oxidized designs. If the design on the bolo tie is a bear, the slide is shaped like a bear. If it's a butterfly, the center of the bracelet is a butterfly. Now his teacher is showing him how to work with turquoise and gold."

He gave her a quick look. "I hadn't thought about it until right now, but you'd be interested in his hallmark."

"Hallmark?"

"Most Hopi silversmiths sign their work with a symbol rather than their actual name. Mahu signs with a half of the petroglyph for *twin*."

Kaya Amy sighed. "Unlike me, he remembered he has a twin."

"Let up on yourself, Hermana. Your father and grandparents never quit talking about you. Besides, you remembered him in the only way your grandmother let you—in your dreams."

"I guess. But Mahu knows who he is. He's not even eighteen, and he knows what he wants to be. I quit school for some half-baked notion of being a potter."

"Mahu's no saint," Diego said. "When I first met him, he was always in trouble—drinking, fighting, causing trouble at school. He dropped out as soon as he could."

"Mahu? The other night he seemed so calm—serene even."

"That's now. After your dad died, Mahu was furious at the world. You can't blame him. Both parents dead, kids at school razing him because he wasn't full-blooded Hopi, his twin kidnapped by a grandmother who didn't want him. He started drinking—pretty heavily."

"What changed him?"

"Your grandparents never gave up. White Bear taught him to play the flute. You know how that music gets to you, makes you believe in the world again. Your grandmother tried to get him interested in pottery.

"He didn't care about that, but he discovered he had a talent for silversmithing. He quit drinking, and he plans to get his GED as soon as he turns eighteen. But he still has his moments."

Amy Kaya watched the monotonous landscape streaming by and felt ashamed. She'd imagined herself as the twin with a hard time. She'd assumed Mahu had it easier. After a while, she turned back to Diego. "You said he saved your life."

"Three years ago. We had just moved to Santa Fe from Lawrence, Kansas, and Dad was eager to see the ruins in Canyon de Chelly."

"Canyon de Chelly?"

"Arizona. Near Chinle. There are some interesting cliff dwellings there." He gave her a quick look she couldn't interpret. "Some people say Ya-Ya originated there."

"Please, don't tell me Mahu saved you from a witch!"

Diego laughed. "Nope. He saved me from drowning on a clear day in the desert."

"Sounds like witchcraft to me."

"A flash flood. Dad was poking around the ruins, so I decided to explore a nearby slot canyon. One minute I was walking beside a muddy trickle that couldn't even be called a stream, and the next I was in water up to my ankles. It had reached my calves when I heard a shout."

"Mahu?"

"Yep. He stood halfway up what looked like a sheer rock face, gesturing to me to climb up. I couldn't see any way to get where he was, but by that time, the water covered my knees, and

8acrCRBE NNAZSUS

I was scared enough to try anything. When I got to the place he was pointing to, I saw a series of toe and handholds going straight up the cliff.

"The rocks were worn almost smooth. That was the scariest climb I've ever made. I nearly reached the top when one of my feet slipped. I thought I was a goner. Not only was water roaring through the canyon, but I would have fallen about forty feet. Mahu grabbed my arm. He hauled me up like a sack of potatoes. We've been friends ever since."

A strange friendship. A rebellious Hopi kid and a studious Chicano. "You're so different."

He gave her a crooked smile. "Maybe not. Just two different ways of learning how to be an amalgam in a single element world."

Suddenly she understood not only Mahu, but also Diego, and maybe what she would become. She even caught a tiny glimpse of their destiny.

They left the interstate at Chambers, an exit with a cement-block gas station with one pump working and a deserted motel, complete with broken windows and weeds that slowly reclaimed the parking lot for the desert.

As they turned south toward the pueblos, the sense of being watched gradually returned. From his silence, Kaya was sure Diego felt it too, but she didn't want to talk about it.

They stopped at a tiny café for lunch in Zuni Pueblo. She caught her first glimpse of El Morro at mid-afternoon, a yellow-gold headland rising straight up from the desert floor. "It looks like a ship pushing through a sea of desert."

"It's a narrow mesa. There are fairly extensive ruins on top. You can see why. It has a great vantage point."

They turned off near the bluff's base onto a one-way track of blacktop that looped around the Visitor's Center. The brick and glass building seemed to fade into the desert around it, nothing more than another inconsequential rock dwarfed by the immense stone upthrust. The Monday after Thanksgiving must not be a day for many tourists because the parking lot was almost empty.

Diego pulled the Jeep into a space near the door and cut the engine but didn't move. "Any ideas?"

She stared at Diego, surprised at his uncertainty. She started to say, "You're the one who wanted to come here," but she saw him polishing his glasses on Mahu's velvet shirt hem. Suddenly, he looked younger, more vulnerable, as scared as she was. "I don't know if it'll work," she said slowly, "but I do have one idea."

Diego put his glasses back on. "I'm listening."

"Your dad's famous around here, right? You suggested we use his name. What do we have to lose? If he doesn't like it, you can always apologize later."

"So, when destiny deserts you, rely on common sense."

"Yep."

He grinned and opened his door.

The Visitor's Center looked as generic inside as it did outside —a glass counter, shelves filled with books and videos, a bucket of posters. Two park rangers, a woman and a man dressed in olive drab, stood beside a cash register talking. The woman, a tall thin redhead, appeared Irish. The man, of medium height and compact build, looked vaguely Hopi.

As Diego and Kaya approached, the rangers stopped talking and turned toward the newcomers. *What do they see?* A college boy with a Hopi girlfriend or Moon Twins on a mission? Either way, the idea was so ridiculous, it calmed her.

The female ranger smiled. "Can we help you?"

Diego smiled back, all signs of his momentary lapse of confidence gone. "I'm Diego James, and this is my friend Kaya Sekatewa. My dad sent us to see Dr. Montoya."

The woman looked surprised, but the man said, "Willard James?" Stepping around the counter, he held out a large hand. "Peter Lacapa. I know your father. An excellent researcher."

Diego shook the ranger's hand. "Dad's talked about you, but I didn't know you were here. I thought you ran the archaeology study center at Chimney Rock."

"I do. Arlene's in charge of El Morro. I just came down for the day to see Rina." He winked at the other ranger. "This must be her day."

"I hope she sees it that way," Arlene said.

The other ranger grinned. "I convinced Rina—just barely—to speak on her research at our next local archaeological meeting. She hates to be interrupted in her work. What's your dad want from her? I'm surprised he didn't come himself."

Diego smiled. "You mean why send a boy to do a man's job?"

Pete laughed. "Not exactly what I meant, but it'll do."

"Dad's at a conference in Mexico City. This weekend an artifact that surfaced on Third Mesa came to the MIAC lab. When I told him about it, he asked me to have Dr. Montoya examine it."

"Makes sense." Pete shifted his attention to Kaya. "*Sekatewa*. That's a name from Third Mesa. White Bear's family name is *Sekatewa*, I think. You wouldn't happen to be the person who helped this artifact surface?"

Kaya hesitated, unsure of how much to say.Nothing secret, except that Dr. James didn't know anything about it. In the back office, a phone rang. Both rangers automatically looked toward the sound. Amy Kaya stole a quick glance at Diego. He gave her an almost imperceptible nod.

Arlene left to answer the phone, and Pete turned back to Kaya.

"It's an old manuscript," she said. "My brother found it. He couldn't get away today, so he asked me to come with Diego." Like Diego's story, almost true.

"Pete," called Arlene. "Phone's for you."

"I've got to take this," Pete said. "Take care, you two. Take very good care."

Back behind the glass counter, Arlene said, "I don't know how much luck you'll have with Rina today, but she's on the mesa by Átsína ruins. You know the way?"

Diego nodded and pulled his wallet out of his pocket. "I've been here a couple of times. It's a great park."

Arlene looked at her watch and shook her head. "Don't pay. You've only got a couple of hours before we close. Just be sure to check in before you leave."

Double glass doors opened into a small courtyard bounded by a low rock wall. Overhead the bluff loomed against a deep blue sky. A stone path seemed to go straight into the rock. As they followed the path, Kaya touched Diego's arm. "What did Pete Lacapa mean? Do you think he knows what's going on?"

"Take a deep breath, Hermana. I don't know, and I don't know."

"Sorry. It's just all so weird. Who is he?"

Diego shrugged. "All I know is he's an amalgam like us— Puebloan on one side, Anglo on the other. Dad says he's the perfect ranger, a protector of the ruins by birth and by training. Come to think of it, Rina Montoya is another amalgam.

"She's another archaeologist with Native blood. I don't know which tribe, but I remember hearing her say she was looking for her roots when she started studying petroglyphs."

"We're collecting archaeologists," Kaya said. "Maybe I'll have to give up pottery and take up archaeology."

"You could learn about pottery from your grandmother and apply what you learned to archaeology.

"You mean instead of archaeoastronomy, I could be an archaeopotter!"

Diego looked down at her and grinned. "You catch on fast, Hermana."

Just ahead on the path, an older Anglo couple stood beside a clear pool. The rock towered over them, throwing them all into a twilight-like shadow. The couple leaned against a waist-high fence studying a string of inscriptions scratched into the sandstone, pointing at first to one and then another.

"I'd like to come back here sometime," said Kaya Hermana. "After this is all over."

"I'll bring you. It's a fascinating place."

*Will the universe tip toward harmony so we can return?* The question came suddenly into Kaya's mind. Shivering, she pushed it away.

Diego pointed to a staircase chiseled into the side of the bluff. "There. Follow me."

At the halfway point, the stairway opened onto a meadow thatched with dry grass. Patches of snow showed white against the north rock face and a few of the tree trunks. To their right, a steep slope tumbled toward the valley floor—red earth dotted with scrub cedar, defined on the north by an indigo line of low mountains split by a black ribbon of road that ran west.

Overhead a lone raven floated in an amethyst sky. Once they heard the shrill cry of a hawk, but otherwise, complete silence. Even their feet, Kaya's in her mother's soft boots and Diego's in athletic shoes, made no sound.

They reached the middle of the open space when she heard the flute song. A puzzled look on his face, Diego stopped abruptly and scanned the little meadow. "You hear it," she said.

He nodded and then pointed to a figure chiseled high on the rock.

"Kokopelli!"

"Mahu told me once that sometimes petroglyphs reveal themselves to people. I didn't believe him."

"The Song of Creation. White Bear said we'd hear it when we're on the right path."

"It doesn't make sense."

She didn't reply. *Mahu? Twin?* He dreamed on, but she thought he stirred.

A second set of stairs appeared in the stone. They resumed

their climb, moving in and out of sun and shadow. At the top, the shadows disappeared, erased by the bright afternoon sun. A few yards from where they emerged, the trail disappeared at a cliff edge. Diego pointed at a sheer limestone wall that closed the near end of the chasm. "That's a box canyon. It was a good source of water for the people who lived here. The trail makes a *U* around it."

In striking contrast to the mesa's bare rock, ponderosa pine dotted the canyon floor, already casting long shadows. "Are the ruins down there?"

Diego shook his head. "Átsína is up on top. Much easier to avoid ambush up here."

They found the trail a few yards ahead, a path marked by parallel lines chiseled into the rock. Wherever it threatened to disappear, whether because of an abrupt turn or a catch basin filled with melted snow, a cairn of three small stones balanced one on top of the other pointed the way.

The path crossed a narrow neck of rock and rounded the end of the box canyon. Another half-mile brought them to Átsína. The ruins lay below them, straight walls of carefully matched stones crisscrossing an area the size of a city block. The square rooms varied only slightly in size, most as large as her grandfather's house.

"We're standing on the second level of what was a three-story structure," Diego explained. "These were storerooms and workrooms and possibly family living quarters. Seven hundred years ago, this was a thriving community with two kivas. That large round structure was one of them. With the top layer gone, you can see how it's dug deeper than the living areas."

"But not the kiva we're looking for?"

"Nope, but I think we've found Dr. Montoya."

Kaya saw the collection of brushes he pointed to, but no linguist.

"See the top of that ladder? I bet she's on it." They looked over the edge. She was there, a petite gray-headed woman clinging with one hand to the ladder and with the other gingerly brushing a small area of the cliff face. Absorbed in her work, she was completely unaware of their scrutiny. Squatting, Diego took firm hold of the ladder. "Dr. Montoya?"

Without looking up, she said, "Go away. I don't have much light left."

"Dr. Montoya! It's Diego James—Willard's son. We need your help."

She looked up. A frown creased her wrinkled face. "Can't it wait?"

"No, ma'am."

"You're sure you're Willard's son?"

"Yes, ma'am."

"Oh, all right." Looking annoyed, she tucked her tiny brush into the pocket of her khaki work vest and started up the ladder, climbing almost as easily as if she were a young woman. "You realize there aren't many people I stop work for," she grumbled. "First Pete Lacapa and now Willard James. What a day!"

At the top, she took Diego's outstretched hand and stepped onto the mesa, a woman with skin the color of a paper bag, wiry and weather-beaten from a lifetime in the desert. She dusted off her jeans with equally dusty hands and looked past Diego to Kaya, then at the otherwise empty mesa. "So where is Willard?" she demanded.

Diego shoved at his glasses and smiled. "He's in Mexico City, ma'am."

Exasperation replaced annoyance on the linguist's face. "Thirty seconds. Tell me what's so all-fired important it's worth using your father's name, or else go away and leave me alone."

"My brother found a lienzo," blurted Kaya. "We need to know what it says. We can't reach Dr. James, and Diego says you can translate it."

"I heard something surfaced in Old Oraibi," Dr. Montoya said, "but I didn't hear it was a lienzo. Who are you?"

"Kaya Sekatewa, ma'am. White Bear's granddaughter."

"The little girl who was taken away? Mahu's twin?"

Kaya nodded.

Dr. Montoya touched her temples and rubbing in little circles. "All right, let's see what you've got."

Diego removed the lienzo in its plastic sleeve out of his pocket and handed it to her.

"You're carrying it in an auto registration folder? Why on earth haven't you taken steps to preserve it properly? Hasn't your father taught you anything, Diego James?"

"It's not his fault," Kaya said.

But the linguist wasn't listening. Using the tiny brush's handle, she opened the sleeve and peered intently at the scrap of cloth inside. After a moment, she looked up and said, "I'll give you thirty minutes. We'll go to my camp."

To Kaya, the word *camp* meant a tent, a table, chairs, and maybe a sleeping bag, but evidently, the word meant something different to this woman. Her camp turned out to be a folding canvas stool, a well-worn backpack, and a large metal box under a stunted and wind-twisted pine. Dr. Montoya let herself down onto the stool with a small sigh. "Pull up a rock and make yourselves comfortable."

"We appreciate your time, ma'am," Diego sat cross-legged on the ground on one side of the linguist's stool. Following his example, Kaya dropped to the ground on the other side.

"Good. Now drop the *ma'am* and call me Rina. I know I seem ancient to you two, but I don't like having my nose rubbed in it. Now, give me my tweezers and magnifying glass. In the outside pocket of the pack over there."

Kaya was closest, so she reached for it. As Kaya searched the pack, Dr. Montoya kept talking. "Old enough to be interesting, but don't get your hopes up too high. The conquistadors were soldiers, most of whom couldn't read or write. The padres who followed were the writers. Probably you've got part of a parish record."

"It's more than that," Diego said. "There's writing on one side, but the other side looks like a copy of pictograph panel."

The linguist looked skeptical, but when Kaya held out the tools, she took them eagerly. Pulling the metal box around to use as a table, she drew the lienzo from the plastic sleeve with the tweezers and spread it out, Spanish script side up. Using the magnifying glass, she peered curiously at the writing. She read slowly, as if she struggled with the script. Gradually her speed increased, and after a few minutes, she turned the lienzo over.

After what seemed a long time, Diego broke the silence. "Not a parish record?"

"No. You've only got a piece of a piece, but whatever it is, it's not a parish record."

## CHAPTER ELEVEN

Diego studied the linguist. "Does the script translate the pictographs?"

Dr. Montoya looked up sharply. "You mean is this manuscript a Rosetta Stone? Not exactly. Though if the rest of it exists and if we can find the panel—"

Kaya looked over the older woman's shoulder. "Please! What does it say?"

"My guess is it's the journal of a young man who came to the mesas with one of the padres. This fragment tells about seeing a pictograph panel that was taboo."

"The figures on the other side?" Diego said.

"Maybe. But this part of the narrative doesn't translate the panel. It just says the panel recorded an important ceremony."

Diego frowned. "Does it say where he saw the panel?"

The linguist shook her head. "I can give you a rough para-phrase of what's here." Moving the magnifying glass slowly across the manuscript, she read. "Today, the girl took me to the kiva where the panel that records the ceremony is. She said the place is taboo because the ceremony was for the banishment of great evil. She wouldn't go inside, but I'm not afraid of their taboos.

"I couldn't read the figures, but they're old, at least five hundred years if the stories are right. I copied the figures so I can talk to their elders about the meaning. Then I'll use the map to come back for a closer study." She stopped reading and looked up. "That's it."

"What about the map?" prompted Diego.

Rina shook her head. "You only have part of the original lienzo. This manuscript was written on more than one piece of cloth. It looks like the stitching gave way on the left, and the right side is ragged as if it was torn."

"What if the map is on the part X got?" Kaya said.

"Yep."

Dr. Montoya looked up sharply. "X? What's this all about? Why do you two have this fragment? It should be locked up at the MIAC Lab."

Diego cleared his throat. "We're taking it there now."

"But my grandfather wants to know what it says first. That's why we came to you." It was almost true. Kaya Moeyha was sure if Ikwa knew what they were doing, he would approve.

"So White Bear's in this? You've got two pretty big guns telling you what to do."

"Yukioma is stirring up trouble," Diego said. "He claims the Committee for Cultural Preservation has jurisdiction, and he wants to burn the lienzo."

Rina raised her eyebrows. "Ya-Ya?"

"Can you read the pictographs?" asked Kaya.

"Maybe a little bit." Rina turned over the manuscript. "Pictograph reading can be tricky. It's usually done in concentric circles with the most important part of the story in the center. The farther from the center, the less important. This configuration is odd, though."

"Those parallel lines," Diego said, "the way they're drawn,

they make the whole thing look more like a *D* than a circle."

"Maybe our conquistador was a bad artist," Kaya said.

"Yep. Or maybe the shape meant something to the people who painted the panel."

"I have no idea," Rina said. "I've never seen anything like it."

"The double lines that make the *D*," Diego pointed to the markings. "They're not in the center, but they must mean something."

"I'm just guessing," Rina said slowly, "but they might represent two roads—the right road and a wrong road. The line with the corn stalks on it would be the Road of Life, the right road. Corn is sacred to the Hopis. Archaeologists often find cornmeal in very ancient kivas. In this dry climate, it keeps. I found some myself right here at Átsína."

"The people are all on the other road," interrupted Kaya. "The wrong road."

Diego pushed at his glasses. "Maybe the ceremony was to get the People back on the right road."

"How did they get on the wrong road?" asked Kaya.

The linguist sighed. "Evidence exists about the wrong road. But no one talks about it." She shrugged. "I've never heard anything but speculation on the topic of how it happened.

*Powáqas?* Kaya looked at the cloth. "The circle at the end of the two roads—could it be the moon?"

Rina gave her an odd look. "Why would you ask that?"

Kaya wasn't ready to talk about the Tokpela Moon or the prophecy, so she said, "Just something my grandfather told us."

"I suppose it might. More likely, it's the sun, but there's no way of knowing."

Diego studied the lienzo over Rina's shoulder. "The cross-hatching on the circle looks like a ladder. Isn't there an extinct ladder dance?"

The linguist nodded. "The theory is that it was similar to an ancient Aztec ritual, but what on earth do you know about the ladder dance?"

"My dad's studying Paquime. He talks about connections sometimes."

"Paquime?" Kaya was confused.

Rina nodded. "Casas Grandes, the Mimbres people—my ancestors."

Diego's eyebrows went up. "Interesting connection."

"What is Casas Grandes?" demanded Kaya. "And what's it got to do with the lienzo? You two are leaving me behind!"

"Sorry," Diego said. "Casas Grandes means 'Great Houses.' It's a huge ruin in Northern Mexico. Its other name is *Paquime*. Archaeologists didn't find it until the 1950s. It's important because it's in line with Aztec and Chaco. Some people speculate it's the Red City of the South referred to in Ancestral Puebloan mythology."

Kaya held up her hand. "Thanks for the info, Professor. What I want to know now is about the ceremony depicted on the lienzo. Four of the figures are headless. Did they decapitate people for this ceremony?"

Dr. Montoya laughed. "Nothing like that. Drawings without heads sometimes represent spirits rather than men and women. These figures might be shamans meant to represent specific mythic characters in a cosmic drama. Possibly the four cardinal directions."

"Yep. I should've thought of that."

"Explain, please, Professor."

"The color of their clothes. It's faded, but you can just make it out. Yellow represents West, blue South, red East, and brown North. See where they're placed?"

"Yellow on the left, blue at the bottom, red on the right, and brown at the top. Okay. The shamans represent the four directions. What does that mean?"

"The totality of creation." Rina absently fingering a scarf at her throat.

Kaya watched her. The scarf was soft blue. Ikwa said shamans would help the Moon Twins. His bandana was yellow.

"Kokopelli?"

"Yes." The linguist gave Diego a steady gaze. "You two know more about this than you're letting on. Don't you think it's about time you told me the story?"

"Long and complicated, but honorable."

"You'll tell me later, I suppose."

"Yep."

"There's another figure." Kaya held the magnifying glass and studied the lienzo. "A side view of two people sitting back to back, hands outstretched, but there's only one hand, one leg."

"Mahu's trademark," murmured Diego.

"Let me see." Rina took the lienzo and the magnifying glass. After a moment, she looked up. "Twins. You and Mahu. And he's the one who found this lienzo. Where is Mahu? Why isn't he with you?"

Kaya and Diego exchanged glances.

"All right, you two. Long and complicated or not, honorable or not, it's time to tell me what's going on. Otherwise, I might have to call the police and report the theft of a priceless archaeological artifact by one Diego James and one Kaya Sekatewa."

"It really is a long story." Kaya sighed.

The linguist shrugged. "See those shadows? I'm out of light. You can tell me while I pack up for the day."

"We'll swap the story for the lienzo." Diego held out his hand.

Dr. Montoya smiled ruefully. "Maybe that's not such a good trade for me."

Diego took off his glasses and held them up. "It is if I throw in the report I give my dad, ma'am. If you keep the lienzo, he'll be the one reporting the theft. If you listen to our story, I tell him how helpful you were. So helpful that he owes you one."

She snorted and handed the lienzo to Diego. "You've got a lot of your father in you, young man. Iron fist in velvet glove and all that."

Diego laughed and put his glasses back on. "Mama says that. She complains that when the two of us gang up on her, there's no winning."

"I'll bet. Okay, but tell your dad he owes me first crack at the lienzo in a laboratory."

"Scout's honor." Diego carefully slipped the lienzo back into its plastic sleeve.

"No doubt you were an Eagle Scout," said Dr. Montoya. "Be prepared and all that."

"Yes, ma'am."

She laughed. "All right, then. Storytime. You talk while I pack up my gear."

"We promised to check out by 5:00," Diego said.

"You're not getting out of the story like that! One of you stays and talks while the other one goes down to the Visitor's Center."

Diego got to his feet. "I'll go. I've got a couple of questions for Dr. Lacapa if he's still here. The Jeep's not locked, Hermana. If you get there first, wait for me."

Kaya looked up. "How much detail in this story?"

"As much as Dr. Rina can stand. She might know something that will help us."

He had noticed the blue scarf too.

"Go then, Diego," Dr. Montoya said. "Kaya, you have my full attention."

As Diego jogged away, the two women rose to their feet. "All right, Kaya. Talk." She moved to where the ladder glowed silver in the last rays of the setting sun.

Kaya cleared her throat. "Mahu and I were together when the man Diego and I call X attacked Mahu and took the lienzo."

"No. Start at the beginning."

"You mean when Grandmother Adams came for me? I don't remember."

"Not that far back. Start with why you came to Santa Fe, with what led you to Mahu."

Amy Kaya started with her dreams, her fascination with pottery, and the fight with her Grandmother Adams. As she talked, Dr. Montoya worked steadily, picking up tools, packing them into the canvas bag. Only when Kaya got to White Bear's prophecy did the linguist interrupt her. "Tell me again," she said. "Try to remember his exact words."

"Ikwa said his grandfather told him the time of the Tokpela Moon would be filled with danger. I don't remember his exact words, but it was something about the universe waiting to tip toward chaos or toward harmony. Modern-day powáqas will help ancient powáqas push toward uncreation, and Moon Twins will sing the Song of Creation."

The linguist pulled up the ladder without comment. Then she said, "Bring my tool bag. After we stow the gear, I have a story to tell you."

Stowing the gear consisted of chaining the ladder to the twisted pine's trunk and putting the tool bag into the metal box they'd used as a table. As Rina snapped the combination lock, she said, "When I was ten, my great-grandmother told me about the Tokpela Moon. She told me about chaos and the Song and the terrible danger. She said I would be sixty when the door to the endless void opened. I turned sixty a couple of months ago."

Together they looked up at the moon. Three quarters. The clock ticked toward Tokpela. Remembering the terrible roar of what waited on the other side, Kaya shivered.

Beside her, Rina folded her stool and slid it under the ladder. "It'll be dark soon, and we need to get down the trail. There's another more direct trail. It's steep, so we'll have to watch our feet. But I can talk as we walk."

In the west, the sky burned orange. The last rays of the

setting sun showed a narrow trail, steeply switchbacked. Rina went first, and Kaya followed, straining to hear. "My grandmother told me I would perform an ancient ceremony to restore harmony to the earth."

"Did she teach you the ceremony?"

Walking quickly, the linguist didn't seem to hear, but she said, "My grandmother said the ceremony had been long forgotten even when her grandmother was a girl. She said there would be seven of us, seven songs for seven stars to rebirth the universe, and she told me it was my destiny to rediscover the ceremony."

Watching her feet, Kaya did her best to keep up. Still, she fell behind. "Wait!"

Dr. Montoya stopped and turned. "Sorry. I walk this trail twice a day, sometimes four times. I forgot you don't know it."

"Please tell me why this ceremony is so important. Ikwa said we needed the proper ceremony for the proper task. I don't understand."

The linguist nodded and started walking again, more slowly this time. "If I have a physical task to perform, I need the right tool. For example, if I need to study something tiny, a hammer won't help me. I need a magnifying glass or a microscope. If I have a spiritual task, I need the right ceremony. A ceremony intended to name a child won't help us keep ancient powáqas from coming through the doorway of the Tokpela Moon."

"So, we need a thousand-year-old ceremony to fight thousand-year-old evil."

"*Fight* isn't the right word. We can't force harmony. What was the word your grandfather used? Do you remember it?"

"I think he said 'invite' harmony."

"Yes. Harmony replaces chaos. We invite harmony."

"Without the ceremony, we can't invite harmony?"

"It's not completely hopeless," said Rina. "Every ceremony strives to bring harmony. No matter the ancient ceremony's details, we need a pipe for Prayers, a feather for Father Sky, clay for Mother Earth, and cornmeal for Life." As she explained, she picked up her pace, starting to talk more to herself than to Kaya. "Diego's moon ladder means something. I must remember more of what my grandmother told me. Something about secrets, secrets of the Tokpela Moon. I've got to go home—to Paquime." They rounded another switchback, and suddenly deep shadow enveloped them. Afraid of missing her footing, Kaya slowed her pace. Rina hurried on, deep in thought. Kaya watched the retreating figure. Wherever she was going, she'd said *we*. Rina's destiny somehow intertwined with theirs. White Bear promised shamans to help, and perhaps Rina was a shaman. That would make two—White Bear and Rina. *Four?* Like on the lienzo—one for each direction?

The trail zigzagged again, giving Kaya a clear view of the parking lot below. Rina reached her green SUV and tossed her gear in the back. At the place where the blacktop loop joined the road, a brown Hummer turned right and sped away. Shadow joined with shadow, lengthening, deepening, dusk becoming night, and for the rest of the hike, Kaya's full attention was on her feet.

By the time she reached the bottom, the last of the daylight dissolved. Overhead streetlights lit the parking lot. The vast expanse of blacktop before her sat empty except for the Jeep and a battered Park Service pickup. The Visitor's Center was dark, a *Closed* sign on the door. There was no sign of Diego, Pete Lacapa, or anyone else. Wondering a little uneasily where everyone was, Kaya crossed to the Jeep and climbed in to wait.

At first, she waited contentedly enough, grateful to rest after descending the steep mesa and glad for time to ponder Rina's words. After an hour, though, she grew impatient. Getting out of the Jeep, she went to see if the outside restroom's door was locked.

It was open, and she went in. She used the facilities, washed her face, rebraided her hair, went back to the Jeep to wait some more. Another hour and worry replaced impatience. She worried Diego had fallen and broken his leg or twisted his ankle, but both she and Rina had come down the same trail. They would have seen him. She worried he was sick, but they hadn't eaten anything for several hours.

By the time the moon rose halfway up the sky, fear had pushed away worry. X has Diego, she thought with certainty. Diego *and* the lienzo. She wanted to do something, look for him, get help. But the Visitor's Center was closed, and the keys to the Jeep were in Diego's pocket. She tried both cell phones, but neither picked up a signal. *Diego?* She called in her mind. *Diego, where are you?* Nothing. Spiritual twin or not, there was no place in her mind where she could sense him.

Late November in the desert, the temperature dropped steadily. By nine o'clock, the moon reached the top of the sky. Kaya huddled in the car coat. By ten, she placed Diego's leather coat on over the car coat. At eleven, fear had worn itself out. She was numb with waiting. Retrieving a flashlight from under the driver's seat, she got out. At first she thought she was walking to get warm, but her feet carried her out of the parking lot, around the Visitor's Center, and to Inscription Rock.

She passed the water pool that had made El Morro important and climbed the paved path to the top of the mesa. The moon, now halfway down the western sky, didn't give her much light. On the parts of the trail that ran close beneath the bluff, she had to switch on the flashlight and follow its pencil-thin yellow beam.

At the top, she stopped to look out at the landscape. Long moon shadows cast by scrub trees sliced the wide, open space into dark and light slivers. The road was almost invisible, a black strand of pavement only slightly darker than the prairie grass. Nothing moved.

Drawn by some yearning for human companionship, no

matter how tenuous, Kaya returned to Dr. Montoya's camp. Her back against the metal box, she looked at the sky. Thousands of stars, pinpricks of light scattered across the dark universe, burned brightly in deep space.

Gemini. The Twins. She'd never learned the constellations properly and didn't think she could find it. The memory came like a curtain lifting to reveal a scene on stage. Their fifth birthday. She and Mahu lying on their backs, gazing at the sky. Mama on her left, Taáta on Mahu's right.

'Orion, the Hunter,' said Mama, tracing the three stars in his belt. 'Now look up, still higher, go left. See Gemini? Twins holding hands. Just like you and Mahu. The night you were born, the full moon passed by Gemini.'

'Your grandfather said it was a sign,' Taáta said.

Off to the east, Kaya found Gemini. The moon had long ago dropped out of sight, but three nights from now it would sail by The Twins again. She wanted to find Mahu, listen to his dream of the Song, but she was afraid. If she pushed on the door in her mind, what would she find? The notes of a red cedar flute, or the cacophony of terror?

Slowly, quietly, the answer took shape in her mind. The terror is part of Tokpela. The ceremony of blessing White Bear performed for the Moon Twins called it up. She didn't understand, but she was comforted enough to open her mind. *Mahu?* He was there, holding out his hand to her. Overhead the stars of Gemini brightened. Lower in the sky, Orion, the Hunter, blazed. *Diego.*

As she slipped toward sleep, a nighthawk cried somewhere close by. A small rodent squeaked, and then all was silent again. Diego—was he hunting or being hunted? Hawk or prey? She dozed and woke and dozed again, trying to dream someone who could help, somewhere she could go, something she could do.

# IV. HOOPO [EAST]

Storytellers say that kachinas, the spirit people, built the Red City. Over the years, it grew from a small village beside a river into a large city with three sections: one for living in, one for storing food, and one for performing ceremonies. For many years, the city grew and prospered. On their migrations, clans stopped long enough to learn the history of the first three worlds, the workings of nature, the pattern of the stars, and the Song that balances creation. Then one day, evil entered the Red City.

Returning from the north, the Spider Clan asked permission to enter the city. But the kachinas knew the Spider Clan had used their power wrongfully in the north, and they refused the request. Angry at being denied admittance, the Spider Clan attacked the city, and a great battle ensued.

The city walls were strong, and day after day, the defenders resisted the attack. On the fourth day of the battle, a great serpent rose up out of the plaza in the center of the city. When it moved, its coils shook the earth so that great cracks split the streets and buildings toppled. By noon thousands of people had died, and half of the city lay in smoking ruins. Only one house remained—the home of twins, a boy and a girl.

*That night, the people made their escape. One by one, the clans left the city to resume their migrations. In all the confusion, the parents of the twins didn't realize their home had escaped destruction. Thinking their children were dead, they left the city with their clan.*

*The next morning, when the twins came outside, they found the city in ruins and all the people gone. Taking some food, a bow, and some arrows, the twins set out to follow.*

*As everyone knows, boy and girl twins have special power; nevertheless, traveling was difficult for the children. Each day it got colder and colder, and each day their food dwindled. Finally, the day came when they were freezing, and their food was gone.*

*Taking the bow and arrows, the boy trailed a deer and shot it. After they cooked its meat and ate, the girl made a sewing awl from the deer's leg bone. Then she made warm clothes for her brother and herself. By helping each other, the two finally reached the thriving pueblo where their clan had settled.*

# CHAPTER TWELVE

**K**aya Amy Hermana woke as the first bit of light washed the sky pearl gray. She was cold and stiff, lying on the ground. Gemini and Orion, along with the rest of the stars, had disappeared. Groaning, she forced her protesting muscles to move and sat up.

Fear returned as memories washed over her. Mahu stabbed. Diego kidnapped. X hunting the lienzo, hunting them. And she had no idea who could help, where to go, or what to do.

Gritting her teeth against panic, Kaya got to her feet and looked around. Rina's camp, the mesa, the trail—nothing suggested a plan. Still, she had to go down. Straightening her two coats and the dress beneath as best as she could, she walked. Not down the longer trail she'd followed in the moonlight, but down the steep switchbacks still in deep shadow. She picked her way, one careful step at a time.

Purple dawn smudged the horizon as she crossed the parking lot to the restroom. It was warm inside. By the time she washed, she'd almost stopped shivering. The reflection that looked back at her from the mirror didn't look like anyone she knew—an odd sort of relief. Kaya, Moeyha, Amy, Moongirl, all of them, none of them—it didn't matter.

Back at the Jeep, she took off Diego's coat to leave if he escaped X and returned. Rina had gone home to Mimbres, much farther south than El Morro. With no idea how to explain to the El Morro ranger when she came to work, Kaya headed for the nearest people, a mile and a half walk.

The two-lane road headed straight east. As she walked, the sky brightened. Sunrise, when it came, was undramatic, a quick flash of gold followed by blue morning. Suddenly, Mahu entered her mind. It was as if the door to the twin room swung open from the inside. No red cedar notes. Mahu dreamed East, dreamed the sun climbed the sky, lighting a path toward Iso.

Moeyha Hermana remembered what Ikwa and Diego told her about her grandmother. Eleanor Naranjo was at Cochiti Pueblo, making storyteller dolls for the tourists. Would she be wearing the shaman's red?

Amy walked faster now that she had a plan, but anxiety stayed with her. She'd escaped X twice, but he would come after her again. She was sure of it—unless she could get to Cochiti.

Who was X? Yukioma knew Mahu had taken the lienzo to Santa Fe. He could have followed, but X hadn't broken into the gallery. Would Mahu have let him in? Yuki had been in Old Oraibi. He could have attacked her, but Diego thought he'd seen a powáqa, and Yuki was obsessed with destroying witchcraft. Or was that just an act? He might have used the Seeing Eye to track them to El Morro and grab Diego.

Who else? The Navajo policeman—Begay? Hermana was sure he was looking for the lienzo when he pulled them over. He could have tracked them to El Morro by his police radio, could have been in Santa Fe. But Mahu wouldn't have let him into the gallery, and Begay couldn't have been her attacker in Old Oraibi. If she and Diego weren't welcome in the ancient pueblo, how much less a Navajo policeman? Besides, a Navajo powáqa didn't make sense. She didn't know what Navajos called witches, but she was sure it wasn't *powáqa*.

Kaya kicked a rock out of her way. What about Walker? He wanted the lienzo, knew more about it than he admitted. He might have followed them from Holbrook to El Morro, but Diego didn't trust him. If Walker had shown up at the Visitor's Center, Diego would have been suspicious. Besides, Mahu wouldn't have let Walker into the gallery. And she couldn't see him as a witch. Black market, yes. Black magic, no.

Frustrated, she called out silently. *Mahu, you saw him— dream of X for me!* But Mahu's dreams were gone.

She reached the tiny town of El Morro a little before seven. The only thing open was the gas station. She needed to get to Cochiti. With a sinking feeling, she realized she didn't have a plan at all. She didn't even really know where Cochiti was. East, but she'd been a tiny child the last time she'd been in Cochiti.

Even if she found out where it was, how could she get there? In her Amy life, she'd always had a car, a ride to wherever she needed to go, or at least enough money for a bus. Hitchhiking was not in her comfort zone. But there was nothing else to do.

Taking a deep breath, she pushed open the glass door and went inside the tiny convenience store. Behind the cash register, a heavy-set Anglo man sat in a metal folding chair, his feet propped on a desk littered with paper. In one hand he had a cup of coffee, in the other a newspaper. He looked up.

"Excuse me," she said, "I need to get to Cochiti Pueblo."

"The bus stops at the McDonald's, Missy, not here."

"I don't have money for a ticket."

"Can't help you with that." He dropped his eyes back to the newspaper. "This ain't no bank, and it ain't no charity."

"I'm not looking for a handout. I'm looking for a ride."

"Does it look like I'm going to Albuquerque?"

"I thought you might know someone who was going there." She felt stupid standing there, practically begging help from a man who wouldn't even look at her. But she didn't know what else to do.

The man sighed and let his chair down with a thud. "You running from the law?"

In a way, that's exactly what she was doing, but not like he meant it. "No, sir. I just need to get to my grandmother's house in Cochiti Pueblo. Family emergency. My brother's in the hospital." That much was absolutely true.

Twisting in his chair, the man opened the center drawer of the desk and pulled out a magic marker. Leaning over, he pulled a piece of paper from the trash can and handed her both items. With exaggerated patience, he said, "Make yourself a sign, Missy. Stand out there by the pump and wait."

Cochiti or Albuquerque? She settled on Albuquerque since the man had assumed that was her first destination. She thanked him, returned his magic marker, and went outside to wait.

The first customer, a grim-faced Navajo man in a dusty pickup, shook his head but didn't speak. The second person to arrive was a teenaged girl with orange spiked hair. Her beat-up station wagon looked like it couldn't possibly run. She parked at the side of the little store and took three boxes of doughnuts from the backseat.

As she passed Kaya, she smiled. When the girl came back outside, Kaya said, "Do you know anyone going to Albuquerque?"

She gave Kaya a curious look. "You a runaway?"

Kaya shook her head. "Family emergency. I need to get to my grandmother's house in Cochiti Pueblo. If I can get to Albuquerque, she can pick me up."

"My brother works in Grants. If you want, I can ask him to take you that far. You can get a ride to Albuquerque from there. Hop in."

"Thanks." Folding her sign, Kaya put it in the pocket of her coat. She got into the passenger's side of the station wagon, settled her feet between empty paper cups and hamburger wrappers, and pulled the heavy door closed.

When the girl was behind the wheel, she said, "My name is Fran."

"Kaya. I really appreciate this."

"I ran away once," Fran said. "It was tough."

Kaya started to object, but the truth was unbelievable. And runaway or not, she was in a tough situation. "Thanks for understanding."

Fran nodded. "There are all kinds of family emergencies. If you're hungry, there's a box of doughnuts open on the back seat. I'm not supposed to eat the merchandise, but the lady at the next stop won't mind if her order's a couple short once in a while."

"Thanks." Kaya was hungry. She reached for one.

"There's a carton of milk back there you can have."

"It must be yours."

"I'll get another one."

"I don't have any money."

"Forget it," Fran said. "You can't always plan for family emergencies. My brother's name is Fred." She grinned. "My parents thought it would be cute to give us all names that started with the same letter. *Fred, Frank, Faye, and Fran.* You got any brothers and sisters?"

"Mahu," said Kaya. "He's my twin." And Diego. He was the closest thing to a brother right now. She knew where Mahu was, but where was Diego?

"Weird. Having a twin would be cool if it was another girl. But a boy? I don't know."

*Stranger than that.* But Kaya didn't say anything about the Moon Twins, just enjoyed the sugar on her tongue and the cold milk sliding down her throat.

Fran pulled into the driveway of a small concrete block house, stopping only inches from a bright red Cougar. "Fred's a good guy," she said. "He doesn't talk much, but he'll give you a ride if I ask him."

"Thanks, Fran. You came at just the right time. I didn't know what to do."

"Forget it. Take another doughnut."

Leaving the car running, Fran got out and headed for the house. Kaya retrieved a second doughnut, ate it, and then and got out to wait. In a few minutes, Fran returned with Fred, a lanky young man dressed in jeans and a blue chambray work shirt.

He was in his late twenties. Like Walker. Like Yukioma. Unlike them, he had small hands. An odd characteristic to notice but reassuring all the same.

"He works at the auto parts store," Fran was saying. "There's a gas station next door where you can pick up a ride into Albuquerque."

"Thanks."

"Same song, next verse," said Fran with a smile. "As I said, I know what it's like. Fred worried about me when I was gone, so he's glad to help out."

"You should've told me what was going on." Fred came up behind his sister and caught her in a friendly neck lock.

"Next time," Fran said. "I learned my lesson."

"That's my girl," Fred, released her. "I gotta go."

Fran headed for her station wagon. "Her name's Kaya. You can talk to her."

Fred grunted and climbed into the Cougar. Kaya got in beside him and buckled her seatbelt. "I really appreciate the ride."

He put the car into gear and watched in the rearview mirror for Fran to back out. "Did you call your brother?"

"He's in the hospital." Where was Diego?

The station wagon out of the way, Fred backed his Cougar into the street. "You should call your brother. Even if he's sick, don't make him wonder where you are. He'll want to help."

Kaya looked at Fred with mild surprise. She suspected it was a long and possibly passionate speech for him. No point in explaining, so all she said was, "I will."

Fred nodded and turned on the radio, filling the car with the notes of a recent country-western song and stopping any possibility of more conversation. A few minutes later, he turned on the heater. Kaya stopped shivering and looked out the window at the drab winter-brown landscape.

She had a brother, but it had been so long. He would help her if he could. Diego had helped. He had been her brother. The names kept time with the rhythm of the wheels on the blacktop. Mahu. Diego. Mahu. Diego. *Mahu* ...

It was thirty miles to Grants. The car clock said 7:45 when Fred pulled into the parking lot of the auto parts store. The gas station was right where Fran had said it would be. Fred got out of the car without comment, but he surprised her by speaking when Kaya got out. "Have to open up or I'd take you to Albuquerque myself. You got a sign?"

Kaya nodded and took it out of her coat pocket.

"Frannie said you're going to your grandmother."

"Yes."

"Be sure you go there. No heading for the bright lights or anything like that."

"No."

"Make sure you call your brother."

"I promise."

Fred nodded toward the gas station. "You can stand inside with your sign. Tell Joe I said it's okay."

"Thanks. I'll tell my brother how much you helped me."

Fred nodded again, locked the Cougar with a remote, and disappeared into the store.

Fran was lucky. Maybe one of these days she would be too.

Whispering prayers for Mahu and Diego, Kaya Hermana

headed for the gas station's connected convenience store. The day was warming up, but she was still glad to go inside.

As Fred had predicted, Joe didn't mind. "Stand over there by the window. Hold your sign so the customers can see. You'll get a ride pretty quick."

The first ten minutes were quiet. A white van with the name of a Grants' security system painted on the side pulled in for gas. Not long after, a Camry that seemed to be a carpool late for school stopped long enough for a frazzled mother to fill the tank. Next came a New Mexico Sheriff's Department patrol car.

Kaya put her sign behind her back and looked at Joe. "It's not illegal to hitchhike, is it?""Up on the freeway. Not here. He just wants gas. He won't care about you."

But the patrol car didn't pull up to a pump. Instead, it stopped just outside the door. A Sheriff's deputy wearing a brown uniform got out and entered the store. Looking straight at her, he said, "Are you Amy Adams?"

Kaya stared at the patrolman.

"Are you Amy Adams?"

"I'm Kaya," she said uncomfortably, not an admission, not a denial.

The officer pulled a small notebook out of his leather jacket and looked at it. "Kaya Seka-something," he said. "That's the other name. You need to come with me, Miss."

"Why? It's not illegal to hitchhike, is it?" She looked to Joe for back up, but he'd disappeared.

"This isn't about hitchhiking, Miss Adams. This is about the fact you're a runaway."

Her heart sank. How did he know—and had he found her?

"Your grandmother's in Albuquerque. It's my job to take you to her."

The wrong grandmother. "What if I don't want to go?"

The patrolman shrugged. "No choice, Miss. You're a minor.

She's your legal guardian. You go voluntarily, or I take you to juvie until a judge sorts things out."

She read the small gold nametag on the brown uniform— Louis Chavez. "I'll be eighteen in three days, Officer Chavez. I won't be required to have a guardian then."

"If you want to spend those days in juvie, it's okay by me."

Kaya considered. Moongirl rejected. She couldn't be in juvie when the Tokpela Moon crossed between the Twins of Gemini. At least with Grandmother Adams, there would be a chance of escape. She shrugged.

"Good choice." Officer Chavez stepped back and waited for her to go first out the door. As she moved, Joe came suddenly out of a door marked Stockroom. "Tough break," he murmured.

"Tell Fred I'll call my brother."

Her brother. That was the connection. It went back to the Delgado Gallery. Becky knew who Mahu was, and she'd thought their grandmother would care about what happened. Somehow the Sheriff had traced Grandmother Adams. Good intentions from someone who didn't know what she had set in motion.

"Hop in," said Officer Chavez, holding open the patrol car's back door.

A man in a brown uniform. Grandmother Adams. Fighting the sense of being dragged into the past, Kaya got in and fastened her seatbelt. But memories held her in their grip.

She wasn't almost eighteen, she was five. She didn't know where they were going, only that Taáta and Mahu weren't with her. And Mama was with the Cloud People. She wondered if Mama could see her. If she could, why didn't she help? Kaya didn't know the red-haired lady in the front seat. The lady said she was her grandmother. But Iso was her grandmother.

"You seem like a nice girl," said Officer Chavez from the front seat. "I'm sorry about all this, but you made the right choice. Spend a couple of days with your grandmother. Then you can leave. All nice and legal. No complications."

His voice brought Kaya back to the present. No red-haired woman in the front seat. A patrolman. She wasn't a child. That was the past. This was the present. Now she was an adult, maybe not by the legal calendar, but by any other measure. She couldn't control what happened at this moment, but she didn't have to cooperate with her grandmother's plan.

Kaya grasped at something small she could do right now. She said, "Do you know how my brother is?" Not her twin, just her brother. She didn't want to drag Mahu into the age question.

"Sorry, Miss. I wasn't told about anything about a brother. Just about a runaway girl I was to pick up on the road from El Morro National Monument and bring to her grandmother at the Airport Hotel."

"He's in the hospital."

"I imagine your grandmother will know."

Won't know. Won't care. "Could you check for me? His name is Mahu Sekatewa. He's at St. Vincent's in Santa Fe."

Officer Chavez shrugged and reached for his radio. "I suppose that information could help confirm your identity."

The reply from the hospital came over the speaker loud enough for Kaya to hear. "Stable. In a coma."

"Tough," said the deputy. "What happened to him?"

It was all out in the open anyway. "There was a break-in at the place I work in Santa Fe. The thief attacked him."

"Probably didn't expect anyone to be there. That's the worst. Perp panics, attacks when running away would have been a better idea. Did they catch the guy?"

"I don't know. I was there too. I ran."

"Santa Fe? I've got a buddy on the force there. Give me some details. I'll see what I can find out."

She knew they hadn't caught X, but she said, "Sunday morning early. The Rebecca Delgado Gallery in Old Town Santa Fe."

While Officer Chavez busied with his radio, she looked out

at the desert streaming by. Acoma Pueblo, the Sky City, was behind now, and they were driving through the Laguna Reservation. The same landscape to outsiders, but home to different peoples with different languages, different cultures.

The deputy's voice interrupted her thoughts. "No idea how the guy got in or what he was after. Nothing taken even though there was a small fortune at hand. It's a weird case. No one can figure out where the arrow your brother was stabbed with came from. It didn't come from the gallery. Turns out, it's an excellent copy of some artifact."

# CHAPTER THIRTEEN

I t was just past nine by the dashboard clock when the patrol car pulled under the Holiday Inn Express portico. "Now, you're not going to try to run away, are you?"

Not now. Soon, but not now. "Three days with Grandmother Adams is better than three days in juvie." She forced a laugh. "Not much better, but a little."

"That's the spirit. It'll go by quick. And if your grandma is anything like mine, she wants you back to make sure you get a big celebration for your birthday. No grandma wants to miss an eighteenth birthday."

She didn't reply, just followed him into the lobby. No longer caught by the past, she was squarely in the present, ready to face the woman who kidnapped her once but couldn't do it again.

The patrolman took his notebook from his pocket and checked it. "Mrs. Quentin Adams," he said to the clerk.

Quentin Adams. He had died while Mama was a senior in high school, so Kaya had never met him, but his pictures showed a heavy-set man without much hair and a wide grin.

When she asked about him, Aunt Eileen smiled. 'Daddy was fun! He loved making people laugh. He had nicknames for everyone. Instead of Lelia, Mama was *Lily*, so he was *Bud*. He called me *Rose* and your mama *Violet*. We weren't the *Adams* —we were the *Flowers*.'

Eileen sighed. 'When he died, Mama became a different person. It was almost as if she thought if she laughed again, it would insult his memory. No more nicknames. Brenda and I had to be serious because we were Daughters of the American Revolution through Daddy's family tree. Brenda and I felt like orphans.'

As Kaya stood in the generic hotel lobby waiting for the wrong grandmother, she considered how she had fit into the picture. Lelia Adams widowed, Eileen in France, Brenda dead, and a granddaughter on the Hopi reservation. No matter that the little girl didn't know her. The child belonged to her. So, Lelia Adams took Kaya and set out to recreate her.

The elevator door opened, and her ash-blonde grandmother stepped out. Tall and determinedly slender, Lelia dressed to match her expensive hair color. Navy wool slacks, white silk shirt and navy and white tweed jacket, leather shoes and purse.

Lelia Adams was a forbidding figure, but this time Kaya refused to be frightened. She knew the truth about who she was now, and nothing Lelia Adams could say would change that.

Her grandmother looked past her and addressed Officer Chavez in her carefully clipped words, "I see my information was correct."

"Yes ma'am, Mrs. Adams. I picked her up in Grants."

Information—Grandmother Adams had contacted the Sheriff's Department about her? Not the other way around? Someone had to have told Lelia where she was. Suddenly Diego's kidnapping and the patrol car picking her up seemed like related events. X wanted them both out of the way.

"Thank you," said her grandmother. "I presume I can take her home now."

Home wasn't in Virginia, and she wasn't leaving here, but

Kaya kept quiet. Now was not the time. Not until the law was out of it.

"Yes, ma'am," Officer Chavez said. As he turned to go, he gave Kaya a searching look, as if he had read her thoughts. "Seventy-two hours," he murmured.

Kaya nodded, but Moongirl knew that the Tokpela Moon would open the door to Endless Space in sixty-three hours. She also knew if she could find it, she would be at the lost kiva doing her best to fulfill the destiny Ikwa believed was hers.

"Come along, then, Amy," Lelia said. "Where on earth did you get that awful coat? And what kind of ridiculous costume have you got on under it? I'm glad I had the presence of mind to bring clothes for you."

Just like she had when she'd kidnapped her granddaughter the first time. Kaya remembered a pink gingham dress with a sash that tied in the back. Scratchy and confining. Not like real clothes. But she didn't say anything about that awful dress. She knew Lelia well enough to avoid a direct confrontation.

Silently, she followed her grandmother onto the elevator and watched her punch the button for the third floor. The doors closed, and the elevator moved up.

Lelia frowned down at her. "What do you have to say for yourself, young lady?"

"I didn't run away."

The elevator stopped with a lurch and the doors opened. "Of course you did. You're still a minor, and you left home without permission."

"You told me to go," Amy said, remembering the confrontation. It had shocked both of them, the only time she'd ever heard her grandmother actually shout.

The clash started with a writing assignment in Freshman English: Draw your family tree for four generations. Identify a relative you'd like to know more about and talk to your family about this person. Write a biographical essay about this relative.

Amy wanted to know more about her father.

'You know his name,' Lelia had said. 'Kenji Nakamoto. It means bright man. That's just what he was, a bright young man studying at William and Mary—like your mother, like you are now.'

'But I need to know about his family. What were his parents' names? What were his grandparents' names?'

'I don't know! It's not important. Write about someone on your mother's side. Write about Zilpha Adams, your great-great-grandmother. Her father was a medical doctor in the Civil War, and her husband bought one of the first cars Henry Ford manufactured.'

But Amy didn't want to know about her great-great-grandmother. She wanted to know about her father. 'What city was my father from? Maybe I could write to his family.'

Her grandmother laughed, an unpleasant sound. 'He was from Tokyo. How many Nakamotos do you think there are in Tokyo?'

Amy gave up on her grandmother, but she went to see her aunt. It was late October, and the trees were changing to red and gold. Usually, the autumn colors entranced Amy, but this time she hardly noticed when the fallen ones crunched beneath her feet.

Her aunt suggested they sit on the porch swing. As the sun slid behind a cloud, Eileen asked about school.

'I have to write a paper about my father for English class,' Amy said. 'Grandmother Adams won't talk about him.'

Eileen went still. Then she got up and headed inside. 'I've got brownies in the kitchen,' she said. 'Come in and tell me about your roommate.'

Amy followed her, ignoring the obvious attempt to change the subject. 'I don't believe my mother didn't tell you anything about my father. You two were close, and she was in love. My mother would want me to know about my father. I'm sure she would.'

Eileen didn't bother with the brownies. She sat down at the kitchen table. 'You're right.' Eileen sighed. 'Brenda was crazy about your father. Daddy was dead, of course, and Mother was completely opposed to him, but Brenda stood up to her. Your mama was a gentle soul, and I think that was the first time she ever flatly refused to obey Mother. That's how much in love she was with your father.'

'Did you meet him?'

Eileen shook her head. 'I was in France. Your mother was in school in New Mexico. She wrote to me about your father, but I never met him.'

'New Mexico? Grandmother told me they met at William and Mary.'

Eileen was quiet for a long time. Then she rose from the table and went into her bedroom. Sitting on the floor in front of her dresser, she opened the bottom drawer and took out a photo album with a quilted calico cover.

Lifting a letter from between the pages, she handed it to Amy. 'It's the only one I have. I moved from Paris to the south of France, and I never got another letter from her. I sent her my new address, but my letter came back. Mother refused to tell me where she was.'

It was the first time Amy had seen her mother's handwriting, small but with tails that swept up as the words flowed across the page. Her father's first name leaped out at her, not *Kenji*, but *Wilson*, not Japanese, but Native American.

The room tipped but righted itself almost immediately. No wonder she'd never been able to find any connection to flower arranging and lacquerware. No wonder she loved pottery and Native American designs.

'Why did Grandmother lie to me?'

'You know how proud she is. She couldn't admit that her

child—a Daughter of the American Revolution—had married an Indian and moved to a reservation.'

'Which tribe? Which reservation?'

But her aunt didn't know—not that, not even Wilson's last name. 'I know she was in college in Santa Fe, but I don't know anything else. Mother would never tell me. I didn't see Brenda again. I lived in Italy when she died. By the time I came back to the States to live, you believed the story about the Japanese father.'

'Why didn't you tell me? Maybe not then, but when I was older.'

Eileen reached out and pulled her close. 'I suppose I should have, honey. But I didn't know how. I couldn't imagine telling you my mother had lied to you all those years. I guess I thought it wouldn't make any difference to you.'

Pushing her aunt away, Amy shouted, 'It does. It matters a lot!'

When she faced Lelia, her grandmother refused to tell her any more than she already knew. 'Thanks to me, you have your own life, Amy,' she said. 'I rescued you from the nightmare of your mother's mistakes.'

'You kept me from my father! You made me believe I was alone in the world except for you. For all I know, I have an entire family somewhere in New Mexico. With or without your help, I'm going to find them.'

'Go then!' Lelia had screamed. 'Leave me just like your tramp of a mother did. But I'm warning you. If you go out to that godforsaken country, the same thing will happen to you that happened to her.'

In the present, Lelia's cultured voice said, "You're daydreaming, Amy. Snap out of it."

It was like waking up in the hallway. Suddenly, she stood beside her grandmother, not in the living room of the house in Virginia, but in front of a hotel room marked 318. Lelia slid the plastic key into the slot and pushed open the door. The room was like the lobby, beige and generic. Except for the turquoise and dusty rose bedspreads, it could have been anywhere in the country.

Sitting on the nearest bed, Amy Kaya said, "What did you mean the same thing would happen to me that happened to my mother if I went to New Mexico?"

Her grandmother blinked but didn't bother to pretend she didn't know what Amy was talking about. "Your mother died there. I was afraid for you." Opening the closet, Lelia removed the expensive tweed jacket and hung it on a hanger.

"My mother died on a reservation in Arizona," Kaya said. "But that's not what you meant, is it? You meant I might fall in love with that part of the country like she did, maybe even find a husband. You cheated me out of my father, Grandmother. He died when I was 12, but he was a good man, a good father. Why didn't you tell me? Why make up such an elaborate lie?"

"I had my reasons."

"Prejudice! Aunt Eileen told me you didn't think my father was a suitable husband for my mother. That was because he was Native American, wasn't it?"

"Not prejudice! Protection for your mother. I didn't want people to make jokes about a Daughter of the American Revolution marrying an Indian!"

"My mother didn't need protection. She loved my father. *You* were the one who was afraid of ridicule. But if your friends make fun of people because of their skin color, they're not worth being friends. And me—why did you tell me my father was Japanese?"

"You were a beautiful child with an almost Asian look to your eyes. And you had your own language. Words no one could understand. I chose Japanese because none of my friends knew that language. I did what I thought was best, Amy."

"My name is Kaya!" She hadn't meant to lose her temper,

but suddenly she was on her feet. Not as tall as her grandmother, but no longer a child.

"Your name is Amy. *Kaya* means 'sister.'"

"That's exactly what it means! You separated me from my twin! How could you do that? If you were so determined to take me, why not take him too? At least we could have been together."

"Mahu was a dirty, wild little boy. Anyone could take one look at him and know precisely what he was. Mahu was everything I meant to take you away from."

"I was five years old! My mother had just died, and you took me away from my father, my brother, my home. You told me so many lies I forgot who I was! I've always known you were cruel, but how could you?"

Amy was so angry she shook, but she could tell by her grandmother's expression that the last shot found its mark.

Lelia's face went white. "I'll tell you about cruel. Cruel is a daughter abandoning her widowed mother. Cruel is an ungrateful granddaughter determined to repeat a history that broke her grandmother's heart."

With a visible effort, Lelia bit back whatever else she might have said. Taking a deep breath, she said, "I have reservations for the two of us on a plane that leaves in three hours, and I don't intend for us to miss it. The next one isn't until morning, and I will *not* stay in this godforsaken country another night."

"I'm not going back to Virginia."

"You will, or you'll go to the Juvenile Detention Center. Is that what you want?"

Kaya Amy wanted to shout that jail would be a relief, but Moongirl's destiny stopped her.

"I didn't think so." Lelia retrieved Amy's William and Mary backpack from the closet and held it out. "Take a shower and put on some respectable clothes."

"These are respectable clothes. They're my mother's clothes."

"They're Indian clothes." The way Lelia spat the words made them a curse.

Kaya didn't respond. She grabbed the backpack, went into the bathroom, flipped on the light with its loud fan, and locked the door. She was furious—not only with her grandmother but also with herself. What had she been thinking? When did her grandmother ever care about anything but her point of view?

Amy Kaya knew giving in to her anger made things worse, if that were possible. Forcing herself to take deep breaths, she turned on the water in the shower. Too numb to think, she took off her mother's boots, removed the turquoise necklace and the red cedar beads, pulled the wool manta over her head, draped it on a towel rack to steam out, pulled her hair out of its braid, ran her fingers through.

When the water was finally hot, she stepped into the shower. The shampoo had a spicy scent, and as she scrubbed it into her scalp, her mind began to work again. Things were bad but not hopeless. Lelia couldn't physically stop her from walking out of the hotel, but she could, and would, call the Sheriff. Open defiance wouldn't work.

The airport would be much easier, offering chances to slip into a crowd and disappear. It would take Lelia longer to realize she was gone, and Officer Chavez would have a harder time knowing where to look for her.

As the hot water beat on her back, she considered the airplane. If she could get Lelia on and keep herself off, by the time her grandmother discovered she was gone, Lelia would be in the air, and she would be back on her way to Cochiti. It wasn't far now.

Though not the one she'd hoped for, her ride had brought her as far as Albuquerque. She needed to find a way to get to

Cochiti, and she needed money. But she could find the one with enough of the other. Lelia always carried plenty of cash.

What she had to do was convince her grandmother she had changed her mind and was willing to go back to Virginia. That would be tough, but at least she had the beginnings of a plan. Kaya Amy turned off the water and got out of the shower. As she toweled off and blew her hair dry, she concentrated on what she could use to convince Lelia of her change of heart.

At first, all she could think of was the list of reasons why she must stay: Mahu in the hospital, Diego missing, Ikwa's faith in her, the Tokpela Moon. Most of all, the choice of destiny. She had to think of something else. Those reasons were all based on love and loyalty—feelings. What she needed was to think like Lelia, focus on what Lelia cared about.

The answer came as she brushed her long, straight hair. Lelia Adams cared about appearances. That was why she hadn't wanted her youngest daughter to live on a reservation. It was why she explained Amy's faintly Asian look with Japanese ancestry rather than Native American.

Lily Adams might have loved happily and deeply, but the widow Lelia only loved where she could be proud. The clothes were an obvious starting place. Lelia had made it clear she was ashamed of the Hopi manta and jewelry. Amy could praise the clothes Lelia brought, even express interest in buying something new at the airport.

School was another opportunity. Lelia was embarrassed Amy had dropped out. If Amy promised to go to her teachers and ask for incompletes so she could be re-instated, her grandmother would believe it, because that was what she wanted to hear. Lelia Adams might lower her guard just enough for Moongirl to follow her destiny.

With the plan as clear as she could get it, Amy Moongirl dressed in the brown chinos and green sweater Lelia had brought. Taking the spiral notebook and pen from the backpack's outside pocket, she bent over the counter and wrote a note.

"I'm borrowing this money from you now, but I'll pay it back. I have a Hopi family emergency. If you want to meet Mahu and see me, come to the Palace of the Governors in Santa Fe on Sunday."

She stood in the entryway of the room in her mind. "Mahu," she whispered, "You'll be okay by then. You will!" She could almost hear a few notes of a red cedar melody, maybe a dream fragment, maybe something more.

"Amy! Hurry up in there!"

Amy folded the note, wrote "Lelia Adams" on the outside, and slipped it in her pocket. "Coming!"

While Lelia was busy in the bathroom, Amy knelt beside her grandmother's expensive leather suitcase. Opening it hurriedly, she felt for the money pouch she knew was stitched in the bottom lining.

'This is a place for carrying a little extra money,' Lelia had told Amy as she tucked a hundred-dollar bill inside. 'It's only for emergencies. We can't know what kind of emergency might arise when we travel. Someone might steal my purse. Or we might need to tip generously for some service we need. In the ten years I've carried my emergency cache, I've never had to touch it. However, it's nice to know it's there.'

This was an emergency. Like Fran said when she offered her a doughnut—there are all kinds of family emergencies. Without a twinge of guilt, Kaya Moongirl exchanged her note for the bill.

CHAPTER FOURTEEN

K okopelli showed Moongirl the way out of Lelia's trap. One foot raised to keep time to music only he could hear, the humpbacked flute player danced across a sign announcing *Pueblo Tours*. The tiny kiosk, sandwiched between Avis Rent-a-car and a traveler's assistance office, stood on the down escalator's left side.

Amy Kaya looked at the up escalator that went to security. "I left my brush in the restroom. You go on. I'll catch up before you get far." The words flowed smoothly. She remembered arguing with Diego over telling the truth. When had lying become so easy?

She knew the answer almost as soon as the question formed. When she was very young, her grandmother taught her. Grandmother Adams wouldn't let Kaya talk about her twin or that her mother was with the Cloud People. She wouldn't even let her tell them she wanted to be called Kaya.

Grandmother Adams taught her to say all sorts of crazy things. Things that confused her.

Brainwashing, Diego called it. Really, it was lying. But when

Kaya turned eighteen, she could live her own life. And she would stop lying.

Lelia frowned. "Buy another one."

"But I like this one. Aunt Eileen gave it to me. I know we're on a tight schedule. I'll catch up before you even get to the line for security. Moongirl, who was Amy, saw her plan start to work.

"Oh, all right. But hurry!"

Amy went back toward the restroom. As soon as Lelia turned the corner, she hurried back to the Pueblo Tours kiosk. A man with salt-and-pepper hair sat behind the desk texting. A driver, maybe.

Moongirl said, "Excuse me. Do your tours go to Cochiti Pueblo?"

The man looked up. "Next one is at 2:00 p.m."

Their flight left at 1:30. It would be close. "I'd like a ticket."

"Cash or credit card. No checks. $35."

Kaya handed him the hundred-dollar bill.

The clerk took it and reached for a clipboard. "Name?"

It was as if he had reached across the desk and slapped her. She couldn't chance giving her real name. If something went wrong and Lelia discovered she disappeared before the plane took off ... Moongirl said the first name that came into her head, "James—Debbie James."

The man wrote the name and handed her a ticket with the change. "Meet the bus at passenger pickup. If you're late, you get left behind. No refunds."

"I'll be there." Moongirl knew it would be true. Shoving everything into her backpack, she sprinted toward the hallway that led to security. When she spotted Lelia, already in line, she slowed to a walk.

"Excuse me," she said to a young mother with a baby in a stroller and a two-year-old tugging on her sleeve. "My grandmother is just ahead of you. Do you mind if I cut ?"

The young woman, her attention on the toddler, shook her

head. "Tommy! Stop pulling on my arm. As soon as we get past the man at the desk, I'll get you a cookie."

"Here I am, Grandmother." Amy tried not to sound breathless.

Her grandmother turned, a mixture of irritation and relief on her face. "I hope you found your brush! I was beginning to think you were trying to run away again."

"No ma'am. I mean, Yes, I found the brush. No, I wasn't running away." One lie and one almost lie. She wasn't running away. She was planning an escape.

"Next time, don't leave your things lying around."

Amy Moongirl shook her head.

As they made their way through the security line and across the airport, Amy wondered how she could get Lelia on the plane without her. When they reached the gate, she spotted the answer.

The waiting area was full, with only a few single seats left. Off to the side, young people sat on the floor. She walked with her grandmother to one of the empty chairs and stood until Lelia sat and opened the paperback she'd pulled out of her purse.

Then Amy Moongirl said, "I see a girl who looks like someone I know. Do you care if I go talk to her?"

Lelia glanced without interest in the direction Amy was pointing. "Don't leave the area. The flight will be boarding soon. There aren't any assigned seats on this flight, and I didn't get the tickets until late. We board with the third group."

Moongirl's heart skipped a beat. No assigned seats—a doorway to destiny. "Sure."

The girl, who didn't look at all like anyone she knew, had long blonde hair twisted in a careless knot at the nape of her neck. She wore a pink turtleneck, jeans, and hiking boots. A battered backpack leaned against the wall beside her. The book she was reading looked like a tour book, but it wasn't in English. German, maybe? A European student traveling in the United

States, someone who might welcome company but who wouldn't care what a stranger did.

Moongirl picked her way through the travelers and their carry-on luggage. When she reached the young woman, she said, "Hi! Mind if I sit with you?"

The girl looked up and smiled. "Please, share this floor with me."

"I'm Amy."

"Britta."

"You're a visitor here, I think. Where are you from?"

"Gothenberg—Sweden. I finish school. This is my adventure. Where is your home, Amy?"

"Old Oraibi," Kaya Amy Moeyha said. "The Hopi Reservation."

"You're an Indian?"

"Native American. Half."

"How interesting! I visited the Sky City when I was in Santa Fe, but I did not speak with any Indian—Native American."

A voice over the intercom announced their flight, warning that boarding would begin soon.

"Which group do you board with, Britta?" Moongirl held her breath. If Britta boarded with the first or second group, her plan could work.

"Group two. What about you?"

"Third. I'm traveling with my grandmother, but if you save me a seat, I'll fix it with her to sit with you. We can talk."

"That will be nice."

A twinge of guilt, but overhead the Tokpela Moon was hours closer to becoming a doorway for ancient evil to enter our world.

Across the seating area, Lelia Adams stood and gestured for Amy to come to her. Amy obeyed.

As the first group boarded, Lelia stood but kept reading. When the second group was called, Britta looked over her shoulder and waved. Amy said, "That's my new friend, Grandmother. She's going to save me a seat. She's from Sweden. She wants me to sit with her so she can practice her English. I told her you wouldn't mind."

"I suppose you're not ready to talk to me."

"When we get home." If her plan worked, *home* would be here in New Mexico, not in Virginia.

"Oh, all right." Lelia turned back to her book.

When they were in line ready to board, Moongirl said, "Go ahead, Grandmother. I hope you find a good seat. I'll let everyone else go first since Britta is saving me a seat. I'll see you later." Sunday—in Santa Fe. If the Moon Twins fulfilled their destiny.

Her grandmother didn't bother to look up. Just nodded and kept reading.

At the airplane boarding door, Moongirl got the opportunity she needed. A late arrival in a wheelchair. A woman angry she'd been left to wait. "Like a piece of luggage," she spat. "And now, where am I supposed to sit? I must have an aisle seat! I need to be up front near the restroom!"

As the flight attendants worked to mollify the woman, Moongirl stepped out of line and hurried back up the jetway. The next opportunity came when a standby passenger insisted the flight attendant recount the seats. There was an extra one now. Without a backward glance, Moongirl sprinted toward the exit that would take her to Passenger Pickup. To Pueblo Tours. To Cochiti. To Iso—her other grandmother, who might be a shaman who could help.

Kokopelli danced across the side of the bus, as he had above the kiosk. With ten minutes to spare, Debbie Moongirl Moeyha climbed aboard and handed her ticket to the driver. The bus was crowded, filled mainly with retirees on holiday. One family occupied three rows on the right side—Mom with a screaming two-year-old girl, Dad with a squirmy four-year-old boy, an older boy sulking behind.

For a moment, she feared she'd have to choose between sitting with the sulky boy or with a middle-aged woman crocheting with yellow yarn. Finally, at the very back of the bus, she spotted two empty seats.

She made her way down the narrow aisle and wondered when Lelia would discover she was gone—and when she'd discover the note she'd left in place of the hundred-dollar bill. For a moment she felt guilty. Stealing was worse than lying.

*I'll pay it back*, she promised herself. *I told her I would in the note, and I will.* Besides, if the Tokpela Moon wasn't a travel emergency, she didn't know what was. Taking the window seat and dropping her backpack on the aisle seat, she leaned back and closed her eyes.

*Mahu?* She groped in her mind for the room where she could feel her twin. She needed him. The melody was there, fainter than before. Snatches of music interwoven with silence that stirred like water on a restless ocean.

*Diego?* It wasn't like with Mahu. Nothing came back, nothing at all.

Panic seized her. How could she face what was ahead alone? Fighting terror, she opened her eyes and leaned her forehead against the seat in front of her. Forcing herself to breathe slowly, she began to count. In, one … two … out, one … two—three. In, one …

With a hiss of airbrakes, the bus pulled away from the curb. At the same moment, a man's voice came on the microphone. "Welcome, folks! I'm Alan, and this afternoon I'm your guide to New Mexico's pueblos—villages where life hasn't changed in a thousand years."

A thousand years! A thousand years since the last Tokpela Moon, and she was caught in a week of nightmare.

Alan, of course, knew nothing about the Tokpela Moon. His placid voice continued. Not exactly a monotone but following the well-worn path of a speech delivered many times. "Like the

Hopi of Arizona, the New Mexico pueblo descended from a group sometimes referred to as the Anasazi, the Old Ones, or simply the Ancestral Puebloans. Sixteen pueblo tribes speaking five different languages live in eighteen villages scattered along the Rio Grande River.

"This afternoon we're going to visit two of the Keres-speaking pueblos, Santo Domingo and Cochiti. Santo Domingo is known for its turquoise jewelry, Cochiti, for pottery figurines called storytellers. Santo Domingo comes first on the road, but our tour starts at Cochiti because the locals close up shop earlier. It's thirty-five miles to Cochiti, so sit back and enjoy the music."

Speech Number One concluded, Alan's voice stopped, and a Native American flute's notes filled the bus. A tape, not the Song of Creation, but faintly reassuring.

Raising her head, Amy Moongirl looked out the window. They were on the interstate ramp. Overhead a large green sign lettered in white read *Santa Fe*, but they weren't going that far. Sunday she would go to Santa Fe, to the Palace of the Governors

Mahu would wake up, and Diego would be found. Together they would live through whatever the Tokpela Moon brought. Maybe Grandmother Adams would be there on Sunday, maybe not.

Either way, after a dozen years of separation, she and Mahu would be brother and sister again. After an intense week of working together, she and Diego would be—what? Friends ... and maybe more?

Or would any of that happen? Under the chatter of the tourists, she considered the details her morning. Someone gave Lelia the information that she could be found in Grants, New Mexico. The Ya-Ya Seeing Eye aside, who could have known or guessed that?

Rina was a possibility, but she'd gone home to Mimbres, and Kaya couldn't imagine how Lelia could have learned about Rina. The El Morro ranger—Arlene—was another possibility. If Lelia had known to contact the El Morro Visitor's Center, Arlene could have guessed where to find Kaya. But it would have been a wild guess, and there was no way Lelia could have known about El Morro.

X was the only answer that made sense. X must have contacted Lelia and told her where to find Amy Kaya. It stood to reason, then, that Lelia might know who X was. As scary as the theory was that her grandmother might be involved with X, it had one good point. No one could read her mind, and only she knew Cochiti was her destination. Lelia knew about Old Oraibi because she'd gone there to snatch her granddaughter. But she didn't know about Iso's connection to Cochiti Pueblo.

That ray of hope cut through her fear. If Amy Moongirl could get to Cochiti, she would be off Grandmother Adams's radar—and off X's.

Fifteen minutes later, with another hiss of airbrakes, the bus exited the interstate onto a two-lane paved road. The passengers sat up and looked interested. In the bus's front stood a squarely built Anglo man with a full head of gray hair. Alan, no doubt. Over the microphone, he said, "Santo Domingo Pueblo, folks, but as I said, we're going on to Cochiti first. The villages are less than ten miles apart, so we'll catch Santo Domingo on our way back."

The middle-aged lady raised her crochet hook. "Cochiti is where they make the storyteller figurines, isn't it?"

"Yes, ma'am. While the tradition of making pottery figures goes back almost 2,000 years, Cochiti potters first made the figures we call *storytellers* in the 1970s."

"What about dances?" asked the dad with the squirmy four-year-old.

"Not today," Alan said.

Dad looked nervously at the sulky older boy sitting behind him. "That's why we signed up for the tour."

"Native American dances are religious ceremonies, sir. The

next one in the pueblos is the Corn Dance on January 1, but you can see traditional dances every Saturday and Sunday at 11:00 and 2:00 at the Pueblo Indian Cultural Center in Albuquerque."

The bus slowed and shook briefly. Through the window, Kaya noticed the road turned from pavement to dirt.

"Remember, we're not visiting an amusement park," Alan said. "We're in a village where people live. You're welcome to go into the church here in Cochiti or the museum in Santo Domingo. There's no admission charge at either place, but a donation is always welcome. You'll find a box for that purpose by the door. Otherwise, don't enter a building unless a resident invites you."

"What about shops?" asked Ms. Crochet.

"No shops. Residents with crafts to sell occasionally set up roadside stands on the pueblo's edge, and some of the artists sell their work from their homes. That's about it for shopping."

"No dances, no shops," grumbled the elderly man. "So, what do we do?"

Alan smiled. "You slow down to the pace of the pueblo, walk around, soak up the atmosphere of a completely different way of life."

The bus slowed even more and pulled into an open field.

Moongirl Moeyha looked out the window with a sort of wonder. She was here. She'd actually made it.

"Three rules while you're in the pueblos," Alan said. "No cell phones, no pictures, no littering. If you break the rules, expect to lose your phone or camera and pay a fine."

The bus driver opened the door, and Alan moved to the steps. "We'll be here for about an hour. I'll be around to answer any questions you have."

Moongirl Moeyha rose to her feet and shouldered her backpack. No questions for him. Lots for Iso.

She was the last one. As Amy Kaya waited her turn to exit, she saw Alan, clipboard in hand, check off each passenger as he or she stepped to the ground. With a sinking feeling, she realized her plan didn't go this far. She didn't know what she had expected when they reached the pueblo, but she hadn't thought she would need to explain herself—or the false name.

When it was her turn, she took a deep breath. "I won't be coming back with you."

Alan's head jerked up. Frowning, he gave her his full attention. "Debbie James?"

She ignored it. "I'm Eleanor Sekatewa's granddaughter. Do you know her?"

"I know an Eleanor, but her name isn't Sekatewa, and it sure isn't James."

Too late, Kaya remembered—her grandmother signed her storytellers with her pueblo name. "I meant Eleanor Naranjo. My grandmother is expecting me, and this tour was the best way to get a ride from Albuquerque."

Alan looked skeptical. "So, where'd you get the name *James*?"

Kaya smiled. "Where does anyone usually get a last name? *Sekatewa* was my mother's name."

"*Sekatewa*—that name rings a bell. You're up to something, Missy. I don't know what it is, but I think I'll ask you to get back on the bus while I check with the Sheriff, just make sure he doesn't need to talk to you." He pulled a cell phone out of his pocket and flipped it open.

Fear gripped Amy Kaya. She'd volunteered information she should have kept to herself. "I'm not a terrorist. I'm Eleanor Naranjo's granddaughter. She'll know me." *Please, God,* prayed Moongirl Moeyha. *Please, let her know me.*

# CHAPTER FIFTEEN

K aya Moeyha stood her ground as the tour guide studied her. Finally, he shrugged and pocketed his phone. "I'll come with you. "Just to make sure Eleanor is home. Lead the way."

She didn't remember the way, but she started walking. It was mid-afternoon, bright and warm. In the slanting sunshine, the red-brown adobe of the pueblo almost glowed. *Mahu! Dream your flute. Lead me to Iso's.*

Only silence, the door in her mind closed. Her steps slowed, and without looking, she knew the man beside her watched. Then she heard the music—not the notes of a red cedar flute, but a steady drumbeat, a gourd rattle, the jingle of tiny bells, a man chanting.

Rounding the corner, they entered the plaza where twelve children danced with ears of corn in their hands, practicing not a ceremony to banish evil, but a ceremony to celebrate life. She wanted to stop, but Alan's impatience urged her on.

*East.* She turned toward the row of houses that bordered the plaza on the east. Memory came suddenly, the way it had in Old

Oraibi. One moment she was walking east, the next she was standing in front of an open door, the door to Iso's house. Memory told her not to knock, not to go in, instead to announce her presence. "Iso," she called, "it's Kaya!"

They waited. But there was no eager response. No response at all. Nothing.

"I thought she was expecting you," Alan said. "If she's not here, I can't let you stay."

Desperately Kaya searched her memory. Ikwa said Iso had gone to Cochiti to make some new storyteller dolls to sell. "Maybe she's firing." But Kaya didn't remember where the kilns were.

Destiny stepped in. Turning automatically, Alan led the way. They found Iso in an open area behind the kiva, a small, sturdy figure in a faded denim skirt, red cotton shirt, and white sweater. Her back was to them as she stacked dried cow patties in a careful mound. Red—She must be the third shaman.

Alan spoke first, "Mrs. Naranjo?"

Her grandmother straightened up and turned. Now completely white, her hair was cut the way Kaya remembered, straight across in a Dutch cut like a child's. In her wrinkled nutbrown face, eyes like jet lit up. "Moeyha!"

*Precious granddaughter*, the same thing Ikwa had said. Iso opened her arms, and Kaya was home again. Five years old, seventeen years old, she was home. Taller than her grandmother now, but somehow Iso cradled her, comforted her.

"Mahu is hurt," she whispered. "Oh, Iso, I don't know what to do."

"Hush, now. White Bear has told me about this."

"So, Debbie James *is* your granddaughter," Alan said.

Iso released Kaya and smiled up at her. "Of course, this is my granddaughter. Who else would she be?"

Kaya smiled back and released the breath she didn't know she was holding.

The guide shrugged. "You got some new pieces there?"

"One for your wife. A bear storyteller like she's been asking for. Next week."

Moongirl looked at the other two. Would harmony sing in creation next week or would the universe tip into chaos, into nothingness where storytellers and even wives didn't exist?

Alan knew nothing about the Tokpela Moon. Smiling, he turned away. When he was gone, Kaya said awkwardly, "I can explain about my name."

"Later you will tell me." Eleanor bent down to balance another cow patty on top of the stack. "Now, tell me what it is that you don't know what to do about."

"Mahu is hurt, Diego has been kidnapped, the lienzo is lost, and we don't know the ceremony. Two nights from now the Tokpela Moon will open, and the powáqas will enter our Fourth World. White Bear is gone, Rina is gone, and I don't know what to do!"

Her grandmother straightened up. "Later we will figure out the big things to do. Now I have to fire these pieces. If I wait, they will be ruined, not fit to sell. Moeyha, sit and breathe."

The calm in Eleanor's voice filtered through Kaya's sense of urgency. After a moment, she dropped her backpack and sat cross-legged on the ground. Eleanor stacked the cow patties, balancing them so they formed a dome around the figurines. It was a careful process, a slow process that depended on attention and balance.

As Moeyha watched her grandmother, she felt her pulse slow. When the dome was almost complete, she said softly, "Iso, I forgot you. Sometimes I cried in my dreams, and when I woke up, I wondered what I had lost. But Grandmother Adams …"

"Hush. She's not what we need to talk about now. Sometime later we can talk about your mama's poor mama. Tonight is for other stories. Do you know my babies?"

Puzzled by the sudden change of topic, Kaya said, "You mean your storytellers?"

"Sure. My kids are all gone. These are my babies now."

"I saw one in Becky Delgado's gallery in Santa Fe where I work."

"I gave her three to sell. Which one?"

Moeyha didn't know how to answer. All the figurines looked similar—a seated adult, arms and lap filled with children, mouth open to tell a story. "It was a woman, not a man."

"They were all mothers I gave to Becky. One had seven children in her lap, and eight in her arms. There was a little girl climbing on that one's head. That mother had on a black dress and a turquoise necklace. The children were wearing salmon-colored clothes. Was it that one?"

"I don't know. I don't think so. You make so many! Do you remember them all?"

"Sure. A mother remembers all her babies. Tell me which one of my babies you met."

Moeyha closed her eyes and did her best to picture the little figure. On a wrought-iron shelf halfway down the left wall. Not so many children. "There was a cradleboard."

"Five kids. Mama wore a red woven belt. The other one I gave Becky was a grandma with her eyes closed. She had gray hair and an orange skirt. Ten kids, listening."

"How do you do it? How do you remember the little details?"

Eleanor struck a match and lit the cow patty kiln. As it blazed, she lowered herself awkwardly to the ground. "You're gonna tell me stories in a minute. You're gonna remember the details. If I ask you what Mahu was wearing when you saw him in Santa Fe, you'll tell me. Each one of my storytellers is a story." She laughed softly. "A story telling a story."

"The stories are important to you, aren't they, Iso?"

"Stories are important to everyone, Moeyha. Without stories, life has no meaning, just a lot of events. We need stories to understand." Beside them the flames of the kiln settled into a steady glow. "This is gonna take a while. Tell me the stories that brought you home to Cochiti."

Stories. A new way to think about what she needed to tell her grandmother. But as she considered, she knew it was true. Story after story—riding with Mama and Taáta through Monument Valley, finding Mahu hurt in the gallery, watching the hawk from the mesa's edge. And other stories—Diego's story of the flash flood. "So many," she murmured.

"We got time. All night if we need it. Start anywhere you want."

She decided to start with Santa Fe. The Virginia stories could wait. Santa Fe was where her stories intersected Mahu's and Diego's. While the embers hardened the clay, Kaya told the stories that began with the flute's sounds and ended running through the snow, clutching the lienzo. "That's how it started. That's how Mahu got hurt and I got pulled into this nightmare."

Eleanor shook her head. "Not pulled into a nightmare. Those are the stories of sipapuni, the place of your emergence into the Moon Twins destiny."

*Sipapuni.* In one way, a comfort, in another a shock.

"You have stories to tell of your journey from sipapuni to Cochiti, but the fire has finished its work. Not one of my babies blew up from the heat, so now we leave them to cool. Can you drive a pickup?"

Moeyha nodded.

Eleanor rose stiffly to her feet. "Good. I knew you would come today. I want to take you into the town of Cochiti Lake to a new restaurant I heard about, but I don't drive after dark anymore. It'll be dark coming home."

Moeyha followed her grandmother past the silent kiva back

to the open field where the tour bus had parked. It was gone now, and the field sat empty except for three pickups. Not quite sunset, in the deep blue eastern sky, the pale moon climbed. Seven-eighths—time running out. Almost fiercely, she pushed away the thought.

Iso stopped in tall weeds at the edge of the field beside a pickup that had once been black. Opening the passenger's door, she pulled herself up into the cab. "The keys are in it."

"Mahu leaves his keys in his pickup. Don't you worry someone might steal it?"

Eleanor shrugged. "Someone might need to drive it."

Someone running from a witch. Moeyha started the engine, and they bumped across the field until, with one final jolt, they landed on the dirt road. The ride was smoother, but only by comparison. "Iso, do you believe in powáqas?"

"What do you mean *believe in*? Powáqas been around a long time."

"But do you think a powáqa could attack Mahu and kidnap Diego?" They hit a pothole with jarring force. Moeyha pulled on the headlights.

"Best not to think too much about powáqas. You think too much about evil, it gets a grip on you. Right now, we think about Mexican food. See that recreation area? Turn right."

The sky was magenta when Kaya found the street. "I don't see a restaurant."

"Not here—a house where you can see the lake. Keep going." A few houses and then the empty road climbed. Finally, Eleanor pointed to a lone house perched on the side of the hill. "There. Pull in next to that fancy gold car."

The sunset faded. Lighted windows beckoned as they made their way up the walk in deepening dusk. A young Hispanic woman dressed in a white peasant blouse and a skirt that was a bright blue swirl opened the door. "Buenos noches, señora, señorita. I am Maria."

They followed her down a short hall into a wide glassed-in porch with a view of the long lake, shining silver in the last of the light. Of the six tables, two were occupied—one by an expensive-looking older couple who probably belonged to the gold Lexus, the other by a family with a busy toddler in a booster chair. The table Maria showed them sat in a corner with windows on both sides.

When they were seated, Maria smiled. "As you know, we're a family business. We have three choices tonight—chicken enchiladas, chile rellenos, and fish tacos."

"Enchiladas for me," Eleanor said.

"Tacos," Moeyha said.

Maria nodded and moved away. A teenage boy wearing jeans and a dark blue velvet shirt set a basket of chips and a bowl of salsa on their table. The chips were warm and the salsa home-made. Eleanor nibbled on a chip. "Now, tell me another story."

"Diego and I went to Old Oraibi."

"West."

Eating salsa, she told the story that began with calling Diego and ended with Yukioma. While she crunched on corn tortillas filled with flaky white fish and fresh cabbage, she told the story that began with her memories of the mesa and ended with White Bear's prophecy.

"See?" Eleanor took the last bite of her enchiladas. "As I told you before, you emerged into the Moon Twins' destiny back there in Santa Fe. My destiny too."

"You're the third shaman, aren't you?"

"White Bear and I make two. I don't know the third one, but I bet it's a story."

Across the room, Maria seated a middle-aged couple who looked like they were from the pueblo. As her grandmother raised a hand in greeting, the teenaged waiter set flan in front of Moeyha. "Which direction did you go after Old Oraibi?" asked Eleanor.

"South—to El Morro."

"Tell me the South stories."

While they ate the vanilla pudding, Moeyha told the story that began with the powáqa with an antelope head and ended with finding Rina. Iso sipped hot tea, and she told the story of the torn lienzo—the shamans and the ceremony to get the People back on the right road. "Who are these powáqas, Iso? Why do they want to tip the Universe toward chaos?"

The old woman with the child's haircut sighed. "Harmony depends on cooperation, on people sharing. Individual power creates chaos, one person doing what he wants at the expense of the others. Powáqas are people who hurt others to get what they want."

"With magic?"

Eleanor shrugged. "Magic, violence, anything that silences the Song of Creation."

"So present-day powáqas want to bring back the ancient witches to get more power?"

"They might be surprised. Might be more dangerous than they think." Iso gestured toward the lake, vast and black, without edges.

Moongirl stared at the water and remembered her vision of Tokpela—not the raucous cacophony but the tentacled silence, silence so deep they could all drown in it.

Maria brought the bill and two squares of chocolate in green foil. "This is a nice place," Eleanor said, putting a twenty and a ten on the little plastic tray. "One of these days, my granddaughter and I will come back. We'll bring her grandfather and her brother with us."

"And Diego?"

Eleanor smiled, settling her face into light-hearted crinkles. "Sure. He'll like it here."

It was cold outside. Wishing for the warm coat Leila had taken, Moeyha Kaya Amy wondered when her other grandmother had found the note, wondered if she would come to the Palace of the Governors on Sunday. But that was for later.

Now she headed the pickup down the hill, back toward the pueblo. As they drove, she told the story that started with Diego putting the lienzo in his pocket and ended with her decision to come to Cochiti.

As Moeyha parked in the open field, Eleanor said thoughtfully, "That was when you started East. Come inside and tell me the East stories."

The pueblo had electricity, and Eleanor switched on a lamp when they entered the house. It was smaller than the one in Old Oraibi, but much was the same—a small square table for eating, two mattresses leaning against one wall, a corner curtained off for privacy. But it was the differences that made this Iso's house —the basket of pot shards, the square aluminum pan filled with clay ground to the consistency of sand, the orange bucket containing wet clay rolled in plastic, the paint stones, the polishing stones, the yucca brushes.

Iso's pottery drew Kaya across the room. Pots in various stages of completion lined up on benches against the walls, some painted with the white slip that would hold the colored paint, some with the fine black lines that would define the design, some ready to fire, some waiting to be sold. Water jars, seed jars, canteens, bowls, a grandfather storyteller with a cigar in one hand and seven children leaning against his legs were scattered among the pots.

"Let's sit at the table."

Moeyha told the story that began with Officer Chavez and ended with Lelia. Then she told her the story that began with a plan and ended on a bus.

"Sipapuni. West. South. East. All you got left is North."

"I feel like I've been wandering, going in circles."

"Mmm. I got a story to tell you. I'll get a couple of blankets. You get the plastic chairs from behind the house."

"We're going outside?"

"Sure. This is a big story, one for under the stars."

The plaza was deserted now. They set their chairs in the middle of the open space, wrapped themselves against the cold, and settled back to look at the night sky. The moon, so close to full it made Moongirl's stomach knot, had climbed almost to its zenith. Across the top of the sky, the Milky Way looked like a million pinpricks of light suspended in endless space. Silence above, beneath, all around—a cold, clear silence, where nothing moved except the slow stars.

Finally, Eleanor spoke, her quiet voice part of the night. "That sky—the same for a thousand years, maybe for ten thousand. The stars follow a plan, a plan so predictable you can map their journey. Even the moon. Wandering Man looks like he doesn't know where he's going, but he does. Just takes him twenty years or so to get there and back. You watch him careful, you can make a moon map too. All of creation is like that. There's a plan."

"For us—for people too?"

"Hmm. I'm gonna tell you a story. This is the way it was. When the People emerged into this Fourth World, the Creator told us to migrate to the four directions. Back then the Hopi and the Pueblo People and maybe some of the other tribes that settled back East were all the Old Ones—the people the Diné call *Anasazi,* the ancestors we call *The Ones Who Went Before.*

"As the ancestors traveled, they found new places and new ways of living. Nothing was comfortable, nothing easy, so they had to depend on the Creator. Kokopelli went too, playing the Song of Creation on his flute to keep the People singing.

"The clans started out in different directions, but each clan had to migrate to the four directions before they arrived at their permanent home—the Center of the Universe, the Place of Harmony. The migrations were purification ceremonies, weeding out the evil that crept in from the first three worlds. For a long time, the clans migrated.

"Then some of them forgot the Plan of Creation. Those clans settled where it was warm, where life was easy. Other clans continued north, all the way to the Arctic Circle. 'This is as far as we can go,' said some of the People. 'This is the back door of the Fourth World, a place the Creator told us not to go through.'

"But some of those wanted to keep going. 'We can use magic to melt the ice,' they said. They summoned all their powers, but before they could use them, the Creator stepped in. 'If you melt this back door,' he said, 'you will flood the Fourth World. You have done wrong, trying to change the Plan of Creation. Give up your magic. Sing the Song of Creation again and return to your migrations.'"

Eleanor stopped speaking, and for a time, they watched the stars following their own migration patterns.

After a while, Moeyha whispered, "You told that story to show me the pattern of Moongirl's story. I've been following the migration pattern. I emerged in Santa Fe and went West to Oraibi, where I found White Bear. Then I went South to El Morro, where I found Rina, and now I've come East, where I found you. To finish the pattern, I have to go North and find the fourth shaman for the ceremony. Will I find the lost kiva in the North too?"

"No, Moeyha. I didn't finish my story. Listen."

A soft word in a soft voice, but Moeyha felt a shiver run down her spine.

"Those people obeyed the Creator and started their migrations again. One by one, the clans finished traveling to the four directions and turned toward the Center—the place of harmony they all sought. They lived there in peace for a long time, but evil had come in the back door, and even in the Center, it found a welcome in a few hearts."

Moongirl remembered the terror of uncreation—the goal of

the banished powáqas. Staring at the seven-eighths moon, so low on the horizon, she thought of Mahu, Diego, and the lost ceremony.

She looked out past the Milky Way into endless space and thought of the dark lake so deep you could drown. Ripples of despair lapped at the edge of consciousness, and she wondered if the Moon Twins had already failed.

# V. KWININGYA [NORTH]

Storytellers say that long ago, during a time of famine, spirit people of the animal kingdom gave Ya-Ya to the Old Ones to make their hunts successful. The ceremony had great power that enabled the members of the Ya-Ya Society to accomplish surprising feats.

They threw a man into the air over the kiva's opening, and he climbed out unhurt. Using a pole twelve feet long and eight inches in diameter, they ground corn easily into meal. They walked barefoot and dived naked into fire pits filled with hot coals without being burned.

Before a big hunt, the Old Ones performed Ya-Ya for four days, singing and making páhos. On the fourth night, just before midnight, the members of the Society went down into the kiva and put on the heads and skins of the animals that had given them Ya-Ya —Bighorn Sheep, Elk, Antelope, Black-Tail Deer, Gray Deer, and White-Tail Deer.

Then they performed the magic fire ceremony. On the fifth day, if they heard the howl of a coyote and the shrill alarm of a raven just before dawn, the Old Ones knew their prayers had been answered. The hunt would be successful.

*When the migrations began again, the Fog Clan took Ya-Ya with them. When they came to a river, they gave a ceremony. On the fourth day, the Animal People appeared and promised to accompany them on the migration if they had a Game Mother to follow.*

*When fog clan leader heard this, he shaped cornmeal into the figure of a woman, covered it with a cloth, and sang over it all night. In the morning, a spirit baby appeared who grew quickly into a Game Mother. That night a heavy fog came in from the river, so dense the clan couldn't see to travel. But using the magic eye, the Game Mother moved easily through the fog. The Animal People followed her, and the Old Ones followed them, resuming their migration.*

*Storytellers Ya-Ya was a good ceremony for many years, used to help the People in times when food was scarce. Then there came a time when the Society profaned Ya-Ya, using its magic for evil purposes. To stop them, the People declared Ya-Ya taboo. But Two Hearts, those with a human heart and an animal heart, refused to give up the ceremony's power, performing Ya-Ya in secret. That was when Two Hearts became* powáqas.

# CHAPTER SIXTEEN

Moeyha Kaya Amy woke to the smell of coffee and bacon. And pancakes—not Lelia's pancakes. Blue cornmeal, like when she was little.

"You awake, Moeyha? Breakfast is almost ready." Eleanor was already dressed, the same skirt and sweater as the day before, but this morning a red gingham shirt.

Moeyha stretched and rolled lazily off the mattress onto the hard-packed dirt floor. "Awake and in heaven, Iso." Swathed in blankets, she retrieved Amy's chinos and green sweater set from the chair where she'd left them the night before. After she dressed, Kaya went outside into fading pink reflections of a chilly sunrise.

Wednesday. Tomorrow night the Tokpela Moon would be full. The despair of the night before was gone, replaced with a terrible urgency. *Hurry*, to the outhouse. *Hurry*, to the pump to wash in water as cold as the air. *Hurry*, inside to breakfast.

As Moongirl spread butter on the hotcakes her grandmother placed in front of her, Eleanor said slowly, "This morning we're gonna grind some special clay."

Moongirl looked up, startled. "But, Iso ..."

"I know. You think you gotta hurry. But what you gotta do is wait."

"Wait! Wait for what?"

"The Moon Twins' destiny."

*Moonboy?* The red cedar flute was silent, but Mahu was there. Not dreaming—restless, uneasy. She turned her thoughts to Diego, but she and Diego weren't twins, not even brother and sister, and there was nothing. Alive? *Please, let him be alive.*

White Bear *had* promised her she wouldn't be alone, but Destiny seemed to have gone off track. How to get back on? *Hurry,* North. "There's no time, Iso. I have to finish the migration pattern."

"You know where to go? Maybe you had a dream last night?"

"North. I've been west, south, and east. To finish, I have to go north."

"North is a big place, Moeyha."

"Yesterday I didn't know I was coming to Cochiti. I didn't even know about the pattern, didn't know I needed to go East. I was walking toward the sunrise when I remembered you."

Eleanor put another cake on Moeyha's plate and sat down with her own. "Was that the way it was? If you tell me that story, is that the way you would tell it?"

Surprised, she looked at her grandmother over her fork. "No," she said slowly. "The story would say I was walking, and Mahu was dreaming East."

"How about the other places—Old Oraibi and El Morro? How did you know to go there?"

"Diego."

"Seems like you're being guided, Moeyha. Anybody guiding you now?"

She shook her head. "So, I wait?"

"Right now, you eat."

Moeyha laughed. "Eat, and all will be well, children."

Her grandmother looked puzzled.

"A joke between Diego and me." *Diego, the hunter, where are you?*

"He's okay," said Eleanor as if she had read Moeyha's mind. "This is his destiny too."

"Like Mahu is okay?" As soon as she said it, she was sorry— or maybe not.

Her grandmother nodded firmly. "Like Mahu. Now eat those cakes before they get cold. You need your strength to grind."

"What do you mean, grind? Don't you just dig up clay?"

"Remember back, Moeyha, you helped me when you were little."

She took another bite and let the crisp sweetness take her back. A flat rock on the floor beside the shelf of pottery she couldn't touch. Iso pounding dried clay on the rock with a smooth stone, adding bits of pottery. She said, "You added broken pieces."

"To connect the new clay to the old, to keep company with the Ones Who Went Before. I got some special pot shards for this special clay. Very, very old. Maybe a thousand years."

They finished eating, and while Moeyha washed the few dishes, Eleanor laid out an old sheet on the floor. Then she brought a bucket of dried clay from outside and set everything up on the sheet. "Come on. You probably remember how to pound this into dust."

As Moeyha knelt and beat the clay with the grinding stone, she recalled the rhythm of the work. *Thump, thump, shove.* Sitting beside Iso, Kaya pounded a small stone of her own. *Thump, thump, shove.* She ran her fingers through the fine sand Iso made.

"Here." Her grandmother placed pieces of a broken pot beside the metaté. Faded black and white pottery painted in geometric designs. "Just grind them into the new clay."

Thump, thump, shove, she ground the clay the same way her

181

grandmother had for sixty years, the way her grandmother's grandmother had—back to the way the Ones Who Went Before had ground clay. Time passed. Centuries or years or minutes.

A voice broke the rhythm. "Eleanor? I need some more storytellers." Becky Delgado stood in the doorway, dressed in one of her elaborate rodeo outfits—leather skirt and hand-tooled vest over a dusty rose shirt with pearl snaps. "Amy! So, this is where you disappeared. You have no idea how I've worried about you!"

"My granddaughter." Eleanor put down the yucca brush she was using to paint a black geometric design on a white bowl. "Kaya Sekatewa."

Becky smiled. "And my employee. But I know her as Amy Adams."

Eleanor gestured to her table. "May we offer you some coffee?"

Becky pulled out a chair., "If it's not too much trouble."

"No trouble." Moeyha brushed clay powder off her hands and rose to her feet.

"So, Amy is your granddaughter. I always think of you as Eleanor Naranjo, but your married name is Sekatewa, isn't it? I feel terrible about what happened to Mahu in my gallery."

Kaya set cups of steaming coffee in front of the two women, got one for herself, and joined them. As Eleanor put both hands around her cup, she murmured, "You did not stab him."

Becky sipped her coffee. "Still, I would have gotten in touch if I'd realized he was your grandson. Why didn't you tell me your Hopi name when you introduced us, Amy?"

"It's complicated. I didn't remember it ."

"Never mind. I'm sorry you had such a scare. The police are still looking for the burglar. If you got a look at his face, it would be a big help."

The coffee was so strong now it was almost bitter. Kaya

shook her head. "It was too dark, and all I wanted was to get away."

"You poor kid. How is Mahu? Has he regained consciousness?"

"My grandson still dreams. He's hurt bad, but he's strong. In time he will recover."

"I'm glad, Eleanor. Really glad." Becky put down her cup. "I hate to dash in and dash out, but I do need some new storytellers."

"You sold Mama Red Sash."

Becky looked puzzled. "It was the last one. But how did you know?"

"Not the Seeing Eye. Kaya told me."

"You're teasing me! Amy, your grandmother knows I'm interested in folk magic."

"I don't tease about Ya-Ya," Eleanor said softly.

"No," Becky said. "Neither do I. Do you have any new story-tellers for me?"

"Just that one over there." Eleanor indicated the grandpa with the cigar. "I fired more last night, but they're still cooling."

"One's better than none. It's not spoken for, is it?"

Eleanor shook her head and got up from the table. "I'll wrap him for you."

"Good." Becky checked her watch, hammered silver set with turquoise. "It's time I got back on the road. I'm headed north, to my new house near Durango."

North.

"It's near a place called Chimney Rock, an Anasazi lunar observatory. The moon will rise between the spires tonight." Pushing back her chair, Becky stood. "Maybe you'd like to go with me, Amy. It might take your mind off your twin."

*Destiny.* "I'd like that."

Eleanor handed Becky a sturdy cardboard box.

SUZANNE BRATCHER

"You don't mind if I steal your granddaughter, do you, Eleanor? I'd enjoy her company." "It's up to Kaya to choose."

"Good. I'll make a quick stop at Manuel's for seed pots and meet you at the car, Amy."

When Becky was gone, Moongirl looked at Iso. "Brown is the color for north, right? She's wearing a brown leather outfit and taking me north. Is she the North shaman?"

Eleanor shrugged and retrieved Amy's backpack from beside the mattresses leaning against the wall. "Not everyone who wears brown is a shaman—or red or blue or yellow."

"Tokpela Moon will rise between the spires at Chimney Rock. Is the lost kiva there?"

"Tokpela Kiva is at the Center." Eleanor took the manta out of the backpack and gave it a shake. "At the place of harmony, at the place of disharmony."

"Chimney Rock is North. You're a shaman, Iso. Do you know where the Center is?"

Eleanor hung the manta over a chair and handed her the backpack. "First, you got to complete your migration pattern."

*Hurry!* Moongirl knew she should be confident. Destiny had stepped in to take her North, but there was so little time left. Thirty-six hours. *Hurry!*

"I'm gonna keep this manta. Needs a good pressing." Eleanor held out her arms, and Moeyha, who was Kaya, who was Amy, who was Moongirl, stepped in.

Iso pulled her close. "Next thing is to finish your migrations. You won't be alone."

With one last look at Iso, Moeyha left the pueblo, walked toward the field behind the kiva. *Moongirl's migrations. Maybe Kaya's. Not Amy's.* She shuddered, took a deep breath, wondered if she would learn who she was at the Center.

Becky sat behind the wheel of the silver Land Rover. As Amy, who was Kaya, climbed in, the older woman said, "I saw you grinding clay with Eleanor. Do you want to be a potter?"

184

Almost as if Becky had read her mind. Moeyha remembered how natural the clay felt in her hands, how the rhythms of pounding felt like the beating of her heart, how she had imagined herself a potter. "If Iso will teach me."

"You're incredibly lucky, Amy. I know potters who would pay thousands of dollars for just a few lessons with Eleanor Naranjo."

"Doesn't she take students?"

"She says teaching interferes with her work."

The sun had almost reached the top of the sky when they reached Santo Domingo Pueblo. Becky pulled into a gas station. "Another quick stop. Marie Paca sent three water jars for me to pick up here."

On an impulse, Moeyha got out of the car. Instead of following Becky inside, she turned and looked back toward Cochiti. The longing in her heart told her she didn't want to go North. Whoever she was, she didn't want to follow Moongirl's destiny. She wanted to go back and learn to work clay.

"Ready?" Becky opened the back of the Land Rover and loaded a third box.

No—but Moeyha couldn't get the word out. Something still pushed, pulled, called to her. Mahu, red cedar notes climbing the scale, a song of harmony. Shrugging, Amy Kaya Moongirl got back into the car.

They traveled north on Interstate 25 toward Santa Fe. "I didn't know you had another house, Mrs. Delgado."

"Not many people do. It's a special house."

"Durango is in Colorado. Is it a ski lodge?"

"No. You remember my special room—my magic room."

*A shaman's room.*

"This is my magic house. I hope that interests you, Amy Kaya."

In her memory, Diego whispered, 'When the teacher is ready, the student will come.' He didn't trust Becky, didn't like the idea of Becky teaching Amy. Still, a shaman might use magic.

"I don't know much about it. Just that there's black magic and white magic." She remembered the terrible roar of Chaos and the Song of Creation.

Becky shook her head. "Magic is just magic. The same the world over. Not black, not white. Have you looked at my Book of Secrets?"

Amy knew about the book, but she hadn't wanted to look at it. Like the picture of Mami Wati, it made her uncomfortable. "Not really."

"One of the entries tells about an explorer named Kincaid. In 1908, he found an underground cavern in the Grand Canyon, the Lost City of the Dead. The cavern was shaped like the spokes of a wheel, and in the central room, he found all sorts of ancient artifacts, including gold statues of Egyptian gods. Kincaid even found tablets engraved with hieroglyphics that told about Anasazi magic and how it linked with ancient Egypt.

"Of course, his discoveries were hushed up, but those tablets proved magic traditions all spring from the same well of power. That's why I've collected talismans from all over the world—all from the same source."

Amy Hermana remembered what Diego had told her. "For long life."

"Life and death, black magic and white magic, they're the same. It just depends on how the practitioner uses the power. And on your perspective."

The Roar and the Song. Not the same. Moongirl didn't answer.

At Santa Fe, they left the interstate and continued north on US 84. "I'm afraid I've made you uncomfortable, Amy Adams. So, tell me why you grew up in Virginia, not knowing your name was Kaya Sekatewa? I've found out bits and pieces of your remarkably interesting history, but I'd like to hear the story beginning to end."

"Okay, but first tell me, you're the one who called Grandmother Adams, aren't you?"

"Of course. I knew Mahu was your twin, and I thought your grandmother would want to know what had happened to him. It's a good thing you never bothered to get a New Mexico driver's license."

The Virginia license. In the pocket of her jeans.

"You weren't honest with me, Amy. Lelia told me you ran away. She didn't care about Mahu, but she wanted to know everything about you. I had to apologize to her, tell her the only address you'd given me was your dormitory. I'm sorry you didn't trust me."

"I didn't know you then, Mrs. Delgado. I was afraid you would send me back, and I needed to find my family."

"But you know me now, Amy Kaya. You know you can trust me. So, tell me this complicated story of yours. It's another four hours to my house."

They crossed the Rio Grande, and Amy started her story where it began—with Brenda and Wilson and then Lelia. They followed the Rio Chama and stopped in Abiquiu for lunch. As they ate tuna sandwiches on toast, she told Becky about trying to connect to her supposed Japanese heritage and her dreams of brilliant blue skies and petroglyphs. As they drove toward Cebolla, she told about finding Mahu, calling Diego, and talking to X.

Almost to Chama, they saw sheep grazing on both sides of the highway, and she told about Yukioma, Old Oraibi, and White Bear. Wondering if Becky already knew, she told about the Moon Twins and the prophecy.

As one of the sheep stepped into the road, Becky slowed down. "Tell me more about the lienzo, Amy. Could your grandfather tell you what it said?"

The memory of White Bear's face held her back. The story of the lost kiva was not hers to tell. So, she shook her head and told Becky instead about Rina's translation of the story of the young man whose girlfriend showed him the petroglyph panel.

The Land Rover climbed toward the Continental Divide, where patches of snow lingered

on the low mountains, and the brown land slept in shadow. A few puzzle pieces fell into place. "Grandmother Adams found me in Grants. How did you know I was there?"

Becky raised her eyebrows. "I have no idea how Lelia found you, Amy. When I finally tracked her down, all I told her was that you were in New Mexico. How could I have known you and Diego were at El Morro?"

*She couldn't—only X knew.*

At Pagosa Springs, Becky turned left onto Highway 160. "I want to tell you about my house. It's in the San Juan National Forest, and my husband, my ex now, pulled a few strings to get me a 99-year lease on the land."

Becky laughed. "I expect to live a long life, but I don't think I'll need more years than that." She turned off the highway onto a narrow two-lane road that climbed through cedar and gray-green scrub.

As two stone spires came into view, Moongirl turned toward Becky. "You said Chimney Rock was an ancient lunar observatory."

"Mmm. Every eighteen years, the full moon rises between the towers. Some ancient fellow noticed and told his son, who told his son. It took generations to track the moon's journey across the sky. To this day, archaeologists haven't discovered another civilization with as full a record of the lunar cycle. Most moderns don't have a clue."

They turned onto a dirt track and followed it into a stand of taller evergreen, spruce. Another half mile and the road ended abruptly in a small clearing, graveled like a parking lot. It was only a little after four, but dusk gathered.

Fading sunlight threaded its way through the branches over-head, touching here and there a pinecone, a stone, or a tree stump with brief fire. A rambling adobe structure with a flat roof and stone-faced windows, the house, new as it was, somehow gave the impression of great age.

Becky pulled the Land Rover under a towering ponderosa and turned off the motor. A small front-loader sat behind the house next to a mound of dirt, a pile of adobe bricks, and a ladder. "See that?" Her voice sounded irritated. "The contractor is three weeks behind schedule. He promised me he'd have it done by today."

Kaya moved uneasily in her seat "The house looks like an old pueblo. Was it already here?"

Becky laughed. "No, honey, it wasn't here. I haven't profaned an ancient site or disturbed any graves. What you see there is the result of painstaking research, unbridled imagination, and a great deal of money. I'm glad you like it."

Kaya didn't reply. She didn't like it. In fact, the more she looked at the structure, the more she disliked it—ancient or not, profaned or not. It was from another time. It didn't belong *now*.

Seeming not to notice her lack of enthusiasm, Becky pulled the keys out of the ignition and opened her door. "Come on in. I'll make a fire, and we can relax for a little while. Tonight's going to be a big night."

Moongirl didn't want to go in. She wanted to turn the car around and drive away. She had wanted to come North, and she was. But something wasn't right. She sensed it. Fighting uneasiness, she got out and followed the woman she hoped was a shaman to the house. The chilly air, heavy with humidity, clung to her.

Moongirl watched Becky put her key in the front door. "Why is tonight a big night, Mrs. Delgado?"

Becky turned, so close the heavy musk of her perfume enveloped Moongirl, making it hard to breathe. "I thought you knew, honey. Tonight we'll see what the ancient astronomers spent their lives for. Tonight the full moon will rise between the twin spires."

A wave of shock ran like electricity through Moongirl's body. Not tonight. Tomorrow night. Tomorrow night!

# CHAPTER SEVENTEEN

The heavy oak door studded with crude nails swung open. Becky threw a friendly arm around Kaya Amy's shoulders, guided her into a wide entryway with a glass wall that looked out into the darkening forest. The opposite wall, rough-cut cedar, held a dozen copper sculptures of petroglyph designs. An over-sized Navajo rug that hung in the gallery with a $3,000 price tag covered the stone floor.

"Come in, Amy. I think you'll like the inside of my house as much as you liked the outside." As the door shut firmly behind them, Becky let Amy go and pushed a wall switch.

An overhead fixture created from chunks of glass sprang to life, littering the floor with angular bits of rainbow light. "I'm going to the kitchen to make cocoa—the real thing with melted chocolate and whipped cream. Sound good?"

Kaya Amy nodded dumbly, paralyzed by the contrast between Becky's casual hospitality and Moongirl's panic.

Becky laughed softly. "You look befuddled, honey. I know it's a big place for one person, but I do a lot of entertaining." Placing a hand in the middle of Amy's back, she gave her a gentle push. "The living room is straight ahead. If you need a powder room, you'll find one down the hall on the right. I'll join you in a jiff." Then she was gone, disappearing down another hall, switching on more lights as she went.

Not knowing what else to do, Kaya Amy followed the hallway to the living room, passing a score of nooks and crannies that held a collection of exquisitely crafted kachina dolls that probably belonged in a museum. She didn't stop to admire, just kept walking.

The room the hallway opened into wasn't like any living room she'd ever seen. A vast space without windows, it was dark except for the wavering light of a fire that burned in an enormous stone fireplace with a raised hearth. The scent of cedar smoke drifted across the room, stirred by a slight movement of the air.

For a moment, she just stood, letting her eyes adjust. The room, more circular than rectangular, and empty except for tanned animal hides scattered on the red Mexican tile floor, felt more like an extension of the clearing than it did a living area.

Becky said she would like the inside as much as she had the outside. She hadn't liked the outside, but she hated the inside—feared it even.

Amy Kaya crossed to the fireplace with an effort and held out her hands to the warm blaze. The heat comforted her, and she relaxed a little. An empty room, she told herself. That's all it is. Becky just hasn't had time to furnish it.

Turning from the fire, she settled herself on the hearth and examined her surroundings. Animal heads mounted on polished wood gazed down from the walls. Heads with glass eyes that seemed to watch her.

The massive head of a mountain sheep with heavy, curved horns. Smaller deer heads with racks that looked too heavy for the animals that had carried them. A delicate antelope head with sharply pointed horns. A grouping of angular elk heads that gave the impression of an entire herd shot and decapitated. On the floor in one corner sat a stuffed coyote with three legs. Between its ears perched a stuffed raven.

Not an empty room at all. A room full of death. She rose, poised to run from the room, the house, ready to take her chances in the dark forest when Becky returned, carrying two pottery mugs. The woman's eyes narrowed. "Going somewhere?"

"Just stretching."

Becky handed Amy Kaya a mug and sat on the hearth. "Sit beside me, honey. Sorry not to offer you a chair, but you know how it is. When in the pueblo, do as the ancestors did."

*Just Becky being Becky?* Amy relaxed enough to take her place and sip the cocoa.

Sweet with cream and spiced with nutmeg, the cocoa comforted her as much as the fire's warmth on her back did. She sipped again, then asked the question the room begged for. "Are you a hunter, Mrs. Delgado?"

Becky looked at the trophies on the walls. "Not exactly. You remember I told you this is a magic house? These animals are part of the old pueblo magic."

Moongirl shivered. A man with an antelope head ... "Ya-Ya?"

"You know that much. Do you know I'm a two-heart?"

Moongirl started so violently cocoa spilled onto her chinos. "You're a powáqa?"

"Does that scare you?"

Moongirl held her breath, didn't answer.

"I didn't have much choice, honey—become a two-heart or die. Two years ago, like some ancient Aztec priest, a surgeon broke my breastbone and pulled my heart out of my chest. He put it back, but now I have a valve from a pig's heart pumping my blood."

Becky stood and set her mug on the wide mantel. Picking up

193

a heavy plastic page protector, she said, "I've got something to show you, Moongirl. You've seen half of it before."

Amy Kaya realized Becky wasn't the North shaman. She was a powáqa who knew Moongirl's destiny. More pieces of the puzzle fell into place. Becky and X. Amy introduced Becky to Mahu, and Becky told X Mahu was at the gallery. X didn't have to break in because Becky gave him a key. Lelia had found Amy because X told Becky she was at El Morro, and Becky told Lelia about the only road from El Morro.

Becky took her mug, handed Moongirl the lienzo, pictograph side up. As Rina guessed, it started as two panels stitched together. They had studied the panel that was now on the right.

The left panel, the one she hadn't seen before, was a map of sorts, but not a normal map. The place where the conquistador had seen the Tokpela Kiva was in the center of the map, a *D* almost the same shape as the ceremony petroglyphs.

There was nothing to orient her to its location. She assumed the writing on the back had guided Becky when she chose top and bottom, north and south, but there was nothing else to show where the Center was. Just a few squiggly lines radiating out at irregular intervals.

"Not much good as a map, is it?" Becky sat beside her. "Unless you know what you're looking for and how they navigated back then." Taking back the page protector, she turned it over and said, "I know you're interested, and after tonight it won't matter what you know, so I'll give you the high points.

"Our young conquistador talks about walking east three days through the desert until his party came to a place where there were many rivers. He talks about a city of cathedrals at the center of the universe. A place where The Ones Who Went Before studied the heavenly bodies."

Becky looked up from the lienzo. "Rivers were key to maps back then, you know. What you might not know is that four tributaries of the San Juan River pass our Chimney Rock observatory on the way to Navajo Lake."

She laughed, a triumphant sound. "We went to so much trouble to get this rag, but we didn't need it! Rivers and an observatory—the center of the universe has to be close. I was guided to this place before your twin ever found the Ya-Ya cave. We didn't need the lienzo for the map, but I'm glad to have the ceremony."

Hope fluttered in Moongirl's heart. This was North, not the Center. And the Tokpela Moon was tomorrow night. Outside, she heard a sound that didn't belong to the forest.

"There's more to the narrative but not a whisper about Moon Twins. We have to know the prophecies to understand that part of the game, don't we, Moongirl?"

Outside, another sound that didn't belong, louder now. "You're working with X! Where is Diego?"

"X?" Becky laughed. "Of course. You still don't know who my lieutenant is, do you? Who are your suspects?"

But Moongirl didn't care about X. "Where is Diego?"

Becky shrugged. "Diego doesn't matter. He's not part of this."

Ice-cold fear ran along Moongirl's nerves like blood in her veins. She jumped to her feet and sprinted across the room.

"You can't get away," called Becky. "They're here."

Moongirl identified the sounds that had been growing gradually louder—a motor whining, metal clattering, rocks skidding. *Hurry!* Before they could get to the house. She reached the door, yanked it open, bolted outside.

At the same instant, a tan Hummer skidded into the clearing, spraying gravel. The driver killed the engine. In the sudden silence that followed, a coyote howled—a long, lonely sound that lingered before it was swallowed up by the forest. Then the cry of a raven.

Like on the mesa just before the powáqa grabbed her.

It only took an instant to stand still and listen, but it gave Becky time to get to her, time to take a firm grip on her arm and keep her from running away. "You really should have gone with Lelia, honey, But I guess destiny is destiny."

The sun dropped behind the long line of the mountains, but enough light lingered for Moongirl to recognize the two men climbing out of the Hummer.

Yukioma said, "Should be good hunting."

Gabe Walker gazed at the sky. "A clear night anyway

Powáqas—more than one. Becky, Walker, Yukioma, and who else?

Becky faced the two men. "You two have an hour before the others get here."

An hour. An hour for what?

Yuki pointed at the mound of earth behind the house. "It's not finished."

Becky shrugged. "No. It's still crude, but maybe that's what was meant to be. Make do with what's there."

Yuki started to object again, but Walker put a hand on his shoulder and turned him toward the mound of earth. Yuki shook off the hand impatiently, but he went.

"Gabe," Becky said. "Do what Yukioma tells you to,"

"I do what *you* tell me," Walker said, but he followed Yuki.

Walker was X, but Yuki called the shots. Yuki hated Ya-Ya and witchcraft. It didn't make sense.

"Come along, Moongirl." Becky turned her toward the forest. "We're going to watch the moon rise between the spires of an ancient kiva."

They hurried through the deepening dusk for several minutes, eventually emerging into an empty parking lot. "This weekend, this lot will be filled with sight-seers," Becky said. "But tonight, it's just us—us and the spirits of the past."

Above them, the two rock outcroppings created a dark *U* in a sapphire sky dusted with pale silver light at the eastern horizon. Becky's voice, so soft Moongirl almost didn't hear, blended with the growing darkness. "Twin spires—another pair of moon twins." Letting go of Moongirl's arm, she headed up a rock-strewn trail.

Moongirl considered turning and running back into the forest, but the moonrise compelled her. Not yet Tokpela—almost, but not yet. The trail climbed steeply to a narrow mesa where once some sort of ancient structure had stood. Almost a D, like on the lienzo. Had Becky found the Center? Was Iso wrong?

Center or North, she followed Becky, skirting tumbled walls until they faced the stone chimneys. Then, they sat on the ground and waited.

Not long. As Moongirl watched, a luminous white disk as large as any golden harvest moon peeked over the edge of the U. Only a hair's width from full, it climbed the sky until the stone chimneys neatly bracketed it. Wandering Man seemed to hesitate there for a moment before sliding slightly south to hide behind the narrower of the chimneys. Three breaths later, the moon reappeared and continued its bright ascent.

Moongirl realized she had been holding her breath, waiting. Waiting for what? The sound of a flute—a red cedar song.

But the night was silent. A small pewter bird flitted moth-like across the moon's face. Then, the night swallowed it. "How-itzko," she whispered, not knowing why she remembered its name. "The sleeping one."

"A nighthawk. This is a night filled with omens."

"The coyote and the raven. Is Yuki here to hunt?"

"He's here to make sure we do the ceremony correctly." Becky rose to her feet and dusted off her skirt, the brown leather skirt that had nothing to do with shamans.

*What does Yuki know about the Tokpela ceremony?* Moongirl stood. *Or is it another ceremony they need tonight?*

She realized the items she'd seen by Becky's house formed a

pattern. The mound of dirt that meant someone had been digging, excavating a subterranean room. The ladder, a way in and out of a kiva.

Moongirl glared at Becky. "The Ya-Ya ceremony is taboo."

The moon hovered partway up the eastern sky, flooding the ancient plaza with silver light. "*Taboo* is just a word, Moongirl. A word used to scare us away from things we don't understand. Ya-Ya is an ancient ceremony to ensure a successful hunt. I think you know what we're hunting."

*Ancient powáqas.* Maybe powáqas too powerful to control, with magic that will tip the universe into chaos and uncreate us all.

"You're going to see something tonight very few moderns get to see."

"No."

"Don't be silly, Moongirl. This is your destiny."

Not tonight. *Tomorrow* night. She didn't say it, but Becky seemed to read her thoughts.

"Destiny has come a night early for you, honey. How can I fulfill my destiny on the night of Tokpela Moon with Moon Twins blocking me?"

Moongirl ran. The trail was steep, straight down the hillside ,not switchbacked like the trail at El Morro. Pebbles slid beneath her athletic shoes, just as ice had slid under her bare feet the night Walker came for the lienzo, the night he attacked her twin. Like that night, she kept running.

A cloud passed in front of the moon, plunging her into deep shadow, a cold breeze whispered against Moongirl's face, and her right foot slipped. Becky reached her and grabbed her from behind with a grip too tight to break. Becky whistled—two notes and a trill, like the call of the nighthawk.

Another whistle answered, and Moongirl saw the dark shape of a man coming up the trail. The moon came out from behind the cloud. Gabe Walker. She jerked hard. It was almost enough.

Her right arm was free, but Becky's fingernails dug into her left. Becky shoved her toward Walker, so hard she stumbled.

Walker caught her, dropped heavy hands on her shoulders, and righted her. "Hello there, Amy. Giving Becky trouble?"

"She needs a cup of tea." Becky started back toward the house and the kiva.

Walker marched Moongirl straight ahead. "We've got just the thing."

She considered running away, but where would she go? Who would help her? Walker pushed her fast enough to keep her off balance.

*Wait. Wait until you have a chance to escape. Make them think you've given up.*

They crossed the empty parking lot single file—Becky first, Moongirl next, Walker last. When they re-entered the forest, branches overhead fragmented the moonlight. No side trails appeared, no places she could duck between the trees and disappear.

Clouds covered the moon again as they emerged from the forest. Behind Becky's house, now a pale outline of a ghostly pueblo, a campfire burned brightly.

Yukioma sat on his heels, feeding long white flowers into an iron pot among the coals. Three other figures squatted around the flickering fire, watching intently. No one spoke.

Walker shoved Moongirl into the ring of the firelight. She recognized one of the three as Henry Begay, the Navajo policeman who stopped had them in Leupp. He dropped a handful of seeds into the brew. The man next to him added powder, the third man tiny fruits like raisins. At the edge of the forest, a fourth figure moved in deep shadow.

Moongirl Hermana wanted to shout, *Where is Diego?* But before she found her voice, the moon emerged from behind a cloud, bathing the scene with silver light.

Becky looked at Yuki. "It's time for moonflower tea."

"Sacred Datura," Yukioma muttered.

The three figures around the fire shifted slightly, making room for the newcomers. Walker pushed Moongirl to the ground with a rough shove and stood over her, blocking any hope of escape. She pulled her knees under her chin, closed her eyes, and waited for whatever was to come.

"Mahu," she whispered. "I'm scared. I need you—I need the Song."

Silence.

The door in her mind was closed, or the room was empty.

*Mahu, Diego, White Bear, Rina, Eleanor. Mahu* ... Around and around in her head, pleas for help from the others caught up in this destiny.

No one answered. Time passed—slowly or quickly—she didn't know, didn't care.

Becky's voice interrupted the loop of her thoughts. "Whenever it's ready."

Moongirl looked up. Becky stood by the fire, dressed now in a flowing white robe. A long silver necklace hung around her neck, and silver bracelets covered her arms wrist to elbow. Lifting the pot from the coals, Yukioma poured steaming liquid into a crude pottery mug and handed it to Becky.

Squatting, Becky pressed the rough mug into Moongirl's hand. An aroma of mint and licorice drifted up from the cup—a wild, dusty desert smell. "This one's for you, Moongirl. Moonflower tea for Moongirl."

"I don't want it." Moongirl turned her head away from the mug. "I know what it is, and I don't want it."

"It will help you understand." Becky's voice raised chill bumps on Moongirl's arms.

"Hallucinations. I won't drink it."

"You will." Becky put her hand on Moongirl's wrist and guided the mug toward her mouth.

"No." Grabbing the mug from Becky's hand, she threw it into the fire. "Whatever is going on here, I want to be awake for it."

Becky slapped her, a hard blow that sent her sprawling backward. "You're going to drink it." She reached for Moongirl and yanked her into a sitting position. "Give me another mug, Yuki."

They forced the liquid into her mouth, hot but not scalding, tasting like it smelled—bitter and minty. When the mug was empty, Walker stayed behind her, still cutting off any possibility of escape. Despair washed over her. *Mahu, Diego, White Bear, Rina, Eleanor ...* Silence.

Becky's quiet voice came again, sending a chill down Moongirl's spine. "Let's all have some."

As the moon slid in and out of the clouds, Yukioma filled more mugs and passed them around. The group was larger now. They stood in silence, watching the fire. She counted. One, two, three, four ... seven ... twelve ... fifteen. Moongirl was sure of the number. She hoped the drug wouldn't affect her.

Gradually, however, the red and yellow flames danced. Gracefully, hypnotically, each tongue different from the others. As she watched the flickering dancers, she knew the hallucinogenic was working. Fear became panic. If she was drugged, how could she escape?

The panic slowly dissipated, dissolving first into uneasiness and then into contentment. After a few minutes, even the contentment dissolved. Moongirl swam through the night sky, among the stars, toward the bright disk of the moon. Behind her, Walker moved away, but she didn't care. She wanted to swim through the stars forever.

A woman dressed all in white appeared beside her, someone she should know but couldn't quite recognize. Moonlight played on her pale hair and shimmered on her bracelets and earrings. A woman made of silver.

The silver woman spoke. "It's time."

Moongirl wondered if she should be afraid. A pair of hands went under her arms and pulled her to her feet. Surprisingly gentle hands. In her ear, a voice whispered, "I'm here."

Hope, so strong and sharp it hurt, sliced through the drug-induced lethargy. *Diego?*

# CHAPTER EIGHTEEN

As hope whispered to Moongirl, insistent hands pushed her toward the ladder. The earth whirled around her. She did not want to move her aching head. But she had to know. Moving carefully, she looked over her shoulder.

In the fire's restless light, she saw not Diego, not a man—an antelope. She screamed, or tried to, but she didn't have enough breath. Rabbit fur filled her mouth and nose. She *had* to scream, or the antelope would fling her over the mesa's edge.

Panic burned in her chest, consuming her scrap of hope.

More hands touched her, rough, insistent hands propelled her along a path lined with fire. Then she descended alone into an underground chamber lit with a soft red glow, climbing down a ladder with shimmering turquoise rungs into the womb of Mother Earth.

The space was round with benches curved along the walls. In the center of the room, a fire sent smoke straight up to a hole in the roof. Two rectangular fire pits filled with glowing embers bracketed the center fire.

Despair wrapped cold tentacles around her throat. The Tokpela Kiva.

The silver woman appeared—a shimmering powáqa.

"Time to get dressed, honey." The silver woman dropped a white robe over Moongirl's head, pulled one arm through, reached for the other one. Frantic to escape from the voluminous folds of fabric that enveloped her like the rabbit fur blanket, Moongirl yanked her arm away and tore at the robe with both hands.

"Gabe! Help me." The woman's voice was shrill, as insistent as her hands with their sharp nails. "I think she's coming out of it."

Before Moongirl could get loose, X was there, pushing her down onto some sort of stool, grasping her chin, forcing her head back. Mug in hand, the silver woman poured more of the moonflower tea into Moongirl's mouth. She didn't struggle, let the liquid fill her mouth, didn't swallow, let it spill out.

In the flickering light, they didn't notice. Finally, X released her head. Bending forward, Moongirl put her forehead on her knees and let the remaining liquid trickle out of her mouth. Still, she knew she'd swallowed some of it. It would renew the effects of the drug, but not as much they intended.

"Now," the silver woman spoke again, "stand up. We're going to fix your robe." The two of them forced her arms into the robe, pulled it straight over her sweater and chinos, forced her back onto the stool.

Already the extra dose of the drug took effect, robbing Moongirl of her will. She forgot why she'd fought the robe, why she feared the kiva. Something about an antelope, but there weren't any animals, just people sitting on the benches along the wall.

The silver woman stood behind her and said, "We've got a little play for you, Moongirl."

The fire burned brightly, blocking Moongirl's access to the ladder, but it didn't matter. She floated above the room, looked down on the scene.

A man wearing a dark brown habit came down the ladder. Silently he made a full circuit of the room. On his second time around, a young woman dressed in animal skins and grass descended the ladder and joined him. He took her hand and they went around a third time, stopping before a slab of sandstone.

He said, "She took me into the Tokpela Kiva."

She said, "My father said it was taboo for foreigners, but my beautiful conquistador was not a foreigner to me."

"I heard the elders talk about it," he said, "the panel that tells the story of Disruption at the Center."

"Power," she said.

"Power," he said. "Power to control nature."

"Thunder."

"Lightning."

"Wind."

"Rain."

She said, "Animals that run."

He said, "Animals that crawl."

"Birds."

"Insects."

"Planted crops."

"Gathered food."

She said, "Men."

He said, "Women."

A white-haired man dressed in the same skins as the young woman came down the ladder. Bent almost double, he shuffled across the room to join the other two. "Power begets power," he said. "We could do whatever we want."

"End life," the young woman said.

"Prolong life," the man in the brown habit said.

Still bent over, still shuffling, the old man circuited the room. When he reached the other two again, he said, "They were jealous. They held a ceremony to banish us. Into Tokpela, into Endless Space."

She said, "For a thousand years."

"Until the next Tokpela Moon," the old man said.

As one, the three actors turned and walked around the room. When they had completed four circuits, they stopped in front of the sandstone slab. The old man said, "They sent those who were left back out on our migrations."

"To the West," she said.

"To the South," he said.

"To the East."

"To the North."

"When the Tokpela Moon is at the top of the sky," the old man said, "build a Moon Ladder at the Center. Stretch it across the opening of the Tokpela Kiva."

"Draw in the power again," she said.

"Take the power for your own," he said.

The rhythm of the words, the slow circular movements, the heat in the kiva—all wove her drug-induced confusion into hypnosis. Moongirl was hardly aware when the silver woman pulled her to her feet and guided her to a place before the fire.

Here the dance of the flames was more intricate than it had been outside. Tongues of fire leaned first one way and then the other, crossed in front of and behind each other with careful precision, stretched high, then bowed low.

As she stared at the red and gold fire, first one flame and then another took on human shape. When every flame had mutated into a tiny, glittering figure, the sturdier of the fire people suddenly leapt with deadly fury on the smaller figures. With growing horror, Moongirl watched the stronger devour the weaker.

Placing both her hands on Moongirl's shoulders, the silver woman forced Moongirl to her knees. "Tonight," she said, "we have our own ceremony. The power of Ya-Ya."

Moongirl shivered. A ceremony. White Bear and Diego. Shamans to help with the next ceremony. Eleanor, Rina, and someone else. Another shaman—the North shaman. Not this silver woman.

"Tonight we perform the old rituals," the silver woman said. "We command the power of Ya-Ya to give us the strength we need for the night to come."

Silently the watchers in the circle rose and climbed the ladder that went up into the night. Moongirl wanted to go with them. She needed to get out under the lopsided moon into the open air where she could breathe.

When she started to rise, X—Walker, she remembered, pushed her to her knees, jerked her head back, poured more licorice and mint into her mouth.

*Moonboy! Twin, why am I here alone?*

The flute answered her, the red cedar notes that sang the Song of Creation. Not alone, then. Still, she felt abandoned.

Time flowed forward, backward, in a circle. Then a procession descended the ladder with the turquoise rungs. First came the silver woman, barefoot and wearing a long cape of soft white leather over the white robe—Becky who had been behind her but just now entered the kiva.

When the silver woman who was Becky stepped from the last turquoise rung onto the beaten earth floor, the white-haired man from the play handed the silver woman a burning torch. Next came a man with the large rounded horns of a mountain sheep on his head. The old man handed him a torch as well.

Then an elk. An antelope. More sheep. Three deer. Two more elk. Another antelope. It was hard to focus her eyes, but as the animals ringed the room, she counted them. One, two three … fourteen in all. The drug was weakening again.

Animals holding flames circled the room, a drumbeat filled it with a steady thump, thump, thump. A gourd rattled, keeping time with the drum. The silver woman danced—on one foot and then on the other.

"I am the Game Mother," chanted the woman. "I lead the

spirits of the animals. We have gathered to perform the fire ceremony that summons the magic eye, the eye that sees in the night, the eye that will show us the Tokpela Kiva."

*Not here?* Moongirl pushed the cobwebs from her mind, tried to understand why it was good news that the animals were still searching for the Tokpela Kiva.

When she found the answer, she understood. Time left for another ceremony. Tomorrow night—the Tokpela Moon over the Tokpela Kiva. Moongirl had to escape, find it herself. She couldn't fail.

As the silver woman continued to chant, a rumbling began inside the room. Thunder. Then the sound of rain, quiet at first, like a distant storm. Then louder and louder until the noise filled her head.

When Moongirl thought her eardrums would burst, the silver woman moved out of the line of dancers. Still keeping the rhythm, she stepped barefoot into the left pit of glowing coals. An elk stepped into the right pit.

Moongirl watched with horrified fascination. *Not me— Please, not me!* Out of the corner of her eye, she saw a hand holding a cloth coming toward her nose and mouth. She caught half a breath before the hand covered her nose and mouth.

Just like the moonflower tea, she couldn't fight it all off. Not as much as they intended, but enough. She slipped into semiconsciousness, barely aware of what was going on around her.

The drumbeat, the shuffling feet, the swaying bodies continued. Time stopped. She lay on her side on the floor, listening to the thump, thump, thump, shuffle, shuffle, shuffle. Counting the dancers—one, two ... fourteen. Strong hands grasped her shoulders, antelope hands, X's hands, Walker's hands.

He rolled her onto her back, and she opened her eyes. Far above, firelight glittered on a slender silver knife. It came closer, closer. She tried to raise her hands to shield her throat, but they were too heavy.

"Moonboy!" she shouted.

Someone screamed. A long, inarticulate scream like a war cry. A heavy weight fell on Moongirl, coming between her and the silver knife.

A deer. Another scream and then another. Rough hands tugged at her shoulders, pulling her from beneath the heavy deer carcass. All around the room, men and women screamed and yelled.

"Wake up, Moongirl! Wake up, Kaya! Wake up, Amy!" An antelope shook her.

X—he was going to drop her over the edge of the mesa ...

"I'm going to take you to Diego," the antelope whispered in her ear. "Don't fight me. This is our only chance."

*Diego?* But Diego wasn't an antelope. Walker was the antelope.

"You have to believe me," hissed the antelope. "If you don't want to die in here, you have to trust me!" Grabbing a mug, he poured hot liquid, not down her throat, but over her head, in her face.

The shock broke through the lethargy that was as heavy as the falling deer had been. She spluttered, quit fighting, groped for his hand.

They ran. Noise and smoke filled the kiva. The drum stopped, but a woman wailed, a sorrowful keening that sounded like it would continue to the end of time. Another woman moaned. A man cursed. Around the room, animals fought in twos and threes.

Struggling to focus her eyes in the flickering light, Moongirl fought to keep from falling over her own feet, fought to keep up with the hand that tugged at hers. Then she was on the ladder. The antelope clambered behind her, pushing insistently.

She climbed, one hand clutching a rung, the other letting go, one foot looking for balance, the other dangling in space. Up, out of the noise, out of the smoke, away from chaos, away from death.

They emerged into an icy fog. Tiny snow crystals stung her face, blown by a sharp north wind, more effective than the hot liquid had been. She was awake, running. It didn't matter where, as long as her feet took her away from the pandemonium, away from the confusion, away from the danger. She ran into a man, ran into him so hard it almost knocked the breath out of her. He reached for her, helped her regain her balance.

"Hermana!" he shouted.

The antelope reached them, breathing hard. He jerked off the grotesque head with its antlers and threw it on the ground. "My office," he said. "You'll be safe there."

Then he was gone, disappeared into the trees in the direction of the stone chimneys.

"What?" gasped Moongirl, who was Hermana. "Who?"

"No time. The Jeep is the other way."

"Diego?"

"Yep. Now come on!"

"Diego!" With a wild kind of joy, she thrust her hand in his.

They ran.

When the long white robe threatened to trip her, she had to let him go and hike up the robe. Still, she ran, following him around Becky's silver Land Rover, past Walker's Hummer, between two pickups, past an SUV, down the road.

The Jeep sat at the edge of the forest, covered with a thin layer of snow, almost invisible in the dense fog. Diego flung open his door and shouted, "Get in!"

As she struggled to get herself and the heavy folds of wet fabric into the Jeep, Diego shoved the old-fashioned gear into four-wheel drive. She pulled herself into the seat. The motor growled into life. They bounced onto the road, and as Diego pulled on the headlights, a rifle cracked, splintering the night into a thousand fragments of fear.

The rifle cracked again. Gravel mixed with snow sprayed the Jeep. They hit a rut. The rear tires skidded, and the Jeep fishtailed wildly. Diego jerked his foot off the gas. They slid for what seemed an eternity, time enough for another crack of the rifle, and then he regained control.

"Hang on!" He jammed his foot on the accelerator. The Jeep lurched forward. They were moving again, picking up speed, careening along the narrow track of road.

As they bounced and skidded, skidded and bounced, she twisted in her seat, doing her best to watch behind them without hitting her head. "Someone's coming. I see headlights."

"Not for long," said Diego. "I was busy while the animals were prancing around the fire down in the kiva."

Fourteen, thought Kaya. Fifteen at the fire. Fourteen animals came down the ladder. "You did something to the cars."

"A little snow in the gas tanks. Look again."

She looked. It was snowing harder now, blurring the shapes into fuzzy outlines. And it was blessedly dark. "No headlights."

With one last bounce, they were out of the forest and back on pavement, back on the road that worked its way down the mountain to Highway 160. Diego pressed harder on the gas. They picked up speed. Clinging to the grab bar beside her head, she said, "Can't we slow down?"

"Can't risk it. Walker and his troops may temporarily be out of commission, but he's got a cell phone and a network.

"Yuki and Begay?"

"No. I was never sure about Yuki, but after what happened in there, I know he isn't Ya-Ya, not one of the powáqas. I think he was there to stop them."

"He wanted to destroy the lienzo to keep them from using it?"

"Something like that."

"So, what happened down there?" She shivered. Reaching for the knob, she turned on the heater. Lukewarm air blew on her legs. Lukewarm, but warmer than outside. "Who had the knife? Were they going to kill me?"

"We didn't expect that, Hermana. If we'd known that was on the agenda, we would have called the police, stopped the whole thing."

"We?"

"Pete Lacapa and me. He was the one who pulled you out of there. I was on the ladder coming back down to help get you out."

"The ranger we met at El Morro?"

"Yep. It's his office we're going to. You'll be safe there."

"You know what happened, Diego. Tell me! I have to know."

He slowed and downshifted as they went around a curve. "Becky had the knife. I'm sure she intended to kill you, but I don't think any of the others, even Walker, knew what she meant to do."

Diego rolled down his window and stuck his head out. Snow blew in, covering the steering wheel, the dashboard, and Moongirl's hands and face.

"There's a road here!" he shouted. "On the left. Do you see it?"

He wore his leather coat, but the cold air overpowered the heater, and suddenly Hermana Moongirl shivered so hard she could hardly see. She leaned forward and stared through the windshield.

The wipers worked hard, pushing at heavy wet snow, and on one of the swipes, she saw a break in the trees. Teeth chattering, she shouted, "There!"

He slowed even more, downshifted again, and made the sharp left turn. Finally, he pulled his head back in and rolled up the window. Snow covered his face and hair. He shook his head, dislodging some of it.

Still shivering violently, she reached over and helped, dusting snow off his hair and neck. Her cold fingers touched his forehead, and for an instant, she was warm all over. She drew her hand back sharply.

Diego gave her a quick look but didn't comment. "Yuki was the one who saved you. I saw him put on that deer head after he finished serving the tea, so that's how I know it was him. As soon as he saw the knife, he jumped Becky."

"He fell on me, and he didn't get up."

"She got him. She was furious, and she went for him. I didn't have time to wait around and watch. I saw Pete get to you, and I wanted to get out of there ahead of everyone else. I was on my way back up the ladder, but I think Walker grabbed Becky and pulled her off Yuki."

"Why would she want to *kill* me? I know she wants to stop the Moon Twins, but to kill me? Did she mean for Walker to kill Mahu?"

Diego was quiet for a long time. Finally, he said, "I don't know for sure. There isn't much to go on about Ya-Ya. Nothing but rumors. It's not supposed to exist anymore."

"Tell me, Diego. Rumor or not."

He sighed unhappily. "It's got to do with long life. Supposedly, when a two-heart kills a human, the powáqa gets the rest of that human's life."

The silver woman with the silver knife. Retching, she rolled down the window and took deep breaths of air so cold it hurt her nose. Snow blinded her, stung her cheeks, swirled so thickly the whole world was white. And would be forever.

# CHAPTER NINETEEN

Hermana rolled up her window to shut out the blowing snow. "My life for hers." She remembered Becky standing in Iso's doorway, a healthy woman dressed in expensive clothes, smiling, praising the grandmother's work, professing concern for the granddaughter.

"Becky wants a long life, and she's willing to kill me to get it." She struggled to believe the woman she'd thought was her friend wanted her dead. But the silver knife—would it forever glitter in her memory?

They passed through a break in the trees, an open area where the snow piled up faster and deeper than it had in the forest. Diego plowed the Jeep in the direction where there might once have been a road.

When they finally drove back under the trees, he let out his breath. "Good twisted into evil, like the Ya-Ya ceremony. Wanting to live is good, but when that desire extends to murder, it becomes evil."

"Maybe the idea that a person could extend one's life by taking someone else's got the Old Ones onto the wrong road."

The track through the woods climbed, not dramatically, but enough. Even with four-wheel drive, the Jeep slid, fishtailing. Diego let it go, then straightened and drove on. "It could be. Or something worse."

"Worse? What could be worse than murder?"

"Cannibalism. Not cannibalism of the dead to keep from starving. Ritual cannibalism."

"You mean eating people as part of a ceremony? That's horrible!"

"Yep. It's a theory no one talks about, but there's evidence of ritual cannibalism around the time the Ancestral Puebloans abandoned their cities."

"Tokpela Moon," whispered Moongirl. "If that's what the powáqas were doing, I understand why the shamans banished them into endless space."

They drove out from under the shelter of the trees again into a parking lot deep with snow. The Jeep slid to a stop. Directly in front of them sat a single-wide trailer. Snow drifted against the north side. In two of the windows, lights burned yellow, spilling out an uneasy glow. Diego turned off the motor. "Boy! Am I ever glad to be here."

"This is the Chimney Rock office? I thought it would be like El Morro."

"The office, a museum, and Pete's living quarters. National Archaeological Sites aren't exactly big draws. Chimney Rock is more about research than tourism."

"North," said Moongirl. "Is Pete a shaman?"

Diego gave her a puzzled look. "I don't know about that, but when I saw him at El Morro, I had a feeling he could help us. Pete Lacapa has one foot in the world of the ancestors and one in the world of the scientists. I was on my way back to the Visitor's Center to show him the lienzo when Walker got me. As soon as I got free, I came here."

Hermana shuddered and held out both hands to Diego. He

took them and squeezed. Bigger hands than hers, warm, reassuring. After a moment, she said, "I knew X had you. I didn't know what to do."

The door of the trailer opened, Pete Lacapa beckoned. They got out and ran. The robe dragged around Hermana's ankles, slowed her, threatened to trip her. Then she was there, shivering and fighting to catch her breath.

Diego was already inside. He grasped her hands, pulled her out of the snow, and into an all-purpose room—part living room with a dark green tweed loveseat and matching chair, part office with a desk and computer, part store with a counter and cash register, even part museum with a glass-fronted case.

"You ought to get rid of that awful robe," Diego said.

She already pulled it over her head. He tugged at it, helping her get free.

"Give it to me," Pete said. "Tomorrow, I'll burn it."

Pete Lacapa—medium height, compact build, almost Hopi. The ranger she'd met at El Morro, the dancer who pushed her up the ladder and out of the kiva. Now, he wore jeans and a brown plaid flannel shirt.

"Are you a shaman?" she blurted. "The North shaman who will help us with our Tokpela destiny?"

"Those are big questions, Moongirl. Not for answering until you're warm."

Surprised, Kaya realized she was shivering violently. She didn't have any dry clothes—not her mother's manta or even the purple sweatsuit. She burst into tears.

Ridiculous to cry over a wet sweater when she hadn't cried about Becky and the silver knife. So ridiculous, she laughed. She stood in Pete Lacapa's living room, shivering, laughing, and crying until Diego put his arms around her.

"You're okay, Hermana," he murmured, pulling her close. "You're safe now."

Mahu's velvet shirt was soft, and Diego's chest and neck

were warm. He rocked her back and forth. Like she was a tiny child. The motion was oddly soothing, almost a dance of mourning.

After a while, she stopped crying and laughing. In the silence, she listened to his heart beating under her ear. Finally, she stopped shivering. From a distance she heard Pete say, "I have a sweat suit you can wear—too big, but dry."

She wondered what color this one was. Not purple.

Over Diego's shoulder, she watched Pete drape the sweat suit on the arm of the loveseat—a soothing, nondescript gray. "I've started a pot of coffee," he said, "and I can scramble some eggs."

Not quite ready to step out of Diego's arms, Moongirl Kaya Hermana nodded her thanks to Pete. Then she looked up at Diego. She wanted to thank him too, but she didn't know how.

He met her eyes and gave her a tender smile. For the length of a heartbeat, she thought he might kiss her. Instead, he sighed, "Ah, Hermana." He gave her a tight hug and released her.

This time she wanted to shout it—*I am NOT your sister.* But of course, it still wasn't the time or the place. But soon. Very soon.

Pete said, "The washroom is at the end of the hall. When you're ready, come to the kitchen."

"Thank you." She managed a shaky smile and headed down the hall.

Kaya felt like a lizard shedding an old skin as she peeled off the green sweater and tan chinos. Not just because they were wet, but also because they were *Amy* clothes. Whatever part of her was Amy, that part didn't belong here or now.

Still, as she struggled with her tangled mess of hair, she looked ruefully at herself in the mirror. Clean and dry, but not the reflection of anyone Diego James would think of as a girlfriend.

She probably imagined he'd considered kissing her because that's what she wished for. With a small sigh, she hung her wet clothes over a towel rack and headed for the kitchen. She heard Diego's voice and the reassuring sounds of cooking—pans clattering, a drawer opening and closing, a knife chopping.

Moongirl Hermana stood for a moment, letting her gaze roam the all-purpose room. Moving closer to the glass-fronted case, she studied its small collection of artifacts. A throwing stick. A stone metaté. Chipped and broken pieces of black and white pottery, so ancient they looked ready to crumble. Like the pieces Iso had given her to grind into the special clay. An arrow, rough cedar with a crude inlay of turquoise. Like the one Walker stabbed Mahu with. But nothing that might give a clue to the lienzo.

The smell of coffee drew her into the kitchen. Pete and Diego were studying a drawing on a piece of plain white paper. Diego tapped the picture with his glasses. "It's a rough sketch of the piece of the lienzo we had. We think the missing piece is a map of where to find the Tokpela Kiva."

"That's exactly what it is," Moongirl said. "I saw the rest of the lienzo. Becky's sure the map means the Chimney Rock area. She says there are four rivers here, so the Center of the Universe has to be close by. Iso told me the old stories say the Tokpela Kiva is at the Center of the Universe. It doesn't make sense. How can we possibly find the Center of the Universe? The idea that it's on earth at all is a crazy myth."

Pete shook his head and opened a bread box. "The Greeks separated body and soul, matter and spirit. They invented the idea of a mythical place as a place that didn't exist in this realm of life.

"The Ancestral Puebloans weren't Greeks. They didn't see the world divided like that. If a story handed down to Eleanor talks about the Center of the Universe, it means a literal place." He dropped two pieces of bread in the toaster. "Can you draw the map?"

Moongirl took the pencil Diego held out to her. "I can. But even if the Center is a real place, the map won't help."

Reaching for another sheet of paper, she sketched what she could remember. "The center of the map, the place I think was meant to show the kiva the conquistador saw, was marked by a *D*. Squiggly lines radiated out in four directions.

"Becky thinks the lines are rivers, rivers that flow beside Chimney Rock. I thought the kiva we were in was the Tokpela Kiva, but she chanted something about the Magic Eye showing them where it is."

Twisting her hair savagely, she secured it with the pencil and looked at Pete and Diego for an explanation.

Pete didn't answer. Instead, he took six eggs from a carton, cracked them into a glass bowl, and whipped them with a fork.

Diego placed his sketch next to Kaya's. "Look. The *D* you saw on the map is the same shape as the ceremony panel."

Fork in hand, Pete came to look. "Interesting. I didn't know that was the design we're looking for."

"Does it tell you where the Center is?" Moongirl said.

"Maybe." Pete went to the stove and bent down to turn on the gas flame and adjust it. Then he put a pat of butter in a cast-iron skillet and set it on the burner. "I need to think about it."

"It's given you an idea, though," Diego said.

"Mmm."

"Are you the North shaman?" Moongirl said. "The one destiny has chosen to help us?"

Instead of answering, Pete picked up the glass bowl, and poured. The eggs sizzled as they hit the hot pan. Sprinkling cheese over them, he stirred.

"What is this about a North shaman?" Diego said.

"You might not have noticed, but we're collecting shamans," she said. "White Bear. Rina. Eleanor. Pete?"

"White Bear, I understand. He told us about the prophecy."

"Rina told us about the ceremony."

"Okay, but what about your grandmother? I wasn't there."

"She told me about Moongirl's migrations to the four directions. Santa Fe was the Sipapuni, the place of emergence into the Tokpela Destiny. Then you took me West to Old Oraibi, where we met White Bear. Then we went South to El Morro."

"Where we met Rina. You met Eleanor in Cochiti, which is East. That's why you keep asking Pete if he's the North shaman."

They both watched the park ranger in the brown plaid shirt scrape scrambled eggs onto plates. He put the filled plates on an old wooden card table and reached for a folding chair. "Moongirl, please pour us some coffee. Diego, get the toast."

When they were all seated and eating, Pete said, "We've known since the Moon Twins were born that the prophecy was meant to happen this year. But we didn't know how it would take shape. The Tokpela stories are a thousand years old, hard to interpret."

"I never heard of Tokpela until White Bear mentioned it," said Diego. "I've been listening to my dad talk for nineteen years, and I've never even heard the word *tokpela,* except to mean *endless void.*"

"We don't tell the Tokpela stories often. They tell of great power gone terribly wrong."

"Cannibalism?" whispered Moongirl.

"Mmm."

"The evidence has been suppressed," Diego said.

"Sure," Pete said. "The Anasazi were the ancestors of the Hopis and the pueblo tribes—all peace-loving people. They were a great civilization with trade routes that stretched all over the known world. No one wants to talk about it."

Moongirl put down her fork. "Why would anyone do that? Diego said it wasn't famine. He said it was ritual cannibalism.

Why would people develop a ceremony around eating other people?"

Pete shook his head. "No one knows for sure. One guess is that it was outsiders showing power over the locals. Maybe from Mexico."

"Aztecs," Diego said. "Aztec Ruins National Monument, Montezuma Castle National Monument, Montezuma Well."

Pete pushed away his empty plate. "Most people believe the use of the word *Aztec* in the Southwest is a misnomer, but sometimes I wonder."

"If we put the stories together," Moongirl said, "the powáqas sent through the Tokpela Moon door were the cannibals."

"Mmm."

"Becky can't know that," Amy Moongirl said. "She's desperate to live, but I can't believe she would willingly let in a bunch of cannibals!"

Pete took a long drink of coffee. "Maybe she knows, but maybe she doesn't really believe it. I've been watching Ms. Delgado for a couple of years, ever since she had her husband pressure the Forest Service to lease that land. He divorced her not long after, maybe because he realized what she was up to. She's one of the dangerous ones."

"What do you mean?" Kaya said.

"She believes in magic enough to dabble in it, but she's too modern to seriously take the dark power. She's the type that's liable to get more than she bargained for—and give the rest of us more than we know how to control."

No one spoke. In the silence, the old fear welled up in Moongirl, who was Hermana, who was Amy. He might be talking about her. On one level she believed what the shamans were telling her, but on another level she still wasn't sure.

Diego interrupted her thoughts. "So, we know more about what we're fighting, and we know who the two sides are. We have an idea of the ceremony they intend to perform. But we still don't know where we need to be tomorrow night.

"I don't know about the two of you, but the fact that they don't know where it is either doesn't comfort me all that much."

"Wait," said Moongirl. "Stop. What do you mean we know about their ceremony? Isn't it Ya-Ya? The one they were doing tonight?"

"We don't think so. Pete thinks I'm right about the cross-hatching representing a moon ladder. He thinks that will be the way the powáqas enter the Fourth World. Beyond that, though, we don't know how the ceremony will be performed, only that it's sure to be taboo.

Moongirl shivered. "You don't think they would commit cannibalism?"

Pete shrugged. "As I said, I don't think Ms. Delgado really believes."

"But where is the Center?" Diego demanded. "Even if it's just a wild guess, Pete."

The ranger nodded. Putting down his coffee mug, he pushed back his chair and stood. "I want to show you something. Bring those two sketches."

They followed him to the main room, where he took a book from a shelf and scanned the index. When he had the page he wanted, he opened the book and laid it on the counter. A drawing on the left-hand page was labeled *Pueblo Bonito*. It was shaped like a *D*.

"Rooms, plazas, kivas." Pete pointed as he talked. "A classic Chacoan great house—a curve that takes in three sides. A long straight wall on the other, lined up with the cardinal directions or with solar or lunar events. Lay your drawings on either side."

"It makes perfect sense," Diego said. "The Tokpela Kiva must be associated with a great house. But there are so many."

"Maybe two hundred scattered across 40,000 square miles," Pete said.

SUZANNE BRATCHER

Kaya groaned. "We'll never find it. We don't even know where to start looking."

Pete held up her drawing. "Maybe we do. Chaco Canyon was the center of the Ancestral Puebloan world. The center of time and space."

Diego nodded. "The center of the universe."

"But what was it?" asked Moongirl.

"A ceremonial center in the middle of the desert," Diego said. "For its time, a stunning accomplishment."

Pete picked up the explanation. "Chaco was a city made of sandstone chiseled into very nearly uniform building blocks and chinked with tiny stones instead of mortar. The builders brought timber for doorways and roofs from mountains seventy miles away—without wheeled carts.

"The Chacoans exported black and white pottery and imported seashells from the coast of California and macaws from Mexico. They had cotton they didn't grow, and bells made of copper they didn't mine. Roads as wide as a modern two-lane highway led to Chaco. The architecture followed the cycles of the sun—and the moon."

"People from all over the Four Corners region made pilgrimages to Chaco Canyon," Diego added. "The builders worked on it for three hundred years, twelve generations. Then one day, they simply started leaving."

"A mass exodus?"

Pete shook his head. "Not at all. People have speculated about it for years. The Ancestral Puebloans moved out clan by clan over a fifty-year period. They left as carefully as they built, closing up doorways and burning kivas. It took a long time and a lot of work to dismantle Chaco."

"But why?" Moongirl said. "If they wanted to leave, why not just go? Why burn the kivas?"

"Purification," explained Pete. "Probably the people believed their kivas had been profaned."

224

"With ritual cannibalism?"

"Mmm."

"But the Tokpela Kiva wasn't profaned," Diego said. "It was used for a sacred purpose, so it wouldn't have been burned."

"Right," Pete agreed. "It's still buried in the earth. We'll be standing at the level of the roof looking for crossbeams covered with soil."

Kaya stared at him. "You mean we're looking for a mound?"

Pete frowned. "Not just a mound—a hidden mound so camouflaged archaeologists have missed it for years."

"Chaco is the right time period." Diego flipped the book's pages until he reached a map of the canyon. "But how do we know where to start? It's a big canyon."

"We're looking for a moon kiva," Pete said. "Seven buildings in Chaco align with the moon, but Casa Rinconada is the most likely. It aligns with the major lunar standstill, the place on the horizon where the full moon will rise tomorrow night."

"That's it, then," Moongirl said.

Pete shook his head. "We won't find the Tokpela Kiva in Casa Rinconada or any of the Chaco great houses. They've all been excavated or studied with laser imaging. If an intact kiva with a mural of a ceremony on the wall had turned up, it would have been big news."

Diego ran his hand through his hair. "This is impossible. You know that, don't you? Maybe Chaco Canyon is the right place, but we don't have enough time."

Moongirl shook her head. "It can't be impossible. It's our destiny."

"You have a suggestion?"

"We go to Chaco Canyon and listen for the Song of Creation."

Diego moved restlessly, not accepting, not rejecting.

"You must choose to believe, Diego James!" Pete said.

"It's hard."

"Sometimes, it's easy. Other times you just have to believe."

"Like now?"

"Like now," murmured Moongirl, who was Hermana, who was Kaya, who was Amy.

# VI. TUWANAASAVI [CENTER]

**S**torytellers say when the People finished their migrations, they came from all directions, converging on the Center of the Universe. At the entrance, they found a great bird with red, yellow, blue, and brown feathers barring their way.

Acting as spokesman, Kokopelli approached the bird. "Will you allow us to go in and live here?" he asked.

"Perhaps," the bird said. "But first, I must test you, Flute Player."

"I'm ready," Kokopelli said.

"The test is this," the bird said. "No matter what I do to you, you must play the Song of Creation."

"Go ahead."

Using a bow and an arrow inlaid with turquoise, the great bird shot Kokopelli. With the arrow sticking out of his side, Kokopelli lifted his flute and began to play the Song of Creation. The notes followed one another up the scale and then down again with a clear sweetness no bird song, even the magic song of a magic bird, could equal.

"You're stronger than I thought," the bird said. "I must test you *again. No matter what I do to you, this time, you must sing your song without your flute."*

*"I'm ready," Kokopelli said.*

*So, the great wild bird shot a second arrow into the Flute Player. With both arrows sticking out of him, Kokopelli put back his head and sang.*

*Ki-tana-po, ki-tana-po, ki-tana-po, ki-tana-po!*
*Ai-na, ki-na-weh, ki-na-weh*
*Chi-li li-cha, chi-li li-cha*
*Don-ka-va-ki, mas-i-ki-va-ki*
*Ki-ve, ki-ve-na-meh*
*HOPET!*

*Kokopelli's voice was even sweeter than the sound of his flute, producing a gentle vibration that sounded like rain, rain that soaked into the hot dry desert, rain that caused flowers to bloom on sharp cacti and frogs to sing in shimmering pools of water. Everyone who heard Kokopelli's song burst into songs of their own, even the great bird.*

*When the canyon was once again silent, the bird said, "You have passed my tests."*

*Pulling a red feather from one wing and a blue one from the other, the bird handed the feathers to Kokopelli. "I am the conqueror of air, the one that inhabits Above. When you put this feather in your páhos, I will come to carry your prayers to the Creator."*

*Then with a bow, the great bird moved away from the entrance and said, "Go in."*

# CHAPTER TWENTY

"I t's time." The voice was quiet but insistent.

Amy opened her eyes in the dark room and tried to remember where she was, more important—who she was. Her head hurt. She wore a sweatsuit that was too big. She was lying on her side, near enough to Diego to feel the reassuring warmth of his body.

She was Moongirl, who was Kaya, who was Hermana —for now.

The two of them lay on the floor with one sleeping bag open beneath them and another over them. Diego slept in sweatpants and a T-shirt. One arm was flung across her shoulder, and his warm breath tickled the back of her neck in a regular rhythm. Time didn't exist.

"Sorry, kids," the voice said. A hand shook her shoulder gently. Pete's hand. Reluctantly, Hermana pushed herself up, every muscle objecting.

Diego groaned and sat. "Is it really morning?"

"Five a.m. You need to leave before it gets light."

Diego yawned and stretched. "Is it still snowing?"

"It stopped a couple of hours ago. Sky's clear, but the moon has already dropped below the mountains. It's cold and dark. No one will see you."

Hermana went to the bathroom first, and by the time she returned Diego was dressed in jeans and green flannel shirt. As they stood beside the door preparing to leave, Pete put a quilted red plaid hunting jacket around Kaya's shoulders. "Too big, but warm."

He gave Diego a canvas tote bag. "Coffee and sandwiches. You'll need to eat."

She knew they both thought it, but neither commented.

Shrugging into his coat, Pete opened the door and went out. Diego was next. Kaya followed, thrusting her arms into the coat's sleeves, and pulling it around her as she shut the door and went down the two steps.

It was as cold and dark as Pete had promised. Dark enough to be night, but somehow morning. It was silent, so still, her athletic shoes crunched on the snow.

As they walked toward the white mound of the Jeep, a clear note in a minor key cut through the silence the way a ray of light cuts through darkness. A second note—a long note that trembled, seeming to wait until a third note joined to climb up the scale. Not a song, just a snatch of melody, so that Kaya wondered if she'd even heard it.

They climbed in the Jeep, slamming doors, shivering. Pete brushed snow off the windshield with a short-handled broom. Diego put the key in the ignition and turned on the motor.

"Did you hear the flute?"

"Yep." Before Diego could say more, Pete tapped on his window.

Diego rolled it down.

"Chaco is about four hours. West on 160. South on 550 to Aztec. Pick up 371. East at Indian Route 9. No pavement from there on. North at Route 12. You'll come in the back door of Chaco."

"We'll find it."

"Good. We'll meet you at Casa Rinconada at moonrise."

Suddenly her headache worsened. He meant the four shamans—shamans ready to fight powáqas with Diego and Moongirl in the middle. Putting her fingers to her temples, she massaged lightly.

*Mahu?* She pushed lightly on the door in her mind. *Moonboy!* Red cedar notes, different ones, part of a new song. Then it was gone.

Pete slapped the side of the Jeep the way he might slap a horse to get it moving. "See ya." Casual words that were anything but casual.

Rolling up his window, Diego pulled on the headlights and shifted into gear.

Hermana turned on the heater, knowing it would blow cold. Still, it couldn't be as cold as the air in the Jeep. "I thought Pete said the Tokpela Kiva couldn't be at Casa Rinconada."

"Yep. But it's our best starting place."

She shifted in the hard seat, tried not to sound as petulant as she felt. "So, we have a starting place. How are we going to find the kiva?"

"You're going to listen for Kokopelli's song. I'm going to go hunt with a compass."

"You and Pete figured something out after I crashed last night."

"I can't say we figured anything out, but we talked about where the Tokpela Moon might rise and set in Chaco tonight. We looked at the alignment of Casa Rinconada and some planetarium software to get azimuth estimates. With my compass, I might be able to locate the center point of that line."

"You think the Tokpela Kiva is there?" Hermana dropped her head slowly to the right and then to the left, willing the tension out of her neck

"I don't know. But we're looking for the Center of the

Chacoan universe. Why not look for the center point of the Tokpela Moon's journey at midnight tonight?"

"The center of time and space—that's what Pete said last night. Did you notice the pattern of the directions he gave us?"

"What do you mean?"

"West, then south, then east."

Diego whistled. "And north into Chaco. The same pattern you've been following."

The headlights cut a bright swath through the untracked snow. Diego found the way back to Highway 160 without making a single wrong turn. A snowplow had cleared the lane they needed, the lane heading west.

Hermana Moongirl reached for the tote. "Ready to eat?"

"You bet. So all will be well."

"I'll settle for so my headache will go away. Caffeine might help."

Diego didn't laugh. "The aftereffects of that wretched brew they forced you to drink. I saw what they were doing, and I wanted to grab you and run. If there had been any way—"

"They would have caught you." She lifted a thermal cup out of the canvas bag, twisted the lid to the open position, and handed it to Diego. The second one was hers. Black, as she'd requested. "Aspirin?"

"Check the bottom of the bag. Pete said you'd need some."

As her hand closed on the bottle, she said, "How long were you there?"

"The whole time. Pete knew what was going on. He's kept pretty close tabs on what Becky was building. When they started digging a kiva, he doubled his surveillance. When I showed up, he put me on watch."

Diego took a drink of his coffee. "I was in the forest behind the house when Becky took you into the house. We thought whatever they were up to would happen tonight. When everything got going a night early, we had to improvise."

Memories crowded in. She trembled. Tossing two aspirin in her mouth, she gulped coffee, burned her tongue, and shocked herself into the present.

"Becky must have planned all along to get rid of me before tonight," Amy Moongirl said. "I'm sure she doesn't know what part the Moon Twins have in this any more than we do, but she wanted us all out of the way." She took swallowed more coffee, slowly this time.

Diego looked at her, but she couldn't see his expression in the darkness.

"Hermana, what do you say we try to forget about all of this for a little while? All these helpful adults have a point. I'm ready to eat."

She laughed shakily and unwrapped the sandwiches—egg salad. The heater finally blew warm, and her headache receded. She gave herself up to the normal.

Not for long. A glance in her side-view mirror showed a pair of headlights. It had begun to snow again, lightly, but enough that Diego was intent on the road ahead. Moongirl felt her stomach knot. The lights kept their distance, and she watched without comment. But when the lights began to close the gap, she broke the silence. "Someone's coming. Do you think the powáqas know where we are?"

Diego checked his mirror. "Don't start with the magic eye."

"Why not? How is the magic eye any different from powáqas and cannibalism and moon ladders? Or even Kokopelli's song?"

For an answer, Diego jammed his foot on the accelerator. The back wheels slid briefly but found traction. The Jeep picked up speed. "I'm going to see if we can outrun whoever is back there. It might not be anyone from Becky's gang, but we can't take the chance. Tell me the second you think he's gaining on us."

The highway stretched ahead of them without so much as a curve to dodge around. On both sides of the road, tall conifers loaded with snow hemmed them in. "It's like being followed in a tunnel," whispered Hermana. "No place to hide."

At first, they seemed to be holding the distance between the two vehicles, but then the other car's headlights grew larger in their mirrors. She fought rising panic. "He's gaining on us."

"We have to find a place to get off. A driveway, a stand of trees, a ditch that won't break the axel."

They drove in grim silence until Kaya pointed ahead. "Slow down! Up there on the left."

"I don't see anything," Diego said, but he took his foot off the gas.

"Back from the road. In that open space. A dark shape—a barn maybe."

An abandoned building with a sagging roof and one wall missing stood off the highway.

"Hang on." Foot on the brake, Diego eased the Jeep onto a rutted trail almost hidden by the snow.

"He'll see our tracks."

"This was your idea. You suddenly have a better one?"

She wanted to snap back at him, but he was too busy to pay attention to anything but wheels bouncing them off the track into rocks or mud or whatever else lay on either side. The collapsing barn loomed in front of them, a space hidden even from the darkness.

Just before they entered the shelter, the back wheels spun in the snow. Diego jammed the gas, let it off, jammed it again. Half sliding, half bouncing, the Jeep skidded inside. At the same instant, the motor died.

Neither spoke. They both held their breath in the sudden silence. Hermana groped for Diego's hand and found it. Fingers entwined, they looked out the back window toward the highway.

A tan Hummer sped past. "He didn't even slow down," she said. "Maybe it wasn't Walker. Maybe it was someone headed into Durango."

"Maybe." Diego released her hand, straightened his glasses, and opened his door. "I'm going to see if anyone else is coming."

She was out almost as fast as he was, hurrying with him to a place where they had a clear view of the road. It stretched dark and empty in both directions. Then far back down the road in the direction of Chimney Rock, a pair of headlights appeared, moving fast.

"Come on." Diego reached for her hand.

They moved as fast as they could with snow underfoot, moving more quickly than they needed to. It would take the vehicle several minutes to reach them, but they ran anyway. Breathing hard, they watched, one on each side of the Jeep. Out on the road, the headlights scraped through the darkness but didn't stop, didn't even slow.

Hermana watched until the taillights of a red pickup disappeared. Then she said, "What will we do if they catch us?"

"You're kidding, right?"

"No."

"If they catch us, sweetheart, this whole thing is over. If they catch us, the powáqas win, the universe careens into chaos, and we probably all die. Them catching us is *not* an option, so don't even think about it."

"Walker caught you, and you got away! Becky caught me, and we got away! They tried to kill Mahu, and he's still alive. It's not a dumb question. I don't appreciate your biting my head off every time I express any anxiety." To her own disgust, she burst into tears.

Diego didn't reply, and she could almost hear him counting to ten. Finally, he said, "Let's start over, Hermana. I'm sorry I snarled. I'm as scared as you are. I have no idea what we'll do if they catch us, but we'll think of something. That's the best I can do."

She wiped her eyes on the sleeve of the coat and took a deep breath. "I'm sorry too. Maybe we should get going."

"Good idea."

Neither one of them spoke, but the silence was companionable. Hermana Moongirl let her mind drift as she watched the white landscape slide by. The snowplow passed them on the other side of the road, scraping a path for cars heading east, throwing snow into the middle of the highway so that it splattered on their windshield. Diego pulled on the wipers but didn't comment.

Green letters on a white sign reflected their headlights—Highway 550. "South," Diego said as he made the turn. "Now, we follow the Animas River for a while."

Hermana Moongirl's head pounded again. To take her mind off it, she said, "What happened to you at El Morro? It was Walker, wasn't it?"

"Yep. I feel stupid now. Of course, I didn't know he was in on it then, but I'd had my suspicions. I should have been ready for him."

"Never mind that. Tell me what happened."

He gave her a look she couldn't interpret. Then he turned his attention back to the road. "When I got down to the parking lot, Walker was there, waiting beside his Hummer. I was surprised to see him, but I went to see what he wanted when he called to me. He had a gun in his pocket, and he told me to get in. I should have refused, shouted for help, but like a dumb jerk, I did what he told me to."

"You're not a dumb jerk. He threatened to shoot you."

"But would he have done it? Who knows? But when I saw Walker, I should have known he wasn't there by accident."

"Just like I should have had better sense than to assume Becky showed up at my grandmother's house by chance."

They dropped out of the high country, headed for the desert. The snow on the road no longer needed a plow. About an hour before dawn now, the sky was perceptibly lighter, and they picked up speed.

"I still feel stupid." Diego shoved at his glasses.

"Okay, you were stupid. So was I. We're even."

"We'd better not be stupid tonight."

"I agree. Tell me the rest of it."

"Once we were in the Hummer, he drove toward the Zuni Mountains. He called me Jim Jim and asked me where the lienzo was. I tried sticking to the story I told him at the McDonald's, that I didn't know what he was talking about, but he told me to quit stalling, that he knew I had it."

"Yukioma."

"Yep. We were far enough into the Zuni reservation that there wasn't much traffic. Walker pulled off on a side road, got his gun, and made me get out. He said that one way or the other I was going to give him the lienzo or tell him where it was. I thought about lying, but I figured he'd work me over and get it anyway, so I let him have it."

"But why didn't you come back to El Morro? You couldn't have been that far away."

Diego slammed his hand on the steering wheel. "He made me get back in the car, and he wouldn't tell me why or where he was taking me. What he did tell me was that he wanted the lienzo for an important customer, and he admitted to following Mahu to the gallery. Now we know the customer was Becky."

Kaya Moongirl sighed. "I introduced Mahu to Becky. I don't know how she knew about the lienzo, but she did. She called Walker and gave him a key to the gallery. This whole thing is my fault."

Diego snorted. "Come on, Moongirl. You're important, but not that important. 'This whole thing,' as you call it, started 1,000 years ago."

"Yes, but I handed Mahu to Becky."

"Walker was already following Mahu. He heard about it when Mahu found the lienzo. He was the one who told Becky. She knew enough to realize its importance. When you brought

Mahu to the gallery, it was just an extra piece of good luck for her. If you want a starting place closer in time than a thousand years ago, it started when that rockslide opened up the cave."

"How did Walker find us in Holbrook?"

"My guess is Yuki realized where we had gone and called his pal Walker."

"What about Henry Begay? He's part of the gang, and he stopped us in Leupp. He could have called Walker."

"Nope. Pete told me Begay infiltrated the powáqas because he's sure they're defacing archaeological sites. He wants to catch them in the act. He thought we were part of the gang."

Behind them, a passenger van came so close its lights reflected harshly in the mirrors. Neither of them commented, but the silence in the Jeep was tense. The van slowed and fell back, accelerated until it was too close, fell back, accelerated.

"Maybe he wants to pass," said Hermana, wishing it to be true.

"Here's hoping. I'm going to pull over, but hang on in case I have to do something fast."

Hermana gripped the grab bar and held her breath. The Jeep slowed and moved onto the shoulder. With a long honk, the van passed them. "Oh, man," Diego said.

She let out her breath and took another one. And then another. When they were back on the highway without a vehicle anywhere in sight, she said, "Tell me the rest of it."

Diego cleared his throat. "We drove a couple of hours, and then Walker turned off onto a series of forest service roads probably meant to confuse me—which they did. Around midnight, he left the road and headed into the forest.

"He must have been following some kind of hunting road because we wound up at an old campsite." Diego paused and cleared his throat again. "He made me get out, and I was sure he was planning to kill me."

*The silver knife.* Diego knew what I felt when he saw it.

Without thinking about what she was doing, she reached over and squeezed his arm. Diego gave her a funny look, and she withdrew it quickly. "Sorry."

He murmured something that sounded like "Don't be," but she wasn't sure enough to believe it. She swallowed hard, struggling to keep her voice level. "Then what happened?"

"He hit me with the gun. I fell but didn't quite pass out. I kept drifting in and out of consciousness. I heard his cell phone ring. He reported, and then he was quiet for a long time. Finally, I heard him say, 'I won't do it, Becky. He's not important enough to kill. Maybe the Moon Twins are important enough for murder, but not this kid. He's just in it by accident.'"

"Thank goodness he convinced her."

"I don't know whether he did or not, but you can guess how I felt when I saw you with Becky. Walker didn't kill me, but he made sure I was out of commission. He had ether or something on a handkerchief.

"I saw it coming, but I was too weak to resist. When I woke up the next morning, I had a humdinger of a headache." He gave her a weak smile. "Maybe you understand now why I didn't make it back that night or the next morning."

She couldn't even pretend it was a joke. "How did you get out of there?"

"Once the sun was up, I started walking east. After a while, I heard a pickup and found my way to one of the forest service roads. Eventually, a white-haired Zuni grandpa came along and picked me up. He told me I was in the Cibola National Forest, about a hundred miles from El Morro. He gave me a ride to the main road, and I hitch-hiked from there."

"I knew something awful had happened to you." Amy Hermana's voice shook, and she stopped.

"While I was walking, I thought about you. I kept wondering what was happening and if you were all right."

Heart racing, she waited for him to speak the next thought.

The tiny town of Aztec was behind them when he said, "While I was walking, I realized I don't know what to call you. You have too many names."

Disappointment washed over her. When she could think again, she had to admit he was right. She did have too many names, but she couldn't choose. They were all her names—none wrong, none quite right. She was Amy, who was Kaya, who was Moeyha, who was Moongirl. But now was the time. She blurted, "Whatever you call me, don't call me Hermana!"

## CHAPTER TWENTY-ONE

Diego touched her knee lightly. "No," he said softly. "I don't want to call you, Hermana. That's what started me thinking. It's probably too soon to call you *Querida*—Darling."

She felt herself blush. "Maybe a little."

He put his hand back on the steering wheel. "So, pick a name that will work for now."

"I can't. All those names are mine. Not *Moeyha*, since that means 'little grandchild.'"

"*Moongirl* seems too formal."

"I guess you can call me *Kaya* or *Amy* then. You pick."

"*Kaya* means 'older sister,' right? I think we're agreed you're not my sister, and you're not older. So that leaves us with *Amy*. Right back to where we started when we met."

"Yep," she said.

They both laughed. The moment passed, but Amy Kaya Moeyha Moongirl wanted to shout good morning to the sun that peeked over the horizon. Its first rays glinted on the surface of the Animas River, turning the dark water silver.

Diego tapped a jerky rhythm on the steering wheel. "Farmington's just ahead. Seventy-five miles to Indian Route 9. If nothing unexpected happens, we'll be at Casa Rinconada by ten. The sun goes down at 4:30, so we'll have about seven hours to find the Tokpela Kiva."

Amy looked out at the blue morning. "Right now, the moon seems like a dream."

"Or a nightmare. Last night was real enough."

Moongirl tried to hold onto the sense of unreality, but it was gone. "Why is Walker doing all this? In a twisted way, I can understand Becky. She's afraid of dying, and she's willing to do anything to live longer.

"But why is Walker willing to do whatever it takes, including assault and kidnapping, to get the lienzo for her? Is he in love with her? Does he want her to live so much?" The feeling that someone was following them returned. She twisted in her seat to look over her shoulder. The road stretched empty behind them.

"I suppose that's possible. But I'm guessing his motivation is plain greed. The lienzo would bring a hefty price on the black market, and if he can find the actual panels, they'll be worth a small fortune."

"How do you sell something painted on a wall in a kiva?"

"You take it down with a chain saw. Lots of rock scars prove it's possible."

"But who would buy something like that? They'd have to know it was protected."

"Yep, but some collectors think they have the right to whatever they can pay for. Even museums have bought artifacts that should have been returned to native peoples. The theory goes something like—'It's already been defaced, or taken from its proper venue, or shipped halfway around the world, better it should be in a museum where people can learn from it than given to locals who don't value it as much as we do.' The real Rosetta Stone is a great example. It came from Egypt, but it's been in a British museum for years."

"So, Walker lets Becky have the lienzo, gets her to lead him to the kiva, and then double-crosses her and takes everything for himself."

"He won't think it's a double-cross. She gets what she wants, and so does he."

A semi pulling two trailers came up behind them fast. The driver honked twice and passed. The trailers bounced, evidently empty. Amy jumped and looked at the road behind them. Still no cars in sight. "I have that feeling that someone's following us."

"Me too."

They rode in silence then, a tense silence that intensified with every mile. Eventually, Amy couldn't stand it anymore. She blurted, "Do you want me to drive?"

"Nope. Sorry."

"Do you mind if I let my seat back and close my eyes?"

"You think you can sleep?"

"Nope. Sorry."

He laughed. "I get it. You want some privacy. Go ahead."

When she was settled, Kaya went looking for Mahu. Red cedar notes in a minor key called her deeper. She found Mahu, awake. *Soon, Moongirl.* The words echoed in her heart. *Soon, soon* ... Comforted, she slept.

Sometime later, the car bounced, waking her abruptly.

"Sorry. The first of many potholes. Welcome to Route 9."

Amy, who was Moongirl, sat up. A narrow two-lane road stretched ahead, paved but badly needing resurfacing. They had it to themselves, and Diego drove around the biggest potholes. In a few miles, the road dipped into a wash, dry now but posted with a flash flood warning.

"A tributary of the Chaco River."

"There's a river in the canyon? This looks like serious desert to me."

"The river was one of the things that made it viable for a settlement. It doesn't run all year. The wash fills in the early spring when the mountain snow melts and again during the late-summer rains. This time of year, there might be some water, but not much."

"So, the rivers on the lienzo map might have been washes draining into the canyon?"

"Yep. If our conquistador visited in the spring or the summer, he would have drawn the washes as rivers."

"And if he came back in the winter, his map wouldn't have been any good."

Diego nodded. "That exact mistake saved a lot of archaeological sites from being plundered."

By the time they found Route 12, the sun was halfway up the eastern sky, climbing inexorably toward the top of the sky where it would pause and then begin its slide toward darkness. Seven hours to find the kiva.

Cattle guards that rattled their teeth interrupted the gravel road. Badly washboarded, it twisted and turned, ran down into dry washes and up onto low hills. Over the clatter of odds and ends sliding in the back, Diego shouted, "Eight miles." Settling his glasses more firmly on his nose, he gripped the steering wheel and drove.

Moongirl reached for the grab bar and hung on.

Twenty noisy minutes later, the road ended in a *T* with a paved road, empty on a Thursday morning in early December. One-way arrows pointed right. Ignoring them, Diego turned left. "We're at the far end of the Park loop. Casa Rinconada is just ahead."

"So, Pete sent us the closest way."

"Nope. Highway 550 would have been a straight shot, south all the way."

Moongirl shivered. "The first part of the ceremony. West, South, East, North, and now the Center." On the right side of the road, shallow water flowed sluggishly in Chaco Wash, a winter river where there shouldn't have been one. On the left a cliff of red rock rose into the blue sky.

The spirits of the ancestors whispered in Moongirl's mind. She shivered again and hugged herself tightly. "What is this place, Diego?"

He didn't answer immediately, and she knew he understood her question. They passed a wide break in the mesa wall, a smaller canyon at right angles to the main canyon.

When the red wall began again, Diego answered. "On the maps, this place is marked Chaco Culture National Historic Park. The rangers say it was a major center of Puebloan culture for four hundred years, from around 850 CE to 1250. They say it was a place of mysterious ceremonies and architectural marvels.

"The tourists say it's a slice of ancient history that should be preserved. They say it's a place of impressive ruins. The Hopis and the Pueblo peoples say it's sacred, a place of power that should be left to crumble back into the dust from which it was built."

Moongirl listened to Diego's explanations, but she knew none of them, not even all of them together, captured the ancestors' whispers.

Diego pulled off the road into a small lot and parked. "Here we are. Casa Rinconada, the house at the corner."

"I don't see a house or a corner."

"*Corner* is because Rinconada is located right where South Gap runs like a street between West Mesa and South Mesa. *House* is a bigger stretch. Here in Chaco, the word *house* usually means *great house*, a ceremonial building of four or five stories with rooms built around a plaza. While great houses all have kivas associated with them, the Rinconada Kiva stands on its own. No great house. Instead, several small houses, probably apartment houses for caretakers, cluster around it."

They got out and walked along a short gravel path that climbed a small hill. The air was cool, but a comforting warmth rose from the sandy soil. They stopped at the top of the rise and looked down into a circular depression as big as a high school gym. "This is the biggest of more than four hundred kivas in Chaco."

Open to the sky and filled with weeds, it didn't look at all like Becky's kiva. "I can't see the kiva."

He pointed. "See the benches around the inner walls? Now imagine all the backfill is gone, put in fire pits, add a roof, and you've got an impressive kiva."

They went down the few steps into the arena, and Moongirl turned a slow circle, following the sweep of the wall. "Now what?"

Diego stretched and then sat on the stone bench, a bench where a hundred people had sat a thousand years before. He stretched out his legs. "Not a clue."

*Mahu?* Surprised, Moongirl realized the door in her mind stood open. Her twin was awake. Now he played his flute, calling Kaya as he had in Santa Fe. "Do you hear it?"

Diego looked up, a puzzled expression on his face. "Hear what?"

"Mahu, playing his flute."

Diego shook his head.

Kaya listened again. At first, all she heard was the sigh of a breeze in Chaco Wash. Then a note, high on the scale. Silence, then another note down low as though one had been, lost from the tune. Then silence again. "It's faint, but I hear it."

Closing his eyes, Diego bent his head, listening. After a moment, he looked up at her. "I don't hear it. Maybe it's in your mind, like before."

Another note, a trill of three, almost a bird song, but not quite. She shook her head. "The sound is coming from deeper in the canyon."

Diego got to his feet and looked the way she was pointing.

"You'll find a half dozen more great houses down there, but the loop doesn't go any farther, just a footpath."

"I don't mind walking." A mile, five miles ... *I'm coming, Twin.*

"You go on then. I'm going to see where my calculations lead me." Taking a compass out of his pocket, Diego squinted at it and gradually lined it up with north.

Moongirl didn't notice.

"You won't get lost as long as you stay in the canyon." He turned to orient his body with the compass. "Stay out of side canyons, though."

She could tell he didn't know whether to believe she heard it or not. But she didn't try to convince him, just reached for him, and gave him a quick hug. Then she turned up the canyon. Three steps. Silence. Four more steps. Two trills down low, a slow slide up.

She looked back at Diego, asking him with her eyes. He shook his head. Taking a deep breath, Moongirl went on alone.

Up the steps out of the kiva, along the road to where it crossed the wash to loop back toward the park's main entrance. A massive red brick ruin, its size exaggerated by the red wall of the mesa behind, rose suddenly before her. Her breath caught in her throat. A cathedral!

Not really a cathedral, of course, but the five-story ruin of the D-shaped great house called Pueblo Bonito. *Cathedrals.* The young conquistador had called the Center of the Universe a city of cathedrals. She wanted to shout with joy, run back to tell Diego.

Her relief was short-lived. Overhead the sun still climbed toward noon, and Chaco was a vast canyon filled with ruins, four hundred excavated kivas. Plus one no one had found.

She walked again, almost immediately passing a second great house, Pueblo del Arroyo. Then a third, Kin Kletso. A little farther on, the canyon seemed to fling out its arms, one to the east and one to the west.

Diego had told her not to follow any side canyons, but how could he know where Mahu sat playing his flute? Stopping uncertainly, she listened. Silence. Even the breeze was still. *Which way, Twin?* No answer.

On the other side of the wash, a single cottonwood stood tall and almost bare. Crossing to it, she dropped to the ground and waited. For long minutes she heard nothing, then the light rustle of the last brown leaves overhead, then nothing again. *Mahu?*

No red cedar notes answered her. The silence in her mind echoed the silence in the canyon. She closed her eyes to listen more carefully. Instead, she dozed.

The sound of footsteps woke her, hiking boots scattering small pebbles. Not Diego in his athletic shoes. Walker?

Moving only her head, she looked. A man had passed, either not seeing her or not caring. Not Walker. Older, heavier, Navajo, looking like he should be wearing a policeman's uniform instead of jeans and a green wool shirt.

If he saw her, he gave no sign. Henry Begay. If he was following the powáqas, they were in the canyon. In the distance, a man followed Begay, furtive. The prey stalking the hunter?

Then she heard the flute again. A clearer tune, now, not missing so many notes. Not now, she wanted to cry. But the powáqa didn't seem to hear.

Turning suddenly, he climbed what looked like a sheer canyon wall. When he was almost out of sight, she walked again, following a line of plaintive notes that called her straight ahead. The song. Silence. Then the song again.

At the great house of Casa Chiquita, she lost the trail of music. Pausing, she spotted a shallow stairway—a line of toeholds going over the canyon wall. Was Mahu up there? Should she climb the stairway?

Moongirl took a step forward when she heard the flute again, not from overhead but deeper in the canyon. Checking over her shoulder to make sure she wasn't being followed, she ran, her feet sliding in the sandy bottom of the wash but getting better traction on a hard-packed path.

She ran faster, ran until she had to stop, gasping for air. Then she saw it—another canyon, a smaller tributary of the main canyon. Diego had warned her about side canyons, but he hadn't known she would find Mahu.

Kaya caught her breath, ready to run again, but the flute went silent, and this time her quick check behind showed someone following. A figure in pants and a shirt—too far back to identify as male or female. Moving quickly.

Not one of the shamans. Someone younger. A ranger, a tourist, another powáqa, Walker, or Becky. Moongirl ducked into the side canyon and watched as the figure stopped beside the stairway and climbed.

She'd missed it. The Tokpela Kiva was up on the butte. She could have been first, but she'd missed it!

Taking a deep breath, she pushed away the panic that threatened. She'd heard the flute. It beckoned her. Now she must wait. Five minutes or five hours later, she heard a line of minor key notes, starting up high, plunging low, finding the middle, and weaving a melancholy song of hope.

Stepping hesitantly out of her hiding place, she checked the wash in both directions. No one, just the line of greasewood interrupted by an occasional cottonwood to show where the water ran. She turned up the canyon and ran.

The melody kept her company, growing stronger with each stride. Not far and the canyon widened perceptibly. The channel of the wash meandered to her left, leaving the ground under her feet firmer and more predictable. She found a pace and settled into a sort of lope that propelled her on.

She ran into a stretch without ruins, a desolate area with nothing but an occasional cliff swallow darting overhead to let her know life could exist here. A swallow whistled, and the red cedar notes stopped abruptly, not as though she'd lost the trail, but as if they'd been deliberately cut off.

Moongirl stopped running and looked around. A small canyon branched off to her right. *Twin?* Where was he? Why had he stopped playing?

As the question flitted across her mind, a shadow fell across her feet. She looked up to see a red-tailed hawk tracing lazy arcs in the brilliant blue sky. The magic eye, given by the animals for the hunt. Could the powáqas see with the eyes of a bird?

If they could see, could they hear? Had Mahu stopped playing for fear of giving away his location to the powáqas as he guided her to him? Right or not, the idea frightened her.

Without making a conscious decision, she ducked into the tiny canyon. The sun had passed the center point, and the canyon was narrow enough that the west wall already cast a shadow. As she waited for her eyes to adjust to the early twilight, she studied her surroundings. Sloping up toward the mesa above, the canyon floor was filled with silt carried by water not strong enough to reach the main channel of the wash.

She started climbing. Easily at first, then watching where she put her feet between rocks tumbled from above, finally looking for handholds to pull herself up and over waist-high boulders with sharp edges. No music now. She wasn't sure why she kept climbing. Something pulled her on through the silence, a melody made of wind.

Suddenly she reached what looked like a solid wall. Leaning her head against the sandstone's cold, rough surface, she closed her eyes and searched in her mind for Mahu. He wasn't there.

She opened her eyes and saw it—a petroglyph pecked into the rock. A pair of flute players, one male and one female, faced each other in a sort of dance. The faint outline of a circle circumscribed the entire design.

"Kaya ..." A sound so faint she thought it was only the wind sighing above her. "Kaya. Behind the petroglyph rock."

Heart pounding, she stepped back and looked at the stone in front of her. Not a wall, a wide slab and behind it a crevice so deep it was almost a cave. Her twin sat there, his flute lying across his knees. "Mahu!"

Smiling, he put a finger to his lips. "They heard too."

Guiltily, Moongirl checked the canyon behind and the rim overhead. Nothing. Ducking around the slab, she settled into the narrow space beside him.

Throwing her arms around her twin, she hugged him tight, hugged him as she had when they were five. "I can't believe it! Are you okay?"

"A headache." He pushed back the brim of his black felt cowboy hat, revealing a wide white bandage.

"Should you be here?"

"Same as you. We were born for this night, Moongirl."

Kaya hugged him again, but this time the hug was for herself, to stop the internal trembling. His heart beat as fast as hers, and he held her until they were both calm.

She released him reluctantly. "How did you get here?"

"Ikwa. He was at the hospital when I woke up. I was afraid I'd let you down, but he said I'd been following Moonboy's destiny while I dreamed."

"What did you dream?"

"I dreamed of you, of migrations, and of my flute. Music I've never heard before."

Moongirl caught her breath. "Sometimes, when I wasn't sure I was on the right path, I heard a flute. Ikwa said if I listened, I would hear Kokopelli's song. Was it you?"

"Maybe it was my dream. I dreamed I was traveling, dreamed I was playing my flute, calling you to me, calling you here to the Kokopelli Kokomana petroglyph."

"Two flute players—male and female. I don't know how to play the flute, Mahu!"

"That doesn't matter. The goal isn't to play the Song. Tonight under the Tokpela Moon, the Moon Twins, male and female, must *be* the Song of Creation."

# CHAPTER TWENTY-TWO

The sun teetered on the west rim of the mesa, brushing the ruins with red light. Across the canyon, the Tokpela Moon rose, as pale as an ancient memory and as round as a great house kiva. Six figures dressed in ceremonial clothes sat in a circle of the Rinconada moon kiva's center.

The women wore wool mantas. Eleanor's was red and Rina's blue. Moongirl wore her mother's black manta with the bands of red and yellow around the hem. The black and white belt cinched her waist, turquoise strands and cedar beads circled her neck. The men wore knee-length kilts and long-sleeved velvet shirts.

Moonboy's shirt was black, his kilt woven with patterns of red and blue, yellow and brown. White Bear wore yellow, Pete brown. All four shamans painted their faces white in the patterns of universal harmony. Each of them had a pouch woven with rain patterns slung over one shoulder.

The ceremonial pipe moved around the circle, hand-to-hand, mouth-to-mouth, sending prayer smoke straight up into the breathless dusk, smoke that requested, entreated, implored. When the pipe had been around once ... twice ... six times,

White Bear said solemnly, "Now from all directions we have come.

"Yellow from the West, Blue from the South, Red from the East, Brown from the West, White from the Zenith, Black from the Nadir. Let us begin."

They knew who and why. But they still didn't know the Tokpela Kiva's location.

The sound of running feet shredded the silence. Diego burst into the Rinconada enclosure. "I've found it—the Tokpela Kiva. Come on! I'll show you."

"Ah … " White Bear's audible sigh released the tension for them all. Unfolding himself, the old man rose stiffly to his feet. "Not yet, Diego James. When it is time, you will take us."

On White Bear's right, Eleanor stood and on his left, Rina. Then Pete and Moongirl. Moonboy reached for a small hand drum. Diego entered the circle between Moongirl and Eleanor.

When the circle was complete, White Bear chanted and stomped his feet. Bells jingled, the drum thumped. They danced, soft leather boots keeping the steady rhythm. Dusk faded into night.

One by one, the stars appeared—Venus, Orion, Gemini. The moon climbed up the eastern sky. Still the drum beat, the bells tinkled, and they kept time with their feet. As abruptly as he had begun, White Bear stopped dancing and nodded to Diego. Moonboy exchanged the drum for a flute and stood.

In silence broken only by a restless breeze stirring in the brush, they followed Diego. Up the steps into the wide expanse of Chaco Wash, around Casa Rinconada, down a path where gravel crunched into a nameless wash where sand slipped under them.

The angle of the narrow canyon cut off the moonlight temporarily, leaving them in silver dusk. When Casa Rinconada was far behind, Diego stopped in front of a dense growth of rabbitbrush. He pointed to a sheer cliff face. "Through here—a fissure in the rock."

The passage was just wide enough to allow them to go single file. White Bear went first. Diego came last. The fissure twisted and turned so, they moved forward, sideways, forward again. When they reached the end, they stepped out into a box canyon no bigger than White Bear's house.

A cloud covered the moon. In a voice of starlight, White Bear spoke into the darkness. "A natural kiva. Is the panel here?"

His voice soft but strong, Diego answered, "Not a painted panel. Petroglyphs etched on the west wall. The story is much more than what the lienzo recorded. I think there are other panels etched on other walls in this canyon. I could see it earlier, but now ..."

"The Tokpela Moon will show us," breathed Eleanor.

Almost as if he obeyed, the Wandering Man came out from behind the cloud, flooding the tiny plaza with silver light. White Bear moved to stand in front of the panel.

Reaching out, he traced the figures his ancestors had chiseled into the stone countless generations before his birth. The other shamans joined him, all of them intent on the ancient record.

The three Moon Twins stood back. "How did you find it?" whispered Moongirl.

"My compass told me it had to be here. I climbed to the top of the mesa, expecting to see a mound, but found nothing—until I looked down. I saw the room, but no way in."

"A ladder wouldn't be long enough," Moonboy said.

"Nope. And I'm not the climber you are. I went back down the way I'd come and followed the canyon wall until I found the fissure. I'm no geologist, but I'd swear it's new."

In the kiva, the shamans turned from the petroglyphs and looked at each other. White Bear said, "The panel is the vision, but a vision has no power until it is performed."

255

"A four-day ceremony," Rina said. "We have only four hours."

No one spoke for a long time. Pete broke the silence. "Time means nothing to the stars—four days, four hours, four minutes. We use the time we've been given."

"We have what we need," Eleanor said. "The Moon Twins are here."

Moongirl's heart stopped. Instinctively she reached for her twin. He took her hand with a strong grip. Behind them, Diego put one hand on Moonboy's shoulder and the other on Moongirl's. For a moment, the three of them stood joined by the warmth of touch.

White Bear said, "Let us begin."

At the same moment, Diego stepped back, Moonboy let go of her hand, and Moongirl stood alone. White Bear stayed where he was. Eleanor moved to his left, Pete to his right, and Rina took her place across. The four cardinal directions.

Opening his pouch, White Bear drew out four páhos, more elaborate, more colorful than the ones he'd set out under the stars at Old Oraibi. The shamans chanted, so quietly at first, Moongirl wasn't sure she heard. The volume increased one decibel at a time.

Walking clockwise, White Bear placed a páho in each corner of the ancient roofless room. "Parrot feathers like the Old Ones used, bright feathers to carry our prayers back to the past, through the present, and into the future."

He stepped back, and Rina stepped forward. The others continued to sing softly, and Moongirl felt time slow. Rina opened her pouch and took out a handful of cornmeal. Walking counterclockwise, she painted the great swastika that symbolized the migration pattern for a thousand years.

"Corn for our life together," she said. "Corn for our common purpose. Corn that draws us together when we lose the way."

Pete stepped forward, and time slowed even more. He

opened his pouch, moved to the center of the kiva, and drew out an arrow. With a start, Moongirl realized it was the same one she had seen on his shelf, the arrow like the one Walker used to stab Moonboy.

He placed it in the center of the cornmeal path. "Arrows signify struggle. They can be used to perform evil or to resist it. This arrow is very old—an arrow from the past to resist evil from the past."

Eleanor was last. Now time had no meaning at all. Opening her pouch, she drew out a black and white pottery bowl and held it up. "Clay combines earth and water. Clay needs air and fire to become pottery. Because we grind old pots to make new, pottery joins past and present. When we break a pot as our ancestors did, we can no longer use it, and it becomes an offering." She dropped the pot.

As it broke, a shadow sliced the moonlight. Not a single shadow, a cross-hatching of the tiny kiva, two parallel lines joined at regular intervals by shorter lines of shadow. Moongirl had never seen one, but instinctively she knew what it was.

Diego breathed, "A moon ladder." Silent agreement ran through the group. As one, they looked up at the mesa rim.

A woman stood there, a dark silhouette against the bright disk of the moon. One arm raised, stretched out as if to command the night. The other held the moon ladder with poles that writhed like snakes.

Eleven powáqas stood around her in a semi-circle. Amy thought, *I don't belong.* Kaya thought, *I can't fight.* Moeyha thought, *I'm sorry.*

Beside her, Moonboy whispered, "The Song. Remember, we must be the Song."

She didn't know what he meant, but it reminded her who she was. Moongirl ran toward the sheer wall where the dark woman stood so far above them. Even in silhouette, she recognized Becky, just as she realized it was Moongirl's destiny to stop

Becky from holding the moon ladder steady for the Tokpela powáqas.

Amy Kaya pulled off her boots at the bottom of the cliff, groping for the stone stairway she knew must be in the wall. Overhead the moon ladder grew darker, larger, threatened to engulf the tiny kiva.

Somewhere in the distance, a chainsaw roared into action. Moongirl heard Diego's yell and the sound of his running feet, but she already gripped the sandstone's rough surface with her fingers, finding the first step with her toes.

Far to the north, lightning slashed a heavy black cloudbank, blacker even than the night sky. In the Tokpela Kiva, White Bear began a wordless chant. Eleanor joined in, then Pete and Rina. The bells on their soft boots jingled an ancient rhythm. As Moongirl climbed, the chanting grew louder, the dancing faster, louder ... faster ... The ceremony continued, weaving them all into its pattern.

*Moonboy!*

The answer was immediate. *Here, Twin!*

She reached the top. Becky stood there, crushing Moongirl's hands with stiff-soled boots. The powáqas were there too, dancing a wild dance without pattern, shouting curses without rhythm.

Moongirl grabbed the dark woman's ankle and held on, unbalancing the older woman. It was enough. The ladder trembled, and the shadow wavered. With a curse Becky stepped back to stabilize the ladder, and Moongirl pulled herself onto the canyon rim.

"Too late," hissed Becky as the moon shattered into ten thousand sharp pieces.

Around and around spun Moongirl, caught in an eddy of time from which she knew there was no escape. In her ears the sound of ten thousand windows breaking, of glass raining onto stone. In her nostrils the smell of sulfur, in her mouth the taste of ash. On her skin the relentless stinging of a sandstorm.

The night sky disappeared. Ten thousand thirsty vines crawled across the mesa toward her, twining around her legs, binding her arms to her sides so she couldn't move, wrapping around her throat so she couldn't breathe. Wind slapped at her face, roared in her ears, filled her nostrils and mouth with dust.

An army of twisted trees with swords for branches and razors for leaves marched behind the vines. Overhead, an avalanche of jagged rocks as sharp as flint and as hard as diamonds tumbled from the sky. A grinning gargoyle with the arms and legs of a great ape rode the avalanche. From its hands dangled two heads held by long black strings of hair.

Behind the gargoyle flew an army of creatures that weren't quite human, men with the beaks of birds, women with the teeth of alligators. Over it all, under it all, reeked the stench of human flesh cooking.

Creation itself gone mad. The sky turned to fire, the earth to mud. Every breath burned her nostrils and her lungs. Her skin was a mass of blisters. When it began to rain, acid fell in great drops from the sky. Through the chaos whirled a mindless power bent on annihilation.

She felt herself begin to break apart. Moongirl losing Kaya, Moeyha losing Amy, Amy losing Moongirl, all the patterns of herself unraveling.

Sliding into unconsciousness, she heard the notes from far below, clear notes that fell like cool raindrops through the burning air, notes of a melody that gave her courage to reach for the threads of herself and weave them together into a new pattern.

*The song!* She remembered they had to *be* the Song of Creation. Somewhere Moonboy played his flute, but the song needed words. She knew it was her destiny to sing them. They came to her, ancient words riding ancient red cedar notes.

Moongirl sang, "Ki-tana-po, chi-li-cha, ki-ve, ki-ve, HOPET!"

In the kiva below, the shamans sang. "Ki-tana-po, chi-li-cha, ki-ve, ki-ve, HOPET!"

The Song of Creation filled the Tokpela Kiva, climbed to the top of the mesa, and spread out across the sky, blowing away chaos like fog in a warm wind.

Overhead the clouds parted, and the great silver moon sailed free. A moment of harmony.

Then beneath Moongirl's feet, the ground rumbled and shuddered. Dropping to her hands and knees, she crawled to the edge of the mesa and looked over. As Moonboy and the shamans looked up, the kiva shivered. Moongirl screamed, but it was too late.

She watched in horror as the walls split. For a moment, the great slabs of sandstone leaned against each other, creating a roof for the Tokpela Kiva, a roof with a narrow sipapuni in the very top, wide enough to let in silver moonlight.

Moongirl leaped to her feet, but before hope could form, the slabs groaned and collapsed in on each other.

Thunder surrounded her—under her feet, over her head, in her ears, even in her lungs. Then silence, but not silence, the sound of rushing water. Water lapped at the sides of the box canyon, rising fast, covering the slabs of sandstone.

The lightning in the north. A flash flood. No sign of Mahu, of the shamans, of Diego.

"Twin!" she wailed, searching her mind frantically for him. No answer. Only silence.

Another voice spoke, a voice that ran like a shiver down Moongirl's spine. "Help me!"

The silver moonlight revealed Becky lying on the ground, surrounded by sticks and splinters, remnants of the moon ladder. "My heart," she gasped. "The others ran. Amy, help me!"

"Why should I?" She shouted, wanting to push Becky over

the canyon's edge, down into the water she had unleashed, the water that covered the Tokpela Kiva. "You tried to kill me twice, and now, you want—" Kaya Amy choked on the words.

"I'm sorry," Becky whimpered. "I didn't understand!"

Kaya turned away and walked away. She wanted Mahu. Now. But she couldn't find the door in her mind. Too much turmoil. She shouted. "Mahu! Diego! Ikwa! Iso! Pete! Rina! Somebody! Anybody!!"

"Don't leave me!" screamed Becky. "They're gone. I'm here!"

Moongirl looked toward her employer. Not a silver woman, a dark woman. Amy hated, hated so much she was sick with it. Becky was alive, and they were all dead. She started toward the powáqa, who hadn't really understood the evil she worked so hard to unleash.

Amy, who was Kaya, who was Moeyha, meant to murder the murderess. Then Moongirl heard a thin line of red cedar notes, not Moonboy's flute, some last whisper of the Song. Just as the chaos had disintegrated, so now her hatred dissipated. Sitting on the ground, she pulled her knees up under her chin and wept into her mother's manta.

The moon had moved halfway down the western sky when Kaya went to Becky. Silently, she helped the haggard woman to her feet. Together they found the trail, a narrow path that zigzagged steeply down the side of the mesa.

Pebbles skittered under their feet, and often they had to stop to let Becky rest. Whenever they paused, Kaya called out, "Mahu! Diego! Ikwa! Iso! Pete! Rina!" Silence. Once she thought she heard Mahu's flute, but the snippet of music ceased, and she decided she had imagined it.

When they finally reached the end of the trail, the flash flood's destructive force was spent. But Rinconada Wash still ran with water, ankle deep and muddy in the moonlight. Behind them, the slot canyon was only a memory, blocked by the great slabs of sandstone collapsed in on each other.

"I can't keep hiking like this," Becky gasped. "My heart."

Hoarse with shouting, Kaya didn't bother to answer. Groping for the door in her mind, she tried again. *Mahu? Mahu!*

The silver moon teetered on the rim of the canyon when they reached Casa Rinconada. Leaving Becky to fend for herself, Kaya went down the steps into the ancient kiva. With a sinking heart, she swept the space with her eyes. Empty.

They were dead. No one could have lived through that crash of stone slabs.

Then something moved in deep shadow.

Mahu stepped into the moonlight. His hair was plastered to his head, and his clothes were caked with mud, but he was smiling. "Kaya! Happy Birthday, Twin."

She stared. How could he smile, think of their birthday?

"They're all drowned," she whispered. "All except for you."

He shook his head. "When the kiva walls collapsed, another way out opened up."

White Bear and Eleanor stepped out of the shadows, just as muddy and bedraggled as Mahu, smiling just as broadly. "Moeyha," they said together.

Pete and Rina were there too. "Welcome home, Moongirl."

She looked from smiling face to smiling face. "Diego?" she whispered.

Mahu put his arm around her shoulders. "He wasn't with us, so we don't know. But I think I would feel it if he had gone to the Cloud People."

Leaving the group, Amy ran back to Rinconada Wash. "Diego! Diego!"

In the early morning twilight, she could just make out two figures coming up the narrow canyon, moving slowly, both plodding as if exhausted.

"Diego?" She ran, and one of the two ran toward her.

"Amy!"

Then they were in each other's arms, laughing and crying. In four days, Diego's beard had grown, and it tickled her face. She kissed him suddenly, surprising herself.

His glasses slipped from his face and fell to the ground. Ignoring them, he kissed her back, not a brotherly kiss. More, so much more.

Pulling her close, he squeezed her so hard she couldn't breathe, but she didn't care. He finally let go and leaned down to retrieve his glasses.

*The left earpiece was gone. He would need new glasses—or contact lens. Those beautiful black eyes.* Silly thoughts, but full of wonder because they meant there would be an after.

She grabbed his hand. "How did you get out?"

"First, tell me about the others. I saw the Tokpela Kiva collapse."

"They're all fine—waiting for us. How did you get out of there?"

Diego gave a long shuddering sigh. Hand-in-hand, they walked. "I wasn't in the kiva. I was farther up Rinconada Wash, chasing the sound of Walker's chain saw. He and I got caught in the earthquake or whatever it was, but we survived."

Out in Chaco Wash, Walker went to Becky and helped her to her feet. "I see they found each other," she said. "Can't we stop them?"

Diego grinned. "We don't need to."

"Henry Begay! I saw him this afternoon."

"Yep, and as soon as they leave the Park, they're on Navajo land, and he can arrest them. Between them, they've broken enough laws—from murder to stealing archaeological artifacts—to keep them in prison until they're too old to do any more harm."

They walked back to Casa Rinconada in silence, not needing more words.

As Mahu and the shamans surrounded Diego, she stepped back. In that moment, she saw her past and her future. Her twin —Mahu, the missing part of her, who would never be lost again. Her family—White Bear and Eleanor, who had given her Taáta and who would teach her that part of her heritage.

Her community—Pete and Rina who were part of a pattern bigger than any of them, a pattern that began long before they were born and would continue long after they died. And Diego— the stranger she had asked for help and the friend who was becoming much more.

She had finished this part of the road of destiny. She was eighteen, and she'd found the missing pieces of her past. Now she wanted to be herself. Not Moongirl or Moeyha or Kaya or Amy. None of them. All of them. Herself.

As the pale Tokpela Moon set behind the magnificent ruins, her name came to her, a name that embraced all the pieces of herself and opened the way for a new future. As she stood listening to the name, Diego moved to her side.

Looking up at him, she whispered, "I know what I want you to call me."

He peered at her through his crooked glasses and waited.

Trying it out for the first time, she said, "Maya. My name is Maya."

"An amalgam name. It sounds good. *Querida Maya*."

In the east, the golden horizon glowed. Maya's heart filled with joy, and Mahu raised his flute. As red cedar notes climbed toward blue morning, the shamans began to dance.

Maya and Diego smiled at each other. Joining hands, they too danced.

# EPILOGUE

The Following Sunday
Santa Fe, Christmas Market

M aya sat in Mahu's pickup, staring at the dumpster. Had it only been a week since she'd climbed into this pickup in a driving snowstorm alone and terrified? A week that had taken her on a journey no one but those who had accompanied her would believe. A week that had shown her who she was and moved her from childhood to adulthood.

Yet today, she was almost as scared as she had been a week ago.

Knuckles rapped on her window. Diego. He looked good. He'd trimmed his beard and mended his glasses. Now, they were only a little crooked. He mouthed, "You okay?"

Her smile came easily. She'd met him, fallen for him, and almost lost him in this week.

Her door swung open. "What are you thinking about so hard, Querida?"

She gave him her hands and jumped down from the pickup. "Whether I want Grandmother Adams to come today or not."

"It's a toss-up. Heads' she's changed and shows up with a smile for Mahu and your grandparents. Tails' she's the same unhappy, prejudiced grandmother and stays home to lick her wounds."

"It's the third option I'm worried about. What if she shows up—and she's the same?"

"Whatever happens, it's her choice. You invited her. I'm sure she understands the invitation is larger than simply meeting Mahu." He drew her into arms. "I think you need a hug."

She leaned in, grateful for the comfort. With her face against his chest, she inhaled the smells that made him Diego—leather, soap, and a spicy scent that must be aftershave. He was right. Whatever Grandmother Adams decided, she was surrounded by people who loved her.

When he let her go, they walked to the plaza hand-in-hand. It lay silent and deserted at a little after nine, a wonderland of tree trunks and evergreens decorated with white Christmas lights that sparkled against a dusting of new snow. Under the portico of the Palace of the Governors, a line of artists from many tribes were spreading blankets on the ground and arranging their goods for sale.

Mahu's silver jewelry flashed in the sun. Ikwa and Iso, too old now to sit comfortably on the ground, perched on low stools, one blanket spread in front of the two of them, waiting for Iso's storytellers and Ikwa's kachina dolls.

Maya looked at Diego. "When do the tourists start coming?"

"Around ten. Maybe a little later this morning because of the snow. The streets will be clear by noon, and traffic will pick up. With Christmas shopping in full swing, I'm guessing it will be a busy afternoon."

Diego's predictions turned out to be right. At one-thirty, after the lunch rush had died down, Maya and Diego went to a small café he knew about that specialized in authentic Mexican food. They ordered take-out for everyone. At three, she wandered over to the Delgado Gallery. As she expected, it was closed, but the sign on the door made her sad.

Where was Becky today? With all her money, she was probably out on bail. But did they give bail to a murderer? Wherever Becky was, Maya hoped never to see her again.

Four o'clock had come and gone. Maya sat beside Mahu under the portico. Only two pieces of his jewelry remained, shining silver against the black velvet cloth. One, a modern interpretation of the squash blossom necklace set with aquamarine gemstones, carried a $2,000 price tag. That one would take a special buyer. The other one, a simple Kokopelli/Kokomana pendant, called her name.

Mahu wanted a hundred dollars for it, a fair price, but more than she could pay. She secretly hoped it wouldn't sell and she could buy it after she found a job and saved up some money. Of course, the first hundred of disposable income would go to repay Grandmother Adams. But the next could buy the little pendant if Mahu still had it.

Iso sat beside Mahu, two storytellers left. A white-haired grandpa held five kids, one holding a basketball. Maya smiled at the story behind the clay figure—a grandpa telling a story to encourage a budding basketball team, maybe a story of when he was young and played the game. The other figure was a bear with three cubs in its lap. She would have to ask Iso about the story behind that one.

Beside her, Mahu picked up his flute and began to play. Not the Song of Creation, but a song of hope. Maya moved into a patch of late sun and settled in to listen. Then she spotted Aunt Eileen.

Wearing jeans, tooled leather boots, and a leather jacket over a coral blouse, Eileen looked like she'd stepped right out of one of the clothing store windows. Warmth radiated from Maya's heart until it filled her to overflowing. Her aunt, at least, was trying to show her she wanted to be part of Maya's new world.

Maya's gaze drifted to an older woman standing so close to Aunt Eileen they had to be together. *Grandmother Adams?* The ash blonde hair and the pale green wool suit with matching blouse were the same, but the woman looked older, thinner. Maya leaned over to Mahu and whispered, "She's here."

The notes from the flute never faltered as Mahu nodded.

Maya looked at Iso and mouthed. "She's here."

"Yes, Moeyha. I see her. The years have not been kind to your mama's mama. She is too skinny. Maybe she is sick."

"What should I do? Should I go to her or wait for her to recognize me?"

"You invited her, so she is here on your land."

Iso was right. Maya took a deep breath and stood. As she walked toward her other grandmother, the one she'd come to think of as the wrong grandmother, she wondered if the old woman would even acknowledge her in her manta. Not hers exactly—another one of her mother's. But somehow that made the confrontation more important. If Grandmother Adams accepted her granddaughter, she would also be accepting her daughter. Too late for Brenda, but not too late for Lelia.

Aunt Eileen recognized her first. "Amy!" Letting go of Grandmother Adams's arm, she hurried across the closed off brick street, meeting Maya in the middle. Throwing her arms around Maya, she pulled her close. "I'm so glad to see you, Amy!"

Maya soaked up the hug, but one important bridge remained to be crossed. Stepping back, she said, "I need to tell you something important, Aunt Eileen. Please don't laugh."

"Never, darling. What is it?"

"I've changed my name. I'm not Amy anymore. I'm Maya."

A look of confusion crossed Aunt Eileen's face. In that breathless instant, Maya realized Diego stood beside her. He'd meant it when he said whatever happened, he would be by her side.

Aunt Eileen smiled, breaking the tension. "It fits you! A name that encompasses all of who you are."

Gratitude washed over Maya. At least this part of her mother's family accepted her. In the next breath, Grandmother Adams joined Aunt Eileen.

Maya swallowed. "Hello, Grandmother. I'm glad you came."

Grandmother Adams opened her mouth, looking for a moment like one of Iso's storyteller dolls.

Maya doubted a story was about to emerge. She held up her hand. "Please, Grandmother. Before we talk, I want you to meet my twin, your grandson."

Mahu, flute still in his hand, had moved beside her. Looping her arm through his, she said, "Grandmother, this is Mahu. He's a phenomenal flute player and an awesome silversmith. Mahu, this is Grandmother Adams."

Mahu held out his hand. For one breathless moment, Maya thought the wrong grandmother would refuse to take it. Then the unexpected happened. Grandmother Adams closed the distance between herself and Mahu and embraced him, awkwardly at first, then more warmly when Mahu put his arms around her.

Iso came to join them. "Welcome, Lelia Adams. We are glad you are here. My name is Eleanor Naranjo Sekatewa. I am Maya and Mahu's other grandmother."

Lelia nodded. "I remember you."

"I remember you as well."

"Iso makes storyteller dolls," Maya said. "Some of them are in the Smithsonian."

Eleanor waved the words away. "Maya told me the story of the nicknames your late

husband bestowed on everyone. She told me your nickname was Lily Flower. In our tradition, we don't have nicknames, but we have ceremonial names. I want to welcome you by giving you a ceremonial name."

Lelia raised her eyebrows. "Thank you, but I'm afraid I don't deserve your welcome. I had a long talk with my daughter Eileen after Am—Maya ran—left me at the airport. I owe you and your family an apology. I only wish Brenda and Wilson were here, so I could apologize to them too."

Again, Iso waved away the words. Something in the motion made Maya look closely at Iso's face. Her eyes twinkled with fun. What was her pueblo grandmother up to?

As if to let everyone know he was in on the joke, Ikwa came to stand beside Iso. Iso took his hand. "My husband, White Bear, and I have consulted the council, and we have chosen your ceremonial name. Welcome, Prickly Pear Blossom."

Maya held her breath. Grandmother Adams stared at Iso, frozen. Suddenly, Aunt Emily giggled. As Maya watched, the unexpected happened for the second time. A smile tugged at the corners of Grandmother Adams's mouth, spread to her eyes, and grew until it burst out into a laugh. A heartbeat later they all laughed.

With one hand Diego grabbed Grandmother Adams's arm, with the other Aunt Emily's. "Group hug!"

As Maya and Mahu joined in, Mahu whispered in Maya's ear. "We invited harmony."

Moongirl smiled. "Invitation accepted."

# AUTHOR'S NOTE

Thank you for reading Kokopelli's Song. I hope you had as much fun reading the story as I had writing it. I first visited Chaco Culture National Historic Park fifteen years ago. As I hiked through the ruins left by an advanced civilization that flourished between the ninth and eleventh centuries, I could hardly take in what I was seeing. I've visited the pyramids in Mexico and read about Machu Picchu in Peru, but I had no idea anything like these massive ruins existed in the United States

I bought a book, which led me to more books. I learned that instead of being a residential center like Mesa Verde, Chaco was a ceremonial center. People came from all over the Four Corners region (what we know as New Mexico, Arizona, Colorado, and Utah) for ceremonies at different times of the year. I also learned that, unlike most ancestral Puebloan centers, Chaco was not abandoned all at once. Instead, it was closed over several years —one section at a time—with each kiva, or ceremonial room, dismantled with the same care used to build it. Then the kivas were deliberately burned.

The more I read, the more intrigued I became. I returned to Chaco. This time I hiked more of the ruins and studied the petroglyphs. I joined a ranger talk and learned about macaw feathers, seashells, and copper bells found in the kivas that proved trade between Chaco, the west coast of North America, and South America. I attended a seminar in Santa Fe and learned about three ceremonial cities (Chaco Culture, Aztec Ruins, and Paquime) that flourished sequentially over five centuries along a north-south meridian.

The last time I visited Chaco, I camped under the stars. Early the next morning I heard the haunting strains of a Native American flute. I followed the sound but couldn't find the flute player. As I drove home to Colorado, a story began forming in my head, a story about Kokopelli and cosmic forces of evil from the days of the Chaco civilization colliding with our present day. Clearly a fantasy, *Kokopelli's Song* is mostly my imagination, but its roots are in my research. I enjoy research, so most of my stories are this mixture. Usually I weave every bit of research carefully into the fiction, doing my best to make it invisible to readers.

*Kokopelli's Song* is a little different. While I wove much of my research into the story, each section of the book begins with a Hopi myth. Because Hopi mythology is an oral tradition and I'm not Hopi, I depended on a retelling of these stories by Frank Waters in *Book of the Hopi* (1963). Exercising poetic license, I invented my own version of his stories to act as a backdrop for Amy's story.

If you want to dig deeper, download the free study guide with questions and writing prompts in the next section.

# STUDY GUIDE

## Chapter 1

Research the museums and artists of Santa Fe, New Mexico. Based on what you learn, predict why the author chose Santa Fe as the sipapuni, or doorway, into this story. When you finish the book, check back to see if your hypothesis is correct.

## Chapter 2

Amy has forgotten all about her twin and how she was separated from him and her family when she was five. Psychologists call this kind of forgetting "repression." Look up *repression* and find out what causes it. Predict how Grandmother Adams' lies contributed to Amy's repression. When you finish the book, check back to see if your hypothesis is correct.

## Chapter 3

Research the Rosetta Stone. Find out
• when and where it was discovered

• what it was originally used for
• why it was such an important find
• where it is now

If the lienzo is a sort of Rosetta Stone as Diego thinks it might be, what secrets would it unlock?

## Chapter 4

Amy's dream is an example of a writing technique called *foreshadowing*. It gives readers a hint about where the story might be headed. Predict what you think her dream about the moon means for the rest of this story. When you've finished the book, check back to see if you were right.

## Chapter 5

Look up the word *archetype*. Diego says that "child carried off by evil beings" is an archetype. Many fairy tales use this archetype. *Snow White* is one. Who is the evil being responsible for Snow White's kidnapping? *Rapunzel* is another example. How is this archetype used in this fairy tale?

What does Diego mean when he says, "a prejudiced Anglo" is an archetype on the reservation?

## Chapter 6

Ikwa says, "Destiny is never a straight line. Destiny is a line with twists and turns, a path both good and evil tread. The traveler steps and missteps, goes the wrong way and then the right way."

In this discussion with Diego, White Bear is using the word *destiny* to mean "an important goal." Think of an example of White Bear's point from a story you've heard or a book you've read. Draw a line to illustrate how the journey unfolded. Mark the places where the traveler came to a twist in the road, where she met evil or good, where he went the right way and then the wrong way. Think about your own life and the road you've traveled to accomplish goal. Or think about goals you have for the future. What twists and turns can you imagine on that road?

## Chapter 7

Start to Learn the Night Sky
• Find a star chart of this month for your area. A good place to start is your state's astronomical society. (You can find one on the internet or by asking your local librarian for help.)
• On a clear night, go outside. Using the chart, find the north star, the Big and Little Dippers, Orion's Belt and Gemini--the twins. Depending on the time of year and where you're located not all of these constellations may be visible.
• Do that several nights until you've learned them by heart.
Another Possibility
If your parents agree, attend a free star party held by a local astronomical society. You can find this information on the internet or from your local librarian.

## Chapter 8

Brother/brother and brother/sister bonds are important to this story. Think of someone outside of your birth family who feels like family to you (a brother or a sister, a parent, or a grandparent). How did this bond form?

## Chapter 9

Several specialties are important to this story:
• archaeology
• archaeoastronomy

- linguistics
- museum curator
- pottery
- silversmithing.

1. Find a definition for each of these.

2. Which one sounds the most interesting to you? Why?

3. If none of them sound interesting, what field are you interested in learning more about? Why?

## Chapter 10

A theme that's starting to develop is Diego's description of himself, Amy, and Mahu as amalgams. In chapter 8 he says, "Like amalgams in chemistry. Two elements that join to make something new. Some people are amalgams. I'm not half and half. And neither are you ... I'm all both, all of the above. Something new. Me." In this chapter, Diego says Tommy Lacapa and Dr. Montoya are also amalgams. The material used in dental fillings is an amalgam of silver and mercury. Mirrors are silvered with an amalgam of mercury and tin.

Most Americans trace their ancestry back to an amalgam. My grandfather was full-blooded German, but my grandmother was a mixture of an amalgam (Scotch and Irish) and British. So, my mother was German, Scotch, Irish, and British. My father was German, Swiss, Cherokee, and English. So, I'm a mixture of six nationalities. When we get to my daughter, it gets even more complicated! So, because the racial heritage of many Americans is so complicated, we've all lumped into "White," "Caucasian," or "Anglo."

Amy, Mahu, and Diego, however, are at the beginning of their families' "melting" into the "melting pot" of the U.S.

- Maybe you're an amalgam. What are the advantages and disadvantages of being an amalgam? (For example, one of my favorite singers is Fernando Ortega. He's an amalgam of

Hispanic and Irish. His music is unique because it draws both from Spanish and Irish rhythms.)

• If you're a more complicated mixture than an amalgam, make a list of your nationalities. If you were going to travel to one country to search for your family roots, where would you go and why?

• Which of your friends are amalgams? What is their heritage? What advantages and disadvantages do they have because their family background is clear?

## Chapter 11

When Kaya was talking to Dr. Montoya, she said, "Please, tell me why this ceremony (the lost ancient ceremony) is so important. Ikwa said we need the proper ceremony for the proper task. I don't think I understand."

We still use special ceremonies for special tasks:

• Graduation
• Wedding
• Baptism
• Doctors taking the Hippocratic Oath
• Swearing in of the President
• Memorial Services
• Awards Banquets

Choose any two (or add your own) and trade out the ceremonies. Explain why that ceremony wouldn't work for a different task.

Here's an example: Explain why the Hippocratic Oath wouldn't work for a Memorial Service.

*Hint*: You'll have to do a little research to discover what specific words are used in the two ceremonies you choose.

## Chapter 12

Find a map of New Mexico. Locate
• El Morro National Monument
• Grants
• Albuquerque
• Cochiti Pueblo
How many miles is there between each place? What direction is Amy Kaya traveling?

## Chapter 13

In this chapter Kaya Amy Moongirl is recaptured by the grandmother who took her away from her family when she was five. To escape, she makes a plan to trick her grandmother. How does this turn in the story mimic the fairy tale archetype Diego compared Kaya's kidnapping to when he told her everyone on Third Mesa knew her story?

Hint: Think about fairy tales like *Hansel and Gretel* or *Rapunzel*.

## Chapter 14

Kokopelli (the flute player) is a motif, or design, that appears throughout the story. When did the design first appear? What does the song represent? When does Amy Kaya hear the song? In this chapter, what does "Kokopelli showed Moongirl the way to her destiny" mean?

Predict what role the song will play in the rest of the story. When you're finished with the book, check back to see if you're right.

## Chapter 15

Early in this chapter Iso says, " Without stories there's no meaning. Just a lot of events. We need stories to understand."

Write the story of an event you've had a hard time understanding. It can be personal (like an unexpected grade you received) or public (like the COVID 19 pandemic). If it helps you get started, begin with "Once upon a time..."
When you're finished, see if you understand anything differently. If you found this activity helpful, start a journal of your personal "I don't understand" stories.

## Chapter 16

The threads of the story are starting to come together. Make a list of what you know about the following:
• Kokopelli
• Kokopelli's Song
• Tokpela Moon
• Moon Twins
• The Ya-Ya ceremony
• Migration pattern of the ancient pueblo people
• Powáqas
Predict what's going to happen in the next chapter.

## Chapter 17

The full moon only rises between the spires of Chimney Rock National Monument every 18.6 years, but it's open every year during the summer. Go to www.chimneyrockco.org to read about the ruins there. Be sure to click on "visit" and "media." If you want a bit more go to www.chimneyrockco.org/full-moon-program to read about the program I attended when I was researching this chapter.

## Chapter 18

Did your attitude toward Yukioma change by the end of this

chapter? What caused the shift? Have you experienced a similar change to someone you know or a character in another book? Remembering Iso's idea of telling a story to understand what happened differently, tell the story of your personal experience.

## Chapter 19

Pete Lacapa says Ms. Delgado is dangerous because "she believes in magic enough to dabble in it, but she's too modern to take the dark power seriously. She's the type that's liable to get more than she bargained for."

What do you think of his statement? Do you agree that dabbling in magic is dangerous? Why or why not?

The *Bible* (1 Thessalonians 5:5) says, "you are all children of light and children of the day; we are not of the night or darkness" and "act like children of light" (Ephesians 5:8). What do you think Paul, the author of these two letters, means? For a more in-depth study, get a *Bible* and read the chapters that contain these verses.

## Chapter 20

Have you (or a friend) ever felt like you had too many identities (maybe you were different at home, at school, at church—or other places). Or maybe you've felt like you didn't have enough identities (part of your personality was ignored or belittled). How did you (might you) resolve the conflict? Tell that experience as a story.

OR

If you've never had an experience like that, find a map of New Mexico. Find the roads Amy Kaya and Diego traveled on to get from Chimney Rock to Chaco. Measure the distances. Estimate times (be sure to consider speed limits and type of road).

## Chapter 21

When Moongirl first sees Chaco Canyon, she says, "What is this place, Diego?" Instead of giving her one answer, he gives her four:
- What the map says
- What the rangers say
- What the tourists say
- What the people whose ancestors built the great houses say

Think of a place you've been that might have several answers to "What is this place?" It might be a special place like a national park, or it might be a specific city, or it might be a building like a school, a courthouse, or a church.

Write out the different meanings different people give to this place. What does it mean to *you*? Why?

## Chapter 22

From what you've learned about the teens, predict …
*next week for*
- Maya and Mahu
- Diego

*next year for*
- Maya
- Mahu
- Diego
- Maya and Diego
- Diego, Maya, and Mahu

### Capstone Activities

1. Go back through your predictions for the story. What was your track record? Did predicting get easier, harder, or stay the same as the story progressed? Why?

2. What are the take-aways from this story for you?

3. Would you want to revisit the story by reading it or listening again? Why or why not?

4. Did anything in the story make you want to do some research of your own? If so, what? How can you find out more about that topic?

# BIBLIOGRAPHY

*Selected Bibliography*

Congdon-Martin, Douglas. *Storytellers and Other Figurative Pottery*. West Chester, PA:
Schiffer Publishing, 1990.

Hill, Stephen and Montoya, Robert. *Kokopelli Ceremonies.* Santa Fe, NM: Kiva Publishing,
1995.

Lewis, Lucy with Lewis-Mitchell, Emma and Lewis-Garcia, Delores. DVD: *Daughters of the
Anasazi.* San Cristobal, New Mexico: Rancho Ventoso Productions, 2005.

Lekson, Stephen. *The Chaco Meridian: Centers of Political Power in the Ancient Southwest.*
Walnut Creek, CA: AltaMira Press, 1999.

Martineau, La Van. *The Rocks Begin to Speak.* Las Vegas: KC Publications, Inc, 1973.

Malotiki, Ekkehart. *Kokopelli: The Making of an Icon.* Lincoln, NE: University of Nebraska
Press, 2000.

Noble, David Grant, ed. *In Search of Chaco: New Approaches to an Archaeological Enigma.* Santa Fe, NM: School of American Research Press, 2004.

Strutin, Michal and Huey, George. *Chaco: A Cultural Legacy.* Tucson, AZ: Western National Parks Association, 1994.

Sutcliffe, Ron. *Moon Tracks: Guide to understanding patterns we see with an emphasis on southwest ancient Pueblo cultures* Pagosa Springs, CO: Moonspiral Press, 2006.

Waters, Frank and Fredericks, Oswald White Bear. *Book of the Hopi.* New York, NY: Viking Press, NY, 1963.

Wright, Margaret Nickelson. *Hopi Silver: The History and Hallmarks of Hopi Silversmithing.* Albuquerque, NM: University of New Mexico Press, 1999.

# GLOSSARY OF TERMS

- adobe—brick of sun-dried earth and straw
- amalgam—element created from a mixture of elements
- amigo—friend
- archetype—a story pattern which occurs in many cultures
- Artemis—Greek moon goddess
- conquistador—conqueror from Spain
- glyph—symbol
- fourth world—our world
- hermana—sister
- hupko—welcome
- Isis—Egyptian goddess of magic
- kachina—Pueblo benevolent spirit being
- kaya—older sister
- Kokopelli—male flute player petroglyph and kachina
- Kokomana—female flute player petroglyph and kachina
- lienzo—manuscript written on linen or cotton
- linguist—person who studies languages

- Mami Wata—African water goddess
- matrilineal—inheritance through the mother's line
- moeyha-little grandchild
- el morro—the bluff
- Nefertiti—ancient Egyptian queen
- overlay—jewelry made from two layers of precious metals
- páho—prayer stick
- padre—early Spanish Catholic missionaries
- parish—local church community
- paso—turning place
- petroglyph—writing on a rock
- pictograph—picture writing
- powáqa—witch
- pueblo—village
- querida—darling
- taáta—daddy
- taboo—forbidden
- tokpela—endless void (in space)
- sipapuni—doorway, entrance, or place of emergence
- Wandering Man—the moon
- Ya-Ya—extinct Hopi ceremony of the hunt

# ABOUT THE AUTHOR

A passionate reader since her first encounter with Dick and Jane, Suzanne J. Bratcher wanted to grow up to be a fiction writer. After college, realizing she couldn't support herself on ten cents a word, she became an English teacher, specializing in writing instruction. Over the next thirty years she taught writing to high schoolers, college students, and public school teachers. She continued her own writing: publishing professional articles, two textbooks, short stories, and poetry. Since retiring from Northern Arizona University in Flagstaff, Bratcher has returned to her childhood dream of writing fiction. *The Copper Box* (2017) and *The Silver Lode* (2019) are the first two books in The Jerome

Mysteries. Watch for the third book, *The Gold Doubloons*, in 2021. *Kokopelli's Song* (2020) is the first book in the Fantasy Folklore series.

Find out more about Suzanne and sign up for her newsletter at https://suzannebratcher.com or connect with her via social media.

facebook.com/authorsuzannebratcher

twitter.com/AuthorBratcher

instagram.com/suzanne.bratcher.5

## ALSO BY SUZANNE BRATCHER

If you enjoyed *Kokopelli's Song*, please leave a review on Goodreads.com and/or Amazon.com. Thank you.

You may also enjoy these books

by Suzanne J. Bratcher:

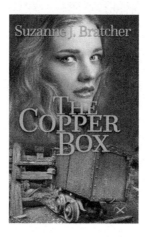

### *The Copper Box*
### Book One of the Jerome Mysteries Series

*Jerome, Arizona: the largest ghost town in America*

Antiques expert Marty Greenlaw comes to Jerome to face the horror that haunts her dreams: Did she kill her little sister twenty-two years ago?

Historian Paul Russell is in Jerome to face his own horror: Was the car crash that killed his wife his fault?

Their lives become intertwined when an old lady dies on a long staircase in a vintage Victorian house. As Marty and Paul search the house for a small copper box Marty believes will unlock the mystery, accidents begin to happen.

Someone else wants the copper box—someone willing to commit murder to get it. As Marty and Paul face the shadows in the house and in their lives, they must learn to put the past behind them and run the race God is calling them to.

**The Silver Lode**

**Book Two of the Jerome Mysteries Series**

*Jerome, Arizona: the largest ghost town in America*

Billion-dollar copper camp alive with rags-to-riches stories

Beneath the ghost town that clings to Cleopatra Hill, a maze of abandoned mine tunnels conceals a vein of silver ore mixed with pure gold. Seventy years ago the discovery of that silver lode caused a murder. Are more coming?

Historian Paul Russell is about to lose his job and the woman he loves. He doesn't have time to search for the legendary silver lode. But when a student drops a seventy-year-old cold case on his desk, a murder connected to the silver lode, the mystery offers Paul the perfect opportunity to work with Marty Greenlaw and win her back.

As Paul and Marty search for the silver lode, suspicious deaths begin to happen. When Paul's son disappears, the stakes become personal.

---

Watch for *The Gold Doubloons*, Book Three of the Jerome Mysteries Series, coming in Fall 2021.

---

Scrivenings
PRESS
Quench your thirst for story.
www.ScriveningsPress.com

*Stay up-to-date on your favorite books and authors with our free e-newsletters.*

ScriveningsPress.com

Made in the USA
Monee, IL
17 November 2020